War Olympus

By Jacob Amos

For Nicola, Poppy & Henry

Foreword

Did you know that every chapter in this book is named after a song?
All the songs listed in order at the end of this book make up the unique soundtrack to accompany this book.
Each song was carefully chosen to evoke an emotional response, to give you the reader, a flavour of how that chapter should feel when you read it.
Some chapters are more uplifting, some are darker, some evoke sadness, and that's why I created a playlist for you to listen to whilst reading, whether you turn it up loud or play it quietly in the background.
I have always enjoyed reading books, but I sometimes wondered how a certain sentence, paragraph or chapter should really feel.
I also love watching films, and without the right music, a scene could be observed completely differently, as music has the power to put you in the moment, so I thought what better way than to combine an action-adventure book with a soundtrack!
Over a thousand songs were considered when trying to find the right feel for each chapter.
Each song once chosen, I listened to again and again as it inspired the writing and feeling at certain points in the book.
You may also quickly work out that some artists feature more prominently than others, as they give the backbone to the feeling.
I hope you enjoy them as much as I did.
Finally, to all the artists and performers of these tracks, your songs inspired me. Thank you.

Chapters

7	Prologue: Birth
8	Supermassive Black Hole
10	Map of the Problematique
12	I Fear Nothing
14	Radius
15	The Wolf
16	Aphelion
19	Sport Vibes
21	Time is Running Out
24	Algorithm
26	Age of Discovery
28	Adventure of a Lifetime
30	Trouble's Coming
32	Equinox
35	Esoteric
38	All That We Are
40	Momenta
43	Anticipation
45	Start of Something Wonderful
48	Rebirth
50	Under Lock and Key
52	Mad Visions
55	These Moments
57	Dark Magic
59	Bring Me to Life
61	Embers
63	Dark Room Yoga
66	From the Deep
68	Leap of Faith
70	Something Human
72	Millennia
74	Try Again Tomorrow
76	Redshift
78	Climb Together
80	Get Up and Fight
82	Reaching
84	Figure It Out

86	Ageless Empire
88	The Handler
90	Ocean Sky
92	When It All Falls Down
94	Our World
96	Try Again Tomorrow
98	Beyond the Clouds
100	Shadowfall
103	Assassin
105	Persecution
107	Choose Your Destiny
111	Eternal Light
113	Compliance
115	Unbroken
117	Reverie
119	Verona
121	Einaudi: Nuvole Bianche
123	The Dark Side
126	Young Blood
128	The Great Unknown
132	Metamorphosis
136	Tails of the Electric Romeo
138	Spectral Dimension
140	Uprising
143	The Devil's Army
145	Another Planet
149	Blockades
151	Kashmir
153	Reborn
156	No Retreat, No Surrender
160	Look to the Sky
162	On the Shoulders of Giants
164	Reign of Vengeance
167	Thunderstruck
169	Invincible
171	Building Smasher
173	Stockholm Syndrome
176	Tantra
180	The Fate of Our Brave

185	Reapers
190	Destructo
193	Thumper
196	Ten Thousand Warriors
199	Sanctus Immortale
209	Mercurial
211	Knights of Cydonia
214	Spiritus Omnia
221	Farewell to Earth
223	Psycho
227	The Final Hour
229	Ground Zero
233	Knock 'Em Dead, Kid
236	Ode to Power
240	Glow
243	Undefeated
245	Rising Dawn
248	Sol Invictus
251	Let the Bells Ring Out
254	Maya
257	Eternal Flame
261	Welcome to the Rest of Your Life
265	The Rock Upon Which All Waves Crash
268	Stand as One
271	Destined for Greatness

Prologue: Birth

In the beginning, there was Chaos. Chaos was everything, the only thing, in the endless expanse of the universe.
Chaos was all there was. No stars. No planets, no galaxies, no cosmos filled with the wonders of space that we know of today.

No time, being, or motion. No need for time. It didn't exist. Then, Chaos reacted, followed by a rumbling, then a flash of light struck across the eternal borders, then the sound of thunder.
Elements inside Chaos collided, creating chain reactions, a fusion process. The noise Chaos made was deafening. Chaos began to dwindle into a tiny dot, as small as the one at the end of this sentence.

The loudest ever explosion occurred, followed by the crashing of particles, with trillions of bright, colourful sparks and particles exploding in every direction. Elements began to combine, creating huge gas giants that were flung out to the farthest reaches of space. These elements bonded together more so, creating great spherical furnaces shining and burning ever so bright. It took millions of years for them to settle in their places. Chaos had now created the stars.

Chaos soon rumbled and sparked again, sending more elements sprawling across the cosmos to join the stars. Some of these elements bonded together tightly to create solid mass. Not all elements bonded equally, but some were still spherical. These new bodies found the stars. The star's gravity drew them near, and they began to circumnavigate them. After millions of years, Chaos created the planets.

Supermassive Black Hole

Chaos continued to roam the universe for millions of years. The need for more creations became apparent to Chaos despite it being pleased with what it had done.
Chaos moved and swirled again. Specks of glimmering elements, beautifully coloured, collided again at ferocious speeds.
Chaos again condensed into a brilliant ball of energy, creating more chain reactions, more collisions, releasing huge amounts of energy.

Chaos ignited, and from Chaos came a giant nebula, dominated by emerald and turquoise, with flashes of aqua, silver and gold. It drifted slowly away from Chaos's body. The new nebula then flashed great storms within and rumbled and moved, turning, and moving majestically.
Chaos had now created Gaia.

Gaia became the Goddess of Earth.
Gaia herself then combusted and convulsed, spitting out her own nebula.
Ouranos, God of the skies and heavens, was now created, coming into existence. Ouranos then fell in love with Gaia, colliding with her, with both nebulas coming together, becoming entwined as one enormous mass. Then, with thunderous noise and flashes of brilliant light, they condensed together and then began the spew out nebula after nebula.

They created Aether, a nebula God who shone so bright, brighter than anything in the cosmos, speckled with brilliant white, gold, and silver elements.
Aether became the God of light, the spark for all life.

Aether now joined Chaos, Gaia, and Ouranos in the heavens of space.

Next came Eros, God of love and procreation.

The next nebula they produce splits in half, creating Hemera, Goddess of day, followed by her twin brother, Erebus, God of night.

Another nebula arrives and splits again. Hypnos, God of sleep, joined by his twin brother Thanatos, God of death. Hypnos condenses and spews out a nebula of his own. Morpheus, God of dreams.

Next is Nemesis, Goddess of retribution, followed by Nesoi, Goddess of the islands.

Next came Ananke, the Goddess of inevitability and compulsion, then Nyx, Goddess of the night.

Ourea was next, God of the mountains, Pontus, God of the seas.

Then, Achylis, Goddess of eternal night and the demon of death.

Aion, God of eternity came next.

Then came Tartarus, God of the underworld, then Thalassa, Goddess of the seas.

The final nebula born was Chronos, God of time.

This was now the time of the Primordia's. the first ever known God to roam to universe and beyond.

Map of the Problematique

It was a peaceful time that spanned many millennia. The nebulas travelled across the cosmos, creating new galaxies, new worlds, and new stars, in all the corners of the cosmos. Over time, though, they became bored, weary through the dullness of existence, creating things that had no sentience, no feeling, no ability to develop and evolve.

Eros decided to act. He moved quickly, sparkling, and twisted faster, spinning so fast, becoming a blur.
Eros ejected a huge amount of energy towards Ouranos and Gaia.
Ouranos collided with Gaia, his nebula, surrounding her, crushing her tight.
Gaia became smaller and smaller, the impact so immense, so tight, crushing her into solid mass, absorbing all the elements that Ouranos offered. Gaia emerged into the planet that we now know as our home, Earth. But the reactions didn't stop there.
Ouranos and Gaia collided again and again, with smaller but more compact and brighter nebulas being spat out, each one falling to Earth, with the gravitational pull of Gaia compacting them into forms of sentient beings.
Other Primordials also created their own bodies of nebulas, too.
Together, they created the Titan Gods.

Rhea, Goddess of fertility.

Oceanus, God of the oceans.

Tethys Goddess of rivers and fresh water.

Hyperion, God of light, and Theia, Goddess of aether and light.

Hyperion and Theia also collided, creating Helios, God of the sun, Eos, Goddess of dawn, and Selene, Goddess of the moon.

Next came Lapetus, God of mortal life.
From Lapetus came Atlas, God of strength, Prometheus, God of fire, and Epimetheus, God of afterthought.

Next came Crius, God of the constellations, then Coeus, God of intellect and rationality and Phoebe, Goddess of prophecy and intellect.

From Coeus and Phoebe, they created Leto, Goddess of protection and Asteria, Goddess of stars.

Themis, Goddess of divine law and order, and the first oracle.

Mnemosyne, Goddess of memory, then Metis, Goddess of wisdom.

The Primordial Tartarus created Typhon, God of monsters, Astraeus, God of the stars and planets, Perses, God of destruction and Pallas, God of WarCraft.

Finally, the last and youngest Titan was born.

He was called Cronus.

I Fear Nothing

At first the Titans were content, roaming the earth, creating the features that we know today.
The mountains and rivers, the seas, the trees. All the landscapes we know today.

Ouranos though kept them from overstepping their limits. He ruled with both cruelty and fairness, rewarding the Gods who created well and punishing those who were fuelled by jealousy and mischief.

Some Titans grew restless of this, wanting to use more of their powers. They wanted more control.
Cronus, the youngest of the Titans, spoke to his siblings, offering to lead them, to be their protectorate against the firm hand of their father.
Some Titans disagreed with Cronus, though. They were satisfied with their life. They were the ones that did not seek to destroy or spoil.

Some Titans, however, followed Cronus. They pledged to support him, with feelings of resentment towards their father and other siblings.
Cronus, with his followers on side, cried out to his father to speak to him, demanding an audience with Ouranos.

"Father, we demand that you show yourself. Why do you seek to punish us when all we do is move through the same circle of events?" Cronus asks of him.
He continues, "All we do is repeat everything over and over. Nothing changes. We build and create, but there is nothing else, nothing more."

Ouranos appeared before Cronus and spoke, "Cronus, you do not build, you do not create. You seek to spoil and damage, to destroy." Cronus hears his words but doesn't care.
Ouranus continues, "Dare not speak to me like that again, know your place."

"What place would that be, then?" replies Cronus sarcastically. "Here? on the wheel of repetition? We will no longer do what you tell us."

This remark angered Ouranos, with rage filling him.
"How dare you speak to your creator like that," thundered Ouranos. "I gave you your life, and yet you scorn this beautiful gift."
He continues his exchange with Cronus, "You shall be punished for your insolence."
Ouranos engulfed Cronus and the siblings that chose his side, crashing down on them with great thunder and lightning, changing their physical forms from what were once great beings, into creatures of the shadows and dark.
He cursed them with disfigurements, giving each one a unique feature that would make them stand out from all others, for all to know what they have done.

Ouranos declares, "I will now banish you from this place and you shall live in the darkness. No longer will you see the sunrise or sunset".
With another fierce crack of thunder and lightning, Ouranos banished them into the darkness of the earth.

Life settled down for a long time. Earth was developing as the years passed, now flourishing.
The Titans who remained loyal to Ouranos created more new life. Flowers and plants grew.
They created new beings of lesser lifeforms, such as many of the animals we know today.

Thousands of years passed by on earth. Evolution took place, and the Gods continued to create more life on the planet and sculpted the earth, moving land and sea, creating the continents known today.
Everything was wonderful. Everything was at peace.

Then, one day, Cronus appeared again.

Radius

Cronus and his followers stand in the shadows of a cave.

He cries out to Ouranos to appear. "Father, we have come here to beg you for your forgiveness". "Please hear us, please show us mercy".

Ouranos appears to Cronus from above and descends to grant him his audience. Cronus continues, "Father, we beg for your divine forgiveness. I know I have wronged you. We have wronged our brothers and sisters. We have wronged our mother, especially our father".

Cronus and the other Gods with him drop to one knee and bow their heads. "Why should I forgive your trespasses?" Ouranos replies. "We have made you this gift as a sign of our repentance," Cronus answers.

Cronus reveals a gift of stunning beauty, much like a giant diamond, that shines brilliantly in the sparse light that manages to penetrate the entrance to the cave that Cronus dwells in.
"Please accept our gift. We cannot walk into the light to give it to you. Remorse and sorrow are our deserved punishment". The gift impresses Ouranos. He's never seen such a beautiful creation before.
He walks across the ground to where Cronus is kneeling and holding out the gift. Ouranos approaches Cronus. "Please take our gift and please grant us mercy" repeats Cronus, his hand held out, keeping it in the dark as he and his followers are still unable to step into the light of the day.
Cronus places the gift on the floor, half of it in the light and half in the shadow. Ouranos walks towards the entrance to the cave. His hands reach into the shadows as he touches the gift.
Cronus and the others watch on as the gift transfixes their father. Their faces quickly change from ones of sorrow to something much different.

The Wolf

Cronus instantly grabs hold of Ouranos's hands, holding them tight. Ouranos is startled, as he looks at Cronus.
He realises that his son has tricked him. Ouranus is now frozen to the spot, unable to move, confusion etched on his face, unable to speak.
Cronus stands up slowly, his face now filled with anger, pulling his father into the cave, slowly, more and more into the shadows. Cronus sneers at him "Fool! Did you think for one moment that we would forgive you for our curses and banishment? I hate you. I hate everything about you".
Ouranos remains stunned, still unable to move or speak, wondering how Cronus could dupe him so easily.
Cronus lets go of Ouranos and steps back, as the elemental curse placed by Cronus holds Ouranos tight where he stands. From within the shadows behind Cronus, the rest of his followers appear, each one holding elemental weapons.
Taking turns, each one steps forward to strike blows into Ouranos, each strike creating a noise that emanates from his body. Ouranos uncontrollably convulses, his elements deforming and phasing out of sync.
Ouranos falls to the ground slowly, his powers being taken away. As his elements fall from his body, Cronus scoops them up to consume them, taking on the powers that his father no longer holds on to.
His siblings behind him all gather to pick up the remaining elements.
Finally, Cronus steps forward, his demeanour is that of rage. "Your time is up, old man." he sneers at his father.
Picking up the gift that had seduced Ouranos, he plunges it into the rapidly beating chest of Ouranos.
This time, Ouranos screams out in uncontrollable anguish. His body emitting light as his elements explode from him.
The elements of Ouranos momentarily hang in the air, and with a swoosh of the weapon held by Cronus, Ouranos is gone.

Aphelion

Cronus and his siblings have now declared war on the other Primordials.
The lifting of the curse assigned by Ouranos has returned Cronus and his siblings' elemental powers, prompting them to head to the skies above the Earth.
They head to the first Primordial they encounter, and in a display of sheer power and brute force, they set upon Ourea, entering the belly of his celestial body, creating thunder and lightning, his elements begin to destabilise and drift apart, unable to keep his form.

Cronus and his disciples appear from within the scattering of Ourea, with hatred etched on their faces.
The other Primordials witnessed the demise of their leader, Ouranos, angrily converge where Cronus and the others are waiting.
Cronus laughs at the chasing Nebulas, before he and his followers turn and head back down to earth.

Above the planet, the Primordial nebulas condense into beams of light and mass, before shooting down to the planet's surface, as one by one they land, like bullets hitting the floor, creating small craters where they stand, sending dust flying.

They now stand in mortal form.
The other Titans have joined to watch the stand-off, amazed, and baffled by the return of Cronus and his followers.
The Gods try to absorb what they see and hear.
Cronus breaks the silence and speaks, "I will give you all this one chance. Join me, and take me as your leader, or become my enemy".
Silence falls on the group again.

Aether screams out, angered by this comment, instantly fashioning a weapon from his elements, and charges towards Cronus and his followers.

Cronus raises his arms high, laughing at Aether. His elements swirl and gather, growing double his size.
Aether lets out a huge amount of elemental energy, firing them at Cronus, but it doesn't have a big effect on him. All it does is push him back several steps, his feet digging into the ground to prevent the push.

Aether stands there stunned, as Aether, one of the mightiest Primordials, is perplexed by what has happened.
Cronus gives off a menacing growl.
He swings his arm, now fashioned into a weapon, at Aether, instantly cutting him in half, his elements spreading and falling to the floor like a shower of tiny gemstones.
Cronus absorbs some of them, the others feasting on his scraps.

Witnessing this left the other Primordials stunned and silent.
Then all hell breaks loose.
The Primordial siblings, Achlys, Aion, Ananke, Nemesis, Nyx, Tartarus, and Thanatos, attack their other siblings.
Fighting breaks out with God vs God. Primordial vs Primordial. Titan vs Titan.

Cronus sits back, grinning. He shouts aloud for all to hear, "Look what happens when you are faced with this simple choice!".
The Titan followers of Cronus then engage in a deadly battle with their Titan siblings.

Lapetus, Atlas, Epimetheus, Typhon, Perses and Pallas set about their Titan siblings, crippling many of them as they try to defend themselves against the onslaught.
The attackers wound or capture some of them as they try to escape.
Rhea goes to Cronus and begs him to stop what he is doing.
"You are killing us all. We are supposed to be family. Please stop," she begs of him.
Cronus reflects for a moment, then shifts his attention back to the battle.

Turning to look back at her again, he responds, "Where was my family when I needed them?".
She looks at him with pleading eyes and cries and thumps on his chest with her hands.
He doesn't laugh or sneer or respond this time, but after she hits him a few more times, he grabs her arms to restrain her.

After being severely wounded, most of the Primordials and Titans who fought against Cronus have just enough energy left to escape, shooting skywards like a flash of light.
Some Titans also try to escape.
Some get away, some do not.

"What do we do now" asks Tartarus.
Cronus thinks for a moment, then replies, "Well, it looks like we need to start a new family" before turning his head slowly to look at Rhea, sneering at her.
Rhea shakes, afraid of what will follow.
Silence falls upon the Earth and the galazy after the battle is over.
Cronus, now the self-declared King, and ruler of the Titans also now commands the Primordial's that joined him.

Cronus then declares that he shall do what his father had always wanted him to do.
"He wanted me to create, so I shall create".
With that, he takes hold of Rhea, dragging her away out of view from the others.
Cronus wants to create his own lineage of Gods, and so he does, but history always has a way of repeating itself.

Sport Vibes

Rhea bore Cronus six children. The other Gods also created their own children, and their children's children, and so on, creating more life on earth.
But it was the children born of Cronus that would become the most powerful, and, by Cronus himself, the most feared.

One day, Ananke comes to Cronus and foretells him, "My Lord, I have seen a vision of your children rising, to challenge your power, to take away from you what is rightfully yours". Cronus listens to her, then thinks about what she has said, contemplating the future.

Hestia was the first child born of Cronus and Rhea, the elder sister to Hades, Demeter, Poseidon, Hera, and, of course, Zeus.

With the birth of each child, Cronus takes each one and imprisons them, ensuring that they will not grow strong enough to challenge his authority.
They may be his children, but Cronus is mindful of the words spoken by Ananke.

Rhea by now has grown weary, and decides to conceal her sixth pregnancy, and when the time is right, she disappears into the night to give birth to Zeus.
She travels to Lyctus in Crete, giving birth to the future Olympian God, before handing him over to trusted friends, and into the custody of Earth herself, Gaia.

Over time, Zeus grows up to become powerful, being guided by Gaia and the others who live on earth with him, notably offspring, bore from the Gods.
They carefully keep Zeus hidden from Cronus and the other Gods.
He learns how to control and master his powers throughout his childhood, leading into his adulthood.

Many women cared for Zeus during his upbringing.
Zeus knew he had great powers, but also that he was handsome and confident, and that he didn't exactly hold back in showing his affections to the opposite sex, either.
Over time, Zeus fathered many of his own children, but only a few would become part of the Olympic dynasty.
He fathered more Olympian Gods.

Athena, who became the Goddess of war and wisdom.

Aphrodite, the Goddess of love.

Ares the God of war.

Apollo the God of the sun.

Artemis the Goddess of the hunt.

Dionysus the God of pleasures, and Hephaestus the God of crafts.

Fuelled by his mother earth Gaia, his powers continue to grow stronger.
Each day, he would test himself in combat with his children, strengthening them along with himself.
Zeus soon became the master of the heavens and skies, employing many elements, notably, thunder and lightning being one of his most favourites.

Zeus became wise and filled with knowledge from his upbringing. He was also very clever.
Zeus also knew that one day, he was going to have to challenge his father, Cronus.
He had been growing, training, and nurturing his children, ready for the day that would surely come in the not-too-distant future.

Time is Running Out

That day arrived.
Zeus decided the time was now to pay Cronus a visit to the temple where he and the other Gods lived.
Zeus dressed himself in a long dark cloak and hood to disguise his identity.
On that day in question, people in the land were to bring gifts to Cronus to show gratitude for his mercy and to show respect to him as their King.
Many people step forward to offer their gifts.
Cronus is quite dismissive of many gifts, his arrogance, barely paying attention to what is being given to him.

When it was Zeus's turn to approach him, Zeus bows down and puts forward his hand holding six small stones.
Cronus takes one look at the gift on offer and scorns at the disguised Zeus, telling him, "How dare you give such a pitiful gift? Who do you think you are!?"
Zeus stands up straight, removing his cloak and hood and then declares before all, "I am the God of thunder, and I will have my vengeance".

Cronus at first is confused, not knowing how to respond, then he laughs at Zeus and stands up from his throne.
Behind Zeus, other people who have gathered around, remove their cloaks and hoods too, showing themselves to be the children of Zeus.
Cronus then flashes a look over at Rhea.
"You are a deceiving witch" he snarls at her, before looking back at Zeus.
Rhea smirks, her eyes fixed on Cronus the whole time, filled with contempt for him.

Cronus again stares back at Zeus.
For a moment, both Zeus and Cronus look at each other, not saying a word, the cogs in their heads turning and thinking different things. Who will make the first move?

Zeus breaks into a wry smile, noting that Cronus is wondering how on earth did he not notice it was a trick, but then again why would he? He thought he had imprisoned all his children.

Zeus's eyes begin to glow ice white, his veins running through his body turning ice white, as his body crackles with static electric around him.
The sound of buzzing emanates from his fingertips as he raises his hands up above him.
Lightning bolts fire down from the sky onto each one of his fingertips, absorbing into his body.
Then, without warning, he thrusts his hands towards Cronus, severely wounding him, sending many of his elements flying around the hall and scattering like raindrops.

Zeus didn't manage to kill Cronus, but he has inflicted enough damage to hurt him badly, with Cronus unable to retaliate properly and fight back in a way that he would want to.

The children of Zeus then set about their foes, using their talents to fight against Cronus and his followers.
They have become extremely powerful whilst they spent their time in hiding, and now they have the chance to avenge their family's birthright.

Cronus is so shocked and wounded that he struggles to fight to begin with, still trying his best to gather himself together to withstand the barrage of attacks being sent his way, desperately trying to defend the attacks.
Zeus and his offspring also inflict severe damage on the followers of Cronus, catching them off guard when they first attacked.
A huge fight ensues as both sides now attack each other ferociously, spilling onto the streets outside the temple.

The battle eventually raged on for ten whole years, known in the pages of history as the great Titanomachy, and with it finally ending with Cronus being defeated, mortally wounded by the Olympians.

His followers also suffer heavy defeats. Their arrogance blinded them into thinking that they were too powerful to be challenged. They were wrong, as each follower of Cronus is crippled into submission.

Zeus had finally got his revenge.

They drag the defeated Cronus and his followers and imprison them inside gigantic mountains and locations where they are unable enough to escape from, where they cannot regenerate or take on the elements that would feed their souls.
The dark gods received their punishment for their sins after the decade of fighting.

Zeus then freed his captive siblings and many others that stood by them.
He then goes to the highest mountain in the land and declares that the mountain shall be the home of the Gods, his throne shall live there. His family shall reside there, to look down upon all that live on earth.

He declared this mountain shall be called Olympus.

On top of Olympus, Zeus and the other Gods built a great city.
Zeus still had his own challenges to his throne though.
His son Ares, a warmonger, hungry for death.
His brother Hades, too, had grown jealous of his power and tried to overthrow and challenge Zeus for control.

Zeus won both battles, and he banished them too, encasing them into the mountains, stripping them of their powers so that they would not challenge him again, for eternal punishment.

The reign of Zeus was now unopposed.
Respected by his family, revered by the creatures of earth.

Algorithm

Prometheus. A Titan.
One of the Titans that sided with the Olympians and survived the great Titanomachy.
Zeus assigned him the monumental task of creating many new roaming species.
This included many animals: the birds, reptiles, and mammals.
However, Prometheus wasn't content, and so he created his greatest masterpiece.

Prometheus, using his own image, created the mortals, and receiving help from his fellow Gods, they assigned attributes to give them characteristics.
Love, compassion, happiness, kinship, belonging, but also fear, jealousy, envy, and rage.

For a time, everything was wonderful, but Prometheus wanted his creations, the mortals, to evolve.
Zeus had commanded that all creations be equal in their dominions.
But Prometheus was proud of his achievements.
He gave them knowledge and the ability to evolve.

He gave them the ability to create fire.
Mortals were once as vulnerable as the other creatures on the planet.
Fire changed everything.
Over time, they grew more knowledgeable, soon becoming the dominant species.
Zeus became angry though after discovering that Prometheus had helped mortals evolve.
He punished Prometheus severely for disobeying him, as it was too late to turn the clock back on their development.
The wheels were already in motion, and even Zeus saw the worth of an evolving species.
The Gods needed their worship as it fuelled them with powers; it strengthened them, plus, they mined for elements to offer to the Gods as gifts.

Mortals revered Gods for a millennium, but they eventually grew tired of them.
In times of need, their prayers went unanswered, for the simplest of things, such as a poor harvest with no food to put on their tables, unclean water to drink.
The mortals felt abandoned by the Gods.
The mortals decided to rebel and revolt against their creators.

Eventually they stopped believing in them. They stopped praying to them, they even took up arms against them.
The mortals tore the statues they had made to honour the Gods down.
Even when Zeus sent a great flood, they survived and started again.

The Gods eventually gave up on them though, deciding to leave the mortals to their own fates.
The Gods even saw conflict coming in the shape of civil wars.
Eventually the great wars broke out on earth between the Gods and the mortals, spanning many years and generations of mortals.

After the wars, the mortals eventually split up their communities up. Many wanted different things, especially now they were free from the control of the Gods. Huge numbers of communities went off in different directions across the lands to settle, creating their own languages, their own identities, and cultures.
The Gods watched on from afar on top of Olympus, saddened by the conflicts they had endured.

Then one day, the Gods vanished. No one knows exactly when. No one knows why. The wars were a great turning point in history for both Gods and mortals, especially when they had fought together against invaders from places far away, but that is for another story.

The age of the mortals had begun.

Age of Discovery

Santorini, Greece.
A huge archaeological dig is taking place in the region.
It is a hotbed of activity.
Many people are working hard in the heat and days of the sunshine, carefully digging up and discovering artefacts from the past.
There are all kinds of mobile structures that inhabit the site, such as gazebos, tents, marquees, caravans, static homes and more.

There had been much excitement when one resident of the town nearby had discovered a rare gold coin in the earth, so rare, and so old that it predated the Lydia Lion that is dated over 2700 years old.

When this newly discovered coin was carbon dated, it came back as over ten thousand years old.
This excited the scientific community.
The World Archaeological Congress sent their best operatives to the area to discover what else they could find.

On one hot day whilst working, Jason and his friends were making new discoveries.
Every day they would find more artefacts, new treasures of the past.
After a hard day's work, they settled down for the night as the sun sets over the horizon.
Inside one marquee, Jason and Hector are surveying the day's finds.

"We've had a good day today, Jason," says Hector.
Jason nodded and replied, "100% we have. It's been great to find so many new things."
Hector adds, "Just think, what history these things must have," as he picks up one find from the dig.
Jason says, "We can only imagine what life must have been like back then".

He stares at it wondering, half smiling.
Hector chuckles in appreciation of his enthusiasm.
"Therefore, we do what we do, why we are here, Hector, my friend!" Jason continues, as he stares at the object he is holding.
It is a spear, gold in colour, with two snakes that entwine near the tip.

As the sun sets and the outside temperature drops, Jason shivers a little as he looks out across the land.
The outside temperature drops even more so as the night sets in.
"Here," says Hector, "Put this on. It's getting cold outside".
He hands Jason a bright yellow fleece.
"I'm not so sure it's my thing, I'm not really a fleece wearing type of person" Jason quips.
Hector chuckles at Jason, clearly seeing that his friend is cold.

They settle down for the night, cooking a meal on the gas burner stoves along with other friends and colleagues that are with them on the dig.

Gabriella, Alex, Isaac, and Elijah turn up with a few bottles of beer and hand them out to Jason and Hector as they all sit and talk about the day's findings.
"Have you worked out what or where that spear comes from?" asks Alex.
Jason looks at her and replies, "I don't know. It looks familiar though. I feel like I have seen it somewhere before". She smiles at Jason and passes over a bowl of soup and a roll for him to eat, as do the others, enjoying the sounds coming from the town below as the locals come out to bring the area to life with music and chatter.

Adventure of a Lifetime

The next morning, Jason and his friends and colleagues continue to dig up more artefacts.
They turn out to be quite unusual, and when carbon dated, lots of them being over five thousand years old.

"Jason!" shouts Alex excitedly.
She grabs Hector's arm tightly, causing him to wince, but he shares in her excitement. "We have just found something you won't believe!"

They hurry over to the carbon dating machine in the main complex.
"Look!" she says with excitement.
"OK, what am I looking at?" asks Jason.
"Look at the carbon dating!" she replies.
"It's ancient yes but it won't show much as it's just metal," says Jason.
Alex counters, "Jason! Look again. The spear we found is not just old, it's stupidly old! The carbon dating machine is still going. So far, it's clocked fifty-five thousand years!".
"How come?" asks Jason, looking puzzled.
"It's only metal though, how come it is giving off these readings still?".
It is the spear that Jason had that they are looking at. The spear looks as new as the day it was created, yet its carbon dating has already reached the upper limit of detection.

Alex says, "This is the best part. We have found traces of DNA on it, around the grip, but that's not the weird part."
She continues "Now try to keep up on this bit!", "The DNA is 99% humanoid, which is normal, but this DNA is the part that's still clocking up the years, and, within it we have picked up several unknown elements that do not register on the periodic table… at all!".
Jason is excited and puzzled at the same time as he stares at the spear.

Alex continues "We have also tested this spear too, and that also contains several unknown elements!".
"So, what are you saying?!" asks Jason.
"Some elements on this spear don't exist!" Alex replies.
"So, exactly how old is it? How did it even get here?" Jason askes her, his face puzzled but excited at the data.
The carbon dating machine now shows a figure of over 500,000 years, and it is still counting. Carbon dating machines only go up to fifty-five thousand years but the machine they have is the most advanced version available and has a predictor function.
"Keep it going, leave the sample in the machine" says Jason excitedly to the others.

At dinner that night, they talk about the spear excitedly.
His colleagues, Nestor, and David, who are part of the expedition and working in a sector next to them, also join them.
Jason tells them, "Have you seen the data so far for the spear that we found? It is off the charts!".
David looks at him excitedly and remarks, "Almost as old as my shoes then!" which makes them all break out laughing.

Gabriella, Isaac, and Elijah come bounding over with glasses and a couple of bottles of champagne.
"Come on you lot, time to celebrate!" Gabriella tells them all. "I am sure we can afford a small tonight" as she pops open the cork on the first bottle.
They all drink to toast and celebrate the finding of the spear and the data they have collected so far, plus tucking into some of the local cuisine supplied by the on-site cooks, along with other local sweet delights.

As they sit together, Jason is deep in thought. He thinks about the spear, about where it came from, why it's so old.
He quickly breaks off from his thoughts as Hector passes him a glass of champagne.

Trouble's Coming

The next day, after they all get up and get ready for the day's work, they eagerly head to the carbon dating machine.
They look at the readings in astonishment.
It is now predicting that the spear is over a million years old… and it is still counting.
They all hug each other in excitement and rush to tell their other colleagues outside who have already started work.
Jason quickly gets his phone out to send a text to his friends and colleagues back at the World Archaeological Congress.

Jason then stares at it and says with excitement, "This is incredible. This will change the face of history".
Alex replies, "This has surely got to be the biggest discovery ever made?!".
Hector chuckles with them as they just stand and watch as the machine keeps clocking up the data.

Alex sees it as an excuse to open champagne, and why not.
Other colleagues from the expedition approach them to come and look at the spear.
Jason tells them the news as they talk to each other with joy and excitement about what is going on, but his colleague Nestor, about twenty meters away, who is working on a patch next to them, is carefully removing dirt around something that he has found.

Jason calls out to him, "Nestor, come join us" but Nestor either ignores him or doesn't hear him.

He seems transfixed on something.
Jason again urges Nestor to come and join them to celebrate, but Nestor remains fixated on the object he has found and continues to dig at it with care.
Jason looks at him with curiosity, then walks over to him to look.
His friends Hector and Alex follow Jason whilst the others continue to talk amongst themselves.

"What is it, Nestor? What have you found?" asks Jason.
"I don't know," replies Nestor, as he continues to remove dirt from the ground to reveal whatever he has seen.
After a minute of careful digging, Nestor stops and just stares.

Jason suddenly feels a strange feeling, something he hasn't felt before. He can't explain it, but it feels like a ghost has walked through him, making him shudder briefly.
Hector sees this and asks him, "Are you OK?".
Jason replies to his friend that he is, then tells him, "Did you feel that?".
Hector looks at him blanky. "Feel what?" he asks.
Jason now looks around the area that they are standing at, as if he is looking for something.
"Never mind" Jason replies after a moment.
Hector looks at him strangely but doesn't give it much thought as they both turn back to Nestor and his digging.

Nestor then says to Jason and Hector, "It looks like some kind of ancient book or tablet, but something is weird about it".
Nestor hunches over more, digging away.
Jason and Hector lean in a bit more to look closer at what Nestor has found.
It is now that they can see something bronze and rectangular in shape, but still unsure as it is still half buried.

"What's weird about it?" asks Jason.
Nestor sits up and looks up at Jason, his eyes now showing a little concern.
Jason can now see the tablet, and his eyes widen as he stares intensely at it. Again, Jason shudders and looks around again to see what is out there, again Hector looks at him. It is not cold, in fact it is very warm, and there is no wind to create a chill either.

Nestor stands up and looks at him with all seriousness as he says, "Books don't usually glow Jason".

Equinox

The tablet glows brighter as Jason and the others gather around and stand there, wondering what it is.
All of them are a little confused, just staring at it, not knowing what to think or do, but then it emits a low rumbling, pulsating bass sound.
Some people back away, understandably, feeling just a little nervous about what is happening, and ask each other why is it glowing and vibrating in the ground?
Isaac quips to Jason, "Well, this is something new!" as Jason nods at him in agreement, as they continue to watch what is happening.

The wind suddenly picks up around them.
Softly at first, then growing stronger, which they think is very odd, as it is a very calm day.
"This wasn't on the weather report?" remarks Hector.
The gusts become stronger still, blowing dust up into the air from the floor.
The winds start to rotate and form a small tornado like shape, no bigger than their own height.

Nervously, everyone backs away a few steps.
Suddenly, the tornado constricts.
Elements from the surrounding earth lift from the floor and bind, creating a shape.
Everyone watches on curiously as they continue to be fixated by the developments taking place.
Some of them put their safety glasses on to stop the dust from hitting their eyes as others shield their faces.
Jason narrows his eyes as he continues to watch on.

At first, they cannot make out what shape it looks like.
The shape then shows more, becoming familiar to them all.
It becomes humanoid in form.
The tornado then disappears, and before them, stands the figure of a woman they have never met before.

All of them just stand where they are, unable to move, unable to speak, their jaws literally dropping to the floor.
"What the hell is going on?!" Gabriella asks Elijah.
The new arrival stands before them, pausing for a moment as she looks at them all, and then she speaks.
"My name is Hemera".
Everyone just stands there, gob smacked, stunned at what they have just witnessed.
"Who speaks for you?" Hemera asks the gathered people.

Some of them look at each other, or towards the floor, anything to avoid being the one to interact through apprehension, scared even.
Jason looks at everyone else then shrugs his shoulders, then slowly steps forward. His friends look on in anticipation.
He walks then stops about two meters away from where she is standing.
A silence falls around the camp as they all watch in wonder.
Hemera looks at Jason and smiles at him.
She is dressed in what looks like traditional clothing from an ancient time, but with a modern twist.
She looks imperious in her clothing that is white with gold trim. She wears boots that look like they are made from metal, gold in colour, and on her wrists she has bracelets made of gold, her neckless too is made of gold, as they reflect the rays of the sun, almost shining and glowing in appearance.

Jason then asks her slowly, "Who are you?".
"I am Hemera, did I not just say that?" she counters softly with a wry smile.
"Yes... sorry!" replies Jason, who, by now, feels a little confused, still in shock that someone has just appeared from out of nowhere, caused by the winds that blew up only moments ago.
"What I meant to say was, how did you do that? How did you just appear like that?!".

He continues to look at her in amazement still.

Hemera replies to him "The question Jason is not how, but why".
Jason thinks about the response she gave.
He then replies, "Then why are you here? And how do you know my name?!".
Hemera says, "I have been here the whole time, and until a few moments ago, I did not need to show myself. It is important now that I do. Come with me, Jason, and I will explain."
Jason looks at her, suddenly thinking about the shudders he felt then he tells her, "I felt something moments before you arrived, was that you?".
She looks at him curiously, as if she has realised something. "Maybe that was the wind" she replies to him, as a half-smile appears on her face, as if she wanted to say that it was her, but she doesn't offer any more information.

She asks him again, "Come with me Jason, I need to talk to you about something very important". He turns to look at his friends and colleagues, then back at her, and then nods in agreement.

Jason and Hemera walk off to find a quiet place to sit as his colleagues excitedly talk amongst themselves about what they have just witnessed.
"I still don't know what the hell is going on?!" Alex says to Hector, laughing as she does so, as Gabriella, Isaac, and Elijah laugh along with her.
Hector laughs, raising his hands as if to say he doesn't have a clue either.

As Jason and Hemera walk off to talk, Hector and the others look on.
"Do you think she is friendly?" he asks them.
"I think so" replies Alex. "She doesn't seem threatening do you think?".
Meanwhile, the focus has shifted to the arrival of Hemera, and no one is looking at the tablet, which by now is starting to vibrate more, making the earth around it fall away from it.

Esoteric

Hemera and Jason find a quiet place to sit, then she tells him everything about why she appeared and how.
"The world used to be full of Gods and mortals. The Gods ruled the earth, the mortals worshiped us. Then, one day, the mortals stopped worshipping. They stopped believing in us."
"Us? are you saying that you are a God?" Jason interjects.
She smiles at him gently but with a look as if to say, please don't interrupt!
Jason takes the hint quickly, smiles at her and apologises, asking her to continue.
She smiles at him as if to suggest it's OK.

She continues, "One day, the mortals rose and fought back. They tore down our statues. They had battles against us. Gods are powerful, but we also relied upon the love and worship from them. Many Gods had children through mortals, and those mortals became powerful, enough to fight the Gods."
Jason stares at her in amazement, listening to every word.

Hemera adds, "One day, someone created the tablet you found, using something that we call Stygian Iron. It takes a God to create Stygian. Someone collected water from the river Styx to make it. The mortals then somehow created the tablet."
Jason listens as she explains the rest.
"Then they turned on the God that helped them. He bled ichor, or blood, as you call it, that spilt onto the tablet, giving it a unique power. Power beyond the mortal realms."

She pauses and looks curiously at Jason.
 "Is something wrong?" she asks him.
"Sorry!" he says, "This is huge. I am just trying to process what you are saying".
She smiles and says, "That's OK, I can imagine this must be strange for you".

Jason continues to listen to her, captivated by what she is telling him, but her charm and calmness also captivates him at the way she responds and interacts with him.

She continues, "The tablet that you have found, it is much more than you know, it is extremely powerful, even more powerful than the Gods. I appeared because I am one protectorate of the tablet."
Jason replies, "One of them?".
She nods at him to say yes.
She continues, "In the wrong hands, the tablet would be deadly to both Gods and mortals."
Jason asks her with a smile, "Then why didn't you just hide it somewhere, like in space or on the moon?".
Hemera chuckles and replies, "Gods cannot hold the tablet. It would harm us. The tablet has the power to give and take life. As Gods, we fear the tablet, but we also revere and respect it too."

Hemera continues, "The problem is, mortals cannot fully comprehend the text and language written on it, and only the Gods can read it correctly as it contains a language no longer spoken by mortals here on earth. However, mortals are the only ones who can hold it for the Gods to read it."
Jason replies, "So for it to be used, it would need both a God and mortal working together to use it properly?".
"Exactly," Hemera replies.

Jason takes the news in, then stands up slowly, chuckling and shaking his head and says, "Is this all real? Are you being serious? Are you really a God? I have so many questions!".
Hemera laughs softly and replies to him she is in fact a God, that she is very serious, and that she will answer his questions.
Jason smiles and apologies to her as she again smiles and nods in appreciation at his enthusiasm.

He tells her, "Please understand, it is not every day that I meet a God and to be told about a magical tablet!".

She laughs again, then replies, "It isn't magic. If you think about what you are like now, compared to the technology from say, three thousand years ago, you would be to your ancestors as Godlike would you not?".
Jason thinks for a moment, smiles, and agrees with her, "I guess you are correct on that point."

She continues, "God is a subjective word. We like to think that we have been around longer than most to evolve over the time. We have had a long time to learn how to use the elements."
Jason nods and considers her points.

They both stand up together, looking at each other as they do so.
A few seconds pass, both waiting for one of them to speak.
It becomes a slightly awkward but an amusing silence.
Finally, Jason breaks the silence and gently laughs, Hemera joins him by laughing too, as they both look into each other's eyes.
"I don't know why I am laughing!" Jason tells her,
"Maybe I am nervous, I don't know, but I am glad that we are here having this conversation".
"As am I," she replies, keeping her gaze fixed on him.

Jason looks down at the ground, smiling as she does the same. Perhaps a little blushing is taking place, they sense.
Jason breaks the silence again.
"So, you were going to prove you were a God!", to which Hemera chuckles.
She says, "I thought by me appearing might have been a good indicator of who I am!".
Jason chuckles and says in return, "I have seen many things in my life but that probably tops the lot!"

All That We Are

Hemera sits down on a nearby rock and motions for Jason to sit with her.
She then opens her hand up slowly.
Small glowing particles come up from it, looking like floating glitter, pieces of gold, silver, and many shades of blue.
She then lifts her hand skywards and circles it around to make the particles gently circle around, a bit like looking at a galaxy in space.
All the sparkling particles drift slowly outwards in the air.

"Once long ago the universe we know today was created. Then the stars and planets were created. Then life here on earth was created".
Jason watches on, fixated at what she is doing, as elements float and swirl around them.
"Then after a long time, the mortals were created" she continues. Jason then pauses and asks, "Mortals, as in us?".
She replies, "Correct. Mortals, along with all other created life, have a lifespan, unlike Gods, who can live forever".

Hemera skin glows as she smiles at Jason, keeping her eyes fixed on him. She has warmed to his kindness and openness.
Jason looks on in amazement, as her appearance changes subtlety.
Once more, she waves her hand in the air to produce more sparkling particles that look as if they have thrown confetti up in the air.
The particles fall to the surrounding ground, creating a dazzling shower of droplets.

Jason and Hemera stand up and look at the surrounding particles that cover the floor around them, now standing a little closer together as they feel more relaxed, looking at each other, smiling.
A few small particles have landed on Hemera's nose, so Jason slowly reaches forward to pick them up to remove them, as she chuckles at his gesture.

She too removes some from Jason's hair that have settled there, as they both continue to giggle.

The sun begins to set on the horizon.
"I must go, Jason. I will be back tomorrow at sunrise".
Jason then asks her why she must leave.
"I will tell you more tomorrow," she counters calmly.
Jason acknowledges by nodding.
He continues to smile at her then says, "I'll see you at sunrise then".
As the sun disappears behind the horizon, Hemera disassembles, her particles and elements slowly breaking away from her, gently swirling, before finally disappearing in the small breeze, as Jason watches on in amazement, but not before she flashes him a smile to say goodbye.

Hector approaches and stands next to Jason. "Where did she go?" he asks.
"I don't know," replies Jason, still looking at where she stood.
Hector looks at where she was standing, then looks at Jason.
Jason is still smiling.
Hector smiles at Jason and says, "Something tells me you're looking forward to seeing her again".
Jason looks sheepish but just smiles back, then says, "Come on, let's see the others. Besides, I could do with a stiff drink after today's events!".

As they walk towards the campfire, Hector laughs and says he needs a double of something stronger, as Jason laughs in agreement.
The others have the campfire already set up outside as they approach, with many people chatting about the day's events.

Momenta

As they all sit around a campfire talking about what they have seen, the wind picks up and swirls and picks up dust from the ground.
The wind continues turning, then forming into a small tornado like shape. "This looks familiar," quips Jason, as they all sit there waiting to see what happens next.
Sure enough, the tornado crackles and elements form into a humanoid shape, then from the settling dust, a man walks forward.

"Oh. My. God" exclaims Alex.
"Not quite yours, but a good guess all the same!" replies the man, stepping forward from where the tornado was.
He then walks towards them slowly, stops and sits down next to them as they look on in astonished again.
They stare at him, all thinking what on earth is going on.
The new arrival speaks to them again.

"My name is Erebus. I am the God of the night".
The others are stunned and just sit their open jawed.
Jason, however, after today's events, is feeling a bit bolder, speaks to him.
"Hello, my name is Jason," offering his hand forward for Erebus to shake, to which Erebus does the same as they greet each other.

Erebus sits with them and tells them a little more about himself, that he too is a God.
He then reveals that he is the twin brother of Hemera.
He goes on to tell them a brief history about himself and his fellow Gods.
"They cursed us during the great war while we were fighting. But they also gave my sister Hemera and I the significant task of protecting the tablet," Erebus tells them.
"Who is they?" Jason asks him. "The mortals" comes the reply from Erebus.

He continues, "When the sun rises, Hemera is here, and when the sun sets, I am here".
Jason sits and listens, intrigued. Then Erebus tells Jason about their past and explains how mortals perceive the creation of the universe.
Erebus also describes how the Gods formed, wandering the galaxies for millions of years.

"You and Hemera are looking pretty good for being a few million years old!".
Erebus laughs and thanks him.
As they sit there, Erebus points to the stars and the constellations and tells him about which one is which.
He then points out to Jason all the constellations that make up the zodiac and how they were all real people once, most of them Demi-Gods, their spirits and consciousnesses, kept alive in the stars.

This revelation amazes Jason, and he points to one of them saying, "So right now we are looking at Aries, and he was actually real?".
"Correct," replied Erebus, "When he and the others fought bravely for the Gods against evil forces thousands of years ago, Zeus promised to keep their conscience alive for when their time would come".
"They were not full Gods so they would not be immortal, but this was his way of rewarding them for their loyalty."
The others at the campfire just sit and listen, mesmerised by what they are hearing.

Alex then breaks the silence by piping up "Do a magic trick!".
The silence changes to laughter from them.
Erebus laughs and replies, "I am a God, not a magician! I'll leave that to your earthly jesters!", then adds "Although Dionysus is great at hosting parties!", to which they laugh.

Erebus then turns to Jason and says, "Jason, I would like to speak to you alone".

At which point they get up and they take a walk whilst the others talk amongst themselves.
Erebus then continues, "Jason, the tablet that you have found, you must find somewhere to hide it. If it fell into the wrong hands, it would be devastating. The power that it can unleash would be unthinkable". Jason replies Hemera has given him the same warning about what it can do in the wrong hands. Erebus nods in understanding and agreement.

Erebus continues, "It can give great power to those who mean well, Godly powers, immortality, resurrection and much more, but it has the power to unleash untold forces of darkness too, and therefore that it is better to protect it by burying it somewhere that no one will ever find it."
Jason asks him what he can do to help.
Erebus says, "Now that they have uncovered it from the earth, to leave it so is too dangerous. Do you have somewhere safe to put it for tonight? Tomorrow, Hemera can help you find a safer place."

Jason thinks briefly, then says, "We have a safe". Erebus smiles and comments that would be a good idea. "Only a few of us know the code, but no one knows that we will take it there," Jason finishes. "Good, let us do that. Thank you, Jason," Erebus replies.

Jason and Erebus go to where the tablet is, then Jason removes the barriers that were placed to protect it, pulling the tablet up fully from the ground, picking it up slowly, then covering it in a cloth to conceal it.

Erebus and Jason wait for the right moment to place the tablet in the complex's safe.
The only problem is, someone was listening, watching, and that someone followed them to the building and watched them put it in the safe.
With no one else around, this person took the tablet from the safe. But we will get to that part shortly.

Anticipation

Jason wakes up, having fallen asleep outside in his sleeping bag, next to the by the now flickering fire as it burns its last embers.
It is still dark outside but not for much longer.
"Did you sleep well?" asks Erebus.
Jason looks at him and says, "So I wasn't dreaming about all of this then!".
"No, it is very real," Erebus replies with a smile.
Erebus looks at the horizon and says, "The night is almost over, the sun will rise soon, and I will have to go."
Jason looks and nods at him. "My sister will join you soon," he concludes.

Jason looks down at the ground as a small smile appears on his face.
Erebus spots this and a small smirk appears on his face and then says, "I see that comment makes you quite happy!".
Jason's smile becomes broader as he gets himself up out of his sleeping bag and sits on a log to deflect the attention away from himself.

Erebus stands up, looks again at the horizon as the sun's rays hit the sky just before the top of the sun appears, then says, "You seem like a good person Jason" as he turns to look at Jason, who smiles and thanks him.

The sun breaches the horizon and in front of Jason, Erebus dismantles, his elements deforming and then gently blow away.
As the last elements of Erebus disappear, he puts his hand up as if to say goodbye.
After a few seconds, new elements begin to form next to where he was standing, and in his place where Erebus stood, Hemera appears again.

For a few moments, they don't say anything.

They stand there looking at each other, wondering who will speak first.

Finally, Hemera breaks the silence and says, "Are you OK, Jason?".
He smiles and replies, "Yes, sorry yes, I am. It's just good to see you again" as he continues to gaze at her, smiling.
Hemera now looks a little sheepish herself and looks away, smiling slightly, before looking back at him, quickly changing the subject and asks him about his night.

Jason tells her about everything from the previous night, his conversations with Erebus, and that they locked the tablet away.
She thanks him for helping and trusting them.
She smiles and tells Jason about how the world around her looks much different to when she was last here, thousands of years ago.
"In what way?" He asks her.
"Everything!" she replies. "The houses you build. The clothes you wear. You have machines that carry you to places much quicker than horses".
Jason laughs and replies, "A lot has changed since you were probably last here!"

Hemera then looks over into the distance to concentrate on two locals talking to each other in another language. She smiles and says to Jason that the two people were talking about their plans for the evening.
"You understood what they were saying?" Jason asks, looking at her, impressed that she could do so.
"Of course!" she replies, "I am Greek don't forget!"
Jason smiles then laughs and replies, "Of course!".
"I speak many languages; I have had a lot of time to learn!" she replies. Jason smiles and nods in acknowledgement.

Jason then says to her, "Would you like a tour?".
Hemera replies she would like that very much.

Start of Something Wonderful

Jason takes Hemera on a tour of the complex, showing her how the technology they use has advanced from many centuries ago and what life is like now.
He shows Hemera the equipment they use as part of their work, and explains how phones and electricity work, as this is a new thing to her.
He also highlights the various discoveries they have made over the decades and centuries as a mortal species.
His words pique her interest as she listens and watches him.

He takes her to show her the local area, the town near where the excavations and complex is, to show her how buildings have changed, showing her the inventions of cars as they drive by.
They walk down to the harbour, and he points out modern day boats and ships and how they use power to propel themselves.

He points to a plane in the sky that is flying up high overhead. He explains how we can reach space and that mortals have been to the moon and continue to explore space.
From this she tells him, "You know, there is more up there than mortals currently realise".
Jason looks at her and asks her what is out there. "Let's just say that you are not alone in the galaxy".

Jason's eyes widen and asks, "As in other beings? Aliens?!".
She laughs and tells him, "You call them aliens, but they would call you aliens!".
Jason laughs with her in agreement then ask, "So what are they like? How far away are they?!".
She replies, "The other life forms are currently too far away for mortals here to reach or contact, but the way you are evolving, It would not be too long".
Jason says, "That is just incredible. To know for sure that we are not alone".

She replies to him, "It's not just other mortals that are out there".
He looks at her with surprise and goes to ask who, but she quickly changes the subject back to what is happening on earth.

"You have come a long way in your development," she tells him.
"Tell me, do mortals live peacefully now with these wonderful things you now have?".
"Unfortunately, there is always someone, somewhere in the world, that still likes to cause trouble," he replies. She nods in agreement. "Some things never change, unfortunately," she replies.

As they leave the harbour area, Jason and Hemera then take a walk along a track that looks over the town below, walking past colourful, beautiful wildflowers and wildlife that buzz and hop around in the countryside.

They sit down next to each other to take in the views.
A family walks past by them, with two children running and playing and laughing together as they play tag with each other.
"Do you have a family?" Jason asks her. Hemera looks at him and says, "The Gods are my family". He then asks her if she has her own family, any children, anyone special in her life. She looks at him, smiles and says, "I do not, not yet anyway". With that, Jason looks down and smiles. "What about you, Jason? Do you have a family or anyone special?" she asks him in return to his question.

Jason tells her he's married to his job, as a scientist and archaeologist, that he hasn't really found the time, but that one day, he would like to. They both sit close to each other, looking out over the ocean, small smiles on their faces, as a gentle breeze blows in from the coast.

"You know we Gods are scientists too. We use the elements that surround us. They make us strong".

Jason tells her that when testing the artefacts, some elements came up as unknown on their data and enquires what they are. "Only in the realms of space will you find some that do not exist on earth," she says.

"One of them is called the quantum photon. It allows us to travel much faster than your speed of light photons. It allows us to travel to galaxies far away in a matter of minutes and seconds".

Her words leave Jason in wonder, and he listens intently to what she is saying, before he adds, "Such as other inhabited worlds?".

She laughs at his attempt to try to pry more information. They sit and talk for hours about the old and new worlds they come from, talking about history and events that have taken place.

After a long day spent together, they head back to the complex as the sun begins to set.

Jason takes her to the main building with the safe that they keep the tablet in.

Jason then says to her they need to do something about the tablet, that it needs to be taken away, put somewhere safe.

"We are out of time for today. Erebus will be back when I go," she says.

Jason then says to her with some seriousness "When we take the tablet to be buried, I will carry it as I know you cannot, but when I do, I think you should blindfold me so that even I will not know its location".

They then walk back outside to a quiet area with no one around.

The sun then sets over the horizon, and as the last rays disappear, Jason smiles and says that he looks forward to seeing her again tomorrow. Hemera smiles at him and says that she, too, is looking forward to seeing him again.

Once again, she disappears, leaving him, as Erebus then reappears in her place just a few moments later.

Rebirth

Jason greets the arrival of Erebus and takes him to the complex and to the specific building with the tablet.
He shows Erebus the other artefacts too, showing him the spear that he discovered, and others too such as a shield, pieces of clothing that look like it could have been a soldier's armour and some coins, amongst other things.

Erebus tells Jason what each item is.
He explains that the spear, in fact, belongs to the famous Olympic God Hermes.
The shield belongs to Athena, known as the Aegean shield.
It amazed Jason to hear this and then asks Erebus if that they all actually existed and are not just myths.
"Of course!" says Erebus, surprised that Jason has asked this.

Jason tells him, "In my world today you were all just myths, tales of legends told thousands of years ago".
Erebus tells him that many wars over the centuries and millennia have led to this current situation regarding their existence.
Erebus goes on to tell him that only Hermes can wield the power of the spear, and Athena the power of the shield, otherwise to anyone else, they are just relics of the past.

Erebus changes the subject back to the tablet and says, "Have you thought about where we can take the tablet to?"
Jason replies, "I told Hemera earlier that someone must blindfold me when we do. We need to find a place to hide the tablet where mortals won't be able to find it."

He tells Jason that he is a worthy man, appreciating what he is doing.
Erebus then asks Jason to walk with him, to show him the life that the mortals lead today.
Even though Erebus and Hemera cannot be present together, he knows that Jason showed Hemera the sites of the area earlier.

Jason tells him that, of course, he will, so they head off to the local town so that he can show Erebus what life is like today.
Jason takes Erebus to a local café and orders a couple of beers, one each.
Erebus takes a sip and remarks, "It tastes better than what you mortals used to brew!".
Jason chuckles and asks for two more, as they informally talk.

They discuss the modern world while locals, tourists, and residents of the complex gather in the town centre.
People drink, eat, talk, and socialise, as laughter fills the night air.

Erebus asks Jason what is that he has in his wrist. Jason chuckles and says it is his watch.
"That is quite a piece of engineering" he tells Jason.
Jason takes the watch off his wrist to show Erebus in closer detail and how it works.
Erebus suddenly tells Jason to stop moving his arm, then he takes hold of it, looking at the underside of his arm and looks closely at his veins.
"Er, everything OK?" Jason asks him, not quite sure what he is doing.
"Sorry Jason, yes. I thought I saw something, but it was my imagination" he replies.
"What did you see? Come on, you can tell me. Are they too hairy" Jason jokes.
Erebus replies, "For a moment I thought I saw that your blood within your veins was a different colour".
Jason jokingly replies, "No, just the usual red!"
Erebus though looks for a moment longer, then releases his arm and smiles. "You're right, I think it must be the beer!" he quips.

Jason and Erebus continue to talk and tell jokes to each other as the town has now come alive with people, as music plays in the local bars nearby and the moon shines its full glow down on the town.

Under Lock and Key

Back at the complex, the wind briefly picks up as dust gets blown around in a small circular space, and a female voice whispers something inaudible that is not loud enough to be heard.
No one hears the voice, as people in the complex have a radio with them, playing music, as they sit and talk to each other around the campfire.

But someone heard it, and it has made them take notice.
This person sits up straight, aware that he heard something, not knowing what it was or where it came from. Slowly he stands up, checking that the others are not watching him, leaving his colleagues to continue their conversations, unaware that he has has left their area to follow the sounds of the whispering.

It is too dark to identify the person.
Even though the moon shines bright, the shadow cast from the buildings and terrain has helped to disguise him.
He then heads towards the main building, slowly looking around, then opening the door, entering the complex, then heading to the room where the safe is.
The figure looks around, checking to make sure that he is not being watched, then approaches the safe.
The figure crouches down carefully and inputs the code to unlock the safe before pulling the door open.

His hand reaches in and carefully removes the wrapped-up tablet.
Content that it is still is the tablet, the figure puts the tablet in to a bag, shuts the safe door and walks out of the building, pushing the door open slowly and quietly to avoid attracting any unwanted attention.
As he exits the building, he looks around to make sure no one was watching him.
He turns walks away and out of the shadows.
Into the faint beams of light coming from overhead lights,

it is revealed to be Nestor, Jason's colleague.
Nestor walks across the complex but taking detours to not walk in areas occupied by his colleagues.
He suddenly hears a noise and ducks down behind some crates of equipment and supplies that are stacked up.
Elijah and a female colleague come out from a building giggling and laughing, arms draped over each other as they walk out to the campfire area to mingle with the others outside by the fire and music.
Once they have left his eyesight he gets back up slowly, checking his surroundings, before walking away slowly.

"Nestor!" Alex calls out.
It startles Nestor when Alex calls out to him, so he quickly grips the tablet tight in both hands as he turns his head around to make eye contact and to speak to her.
"Are you OK?" she asks him.
He thinks for a moment, looking for an excuse to use, then replies, "Hi Alex, I'm fine thanks. I've had a little too much to drink. I needed some fresh air and a quick walk to go to the toilet".
Alex chuckles and says, "The toilets are that way!", but he quickly replies that he quite fancies a fresh air version.
She laughs and says, "We've all been there!" then reminds him to not fall over in the dark.
He laughs along with her, but only to get rid of her quickly so that he can continue.
She leaves him to it as he then walks off into the dark, following the voice that he can hear.
He doesn't know where he is walking to. He is caught in a bit of a daze as to what he is doing and why he is doing it.

He finds himself walking around the perimeter of the complex to a quiet location on its grounds, away from everyone else and where no one would be at that time of night.

Mad Visions

Nestor takes the tablet to the part of the complex grounds where he is alone, outside, and away from people who may interrupt him.
He takes the tablet out of its wrapping and stares at it.
He seems to be very curious and anxious as he opens it up, looking at the text on the pages within it.

Suddenly, a ghostly whisper talks to him.
It is the female voice again, calling his name, giving him a set of instructions to follow.
It compels him to do so, not sure why he is following the instructions, but the influence is strong.
Nestor goes to a specific page in the tablet and reads the text, reading what the voice whispering is telling him to do.
Once he has finished reading the text, a breeze picks up, then elements start to swirl to form a human shape, as Nestor stands and watches.
Before him stands a beautiful, intoxicating woman.

She has long, black hair with red lips and dark eyes. Her body dressed in ancient clothing. He glares at her body, moving up from her legs to her chest and up to her face again.
His facial expression suggests that he finds her extremely attractive.

She speaks in a sultry tone to him, "Hello Nestor, my name is Nemesis. I have been watching you, waiting to meet you" as she moves over to where he is.
Nestor stays frozen to the spot but his mouth slightly open, just gazing at her and transfixed at her beauty.
She continues, "You look like someone who deserves more than what you are doing with these people. They do not appreciate you. I know what you are worth, Nestor. Would you like me to show you?".

Nestor ponders her comments, now caught up in her spell, then replies, "I deserve more. They all seem to hold Jason up on a pedestal. I deserve more!".
Nemesis replies to him, "That you do, Nestor. Let me show you, I can show you what true power feels like... and, let me show you what genuine pleasure feels like too".
With that, Nemesis slowly embraces Nestor, her elements phasing slightly, moving into Nestor.

He takes in a small gasp of air and then a grin covers his face, experiencing the power and intimacy that Nemesis has made him feel.
After a few seconds, she moves away, facing him the whole time.
"How was it for you?" she smirks.
Nestor doesn't move, but then gathers himself and declares, "I want more!".

Suddenly there is a noise from behind them, as David, one of his colleagues, appears.
"Nestor! What are you doing out here? Who is she? What are you doing with the tablet?". Nestor tries to mumble some excuse, but David is having none of it. He grabs hold of the tablet from Nestor and steps backwards, whilst facing Nestor.
"I'm not sure what you're doing with this, but it doesn't look right to me. I think Jason needs to know about this," David says.
He turns around slowly to walk away, whilst Nestor stands there, not quite knowing what to do, confused.

"Stop him!" Nemesis calls out to Nestor. "If you don't stop him, you cannot get those feelings back!". Nestor looks at her, then turns to David and immediately chases after him. David turns to see Nestor in pursuit, and he runs, but Nestor quickly catches up with him, pushing David to the floor.
Nemesis tells Nestor "Take it back, take back what is yours!".
Nestor wrestles the tablet back from David, but David grips it.
"Stop him, Nestor!" Nemesis says again.

"Nestor! get off me. What has come over you?!" David shouts at him, but Nestor ignores his comments as he continues to try to wrestle the tablet back.

From the floor, Nestor then picks up a blunt rock and hits David on the head.
David stops struggling, now motionless on the floor, as Nestor holds the tablet in his hands.
At first, Nestor looks at David then says to himself, "What have I done?" as he looks down at the lifeless David, as a small pool of blood beneath his head begins to pool.
Nemesis quickly moves over to Nestor and phases her elements into him. He feels her power and suddenly forgets about David, as he is now filled with power and pleasure again.

As he looks upwards to the sky, the whites of his eyes turn black, his expression turns to a grin, then slowly, he stands back up whilst holding the tablet.
Nemesis then turns to him and says "Now, let me fill you with real power and pleasure beyond what you have ever felt before", before moving to embrace Nestor in a clinch, then moving her hands over his body, kissing his neck, and then moving to his chest.
She then pulls one strap down from her clothing to reveal some of her naked flesh.

Nestor then steps back, now immersed in her charm, removing her garments as she stands there naked.
She has fully captivated Nestor, as he stares at her naked body, his hands twitching, aching to stroke her flesh. She looks at him with a seductive grin as she puts her hand out to beckon him over to take her.
He steps forward to embrace her again.
As they do so, she takes hold of Nestor's hand and places it in David's blood.
Moving it back up, she puts his hand on the tablet.
As they continue in the throes of passion, the tablet starts to glow and vibrate, as the text turns from gold to black.

These Moments

The next morning, Jason wakes up in his bed, nursing a slightly sore head from the night before, having been out on the town with Erebus.
He reaches to take a sip of water to quench his thirst.
Looking out of the window, he realises the sun has now come up.
He suddenly sits up straight, gets dressed quickly, and runs outside to see if he can find Hemera.

He looks around, but he sees no sign of her.
He walks around the camp looking, but all he sees is the staff and colleagues prepping themselves for the day's work or at those that have already started.
Hector sees him and comes over and says, "Everything alright Jason?".
His eyes scan the compound as he replies, "Yes, yes, all good".
Hector can see that Jason is looking around the area and smiles before adding, "Looking for anyone in particular, are we?".
Jason chuckles and flashes him a smile before continuing to walk around looking still.

After a couple of minutes, he stops, as he looks down at the ground with disappointment, then nudges a few small stones on the ground with his feet and turns back around to walk back to the building.

"Did you miss me?" asks Hemera, head slightly tilted to one side and smiling.
Jason suddenly looks up and stops what he is doing and smiles back.
"Hi! I didn't think you were coming back," he says.
"And miss all this?" she says with a smile.
They stand there, looking at each other, wondering who will speak next.

A recurring theme for them both over the last couple of days it seems, but only because they feel an attraction towards each other, something that they realise but have not spoken about.

Gabriella comes over to ask Jason a question.
She greets Hemera, who greets her back, before then realising that they might want to be alone, as Jason and Hemera look at her as if to say they would like to be alone.
"Sorry!" she says, taking the hint, as she backtracks and walks off, giving them both a little wink.

After a few seconds, as they stand there looking at each other, just smiling, Hemera clears her throat and finally breaks the silence by asking him, "How was your night?".
Jason chuckles and says, "I think your brother enjoyed it more than me!", to which Hemera laughs.
"He is quite fond of sampling the local refreshments on offer" she says, as Jason chuckles and replies that he does indeed.

Hemera then shifts the conversation back to the tablet and tells Jason that they need to retrieve it, as she has found a good location that they can take it to.

"Will you still help me?" she asks him.
Jason replies, "Yes, of course. Tell me what I need to do".
She smiles and thanks him.
They walk back to the complex as she tells him of what they need to do as he nods along.

"I have found a place that no one will be able to access. No one will ever know to look for it there".
Jason replies with, "Sounds good to me, let's do it".

As they walk side by side, their hands accidentally brush. A small particle lights up on her hand. Jason notices this and looks at her hand for a moment. Hemera blushes but she doesn't try to conceal it from him, as he smiles at her as they continue their walk.

Dark Magic

"Jason!" shouts Hector, with urgency in his voice.
Hector and Alex run quickly over to him with expressions on their faces that suggest that not all is well.
They arrive to greet Jason and Hemera quickly, catching their breath as they do so, before being able to speak to tell them some startling news.
"Jason, we've got some bad news," Alex tells him.
"Last night, David and Nestor went missing. They didn't check in this morning. And when we searched the site and…" as she pauses, not wanting to say the rest.
Hector finishes for her, bluntly declaring, "David is dead."
Hector walks them to the area where David's lifeless body rests, covered by a sheet. Jason lifts the sheet gently to see his friend lying there lifeless in a pool of dried blood. "We found him about ten minutes ago,"
Hector tells him, while staff members who had gathered around talk amongst themselves at the discovery of the unfortunate David.

The local police are present, having arrived earlier, with the area cordoned off. Barrier tape is up to protect the integrity of the crime scene. They head to the edge of the tape and stand by the barrier to look over.
Jason turns around to look at Hemera. He is visibly upset at losing his friend, and so unexpectantly too. Hemera looks at him, not knowing what to say, as her face fills with sadness for him.

Alex beckons them away from the area, to stand a few meters back from the crowd of people that have gathered. "There's something else too," continues Alex. "Nestor. He is nowhere to be seen, and when we checked the buildings to look for him, we saw the safe was unlocked, and empty."
Jason's eyes suddenly widen with a very concerned look on his face. "What do you mean? Are you saying you think he killed David and took the tablet?".

Hemera's expression is now one of concern. Hector says them, "Apart from poor David, the only person missing is Nestor. With the tablet gone at the same time... coincidence? ".

Jason and Hemera look at each other, knowing that this is not good news at all. "How the hell did he know?" Jason says rhetorically. "Erebus and I were so careful when we took it to hide it".

Hemera steps forward to Jason and says, "The tablet, Jason, we must get it back. If it falls into the wrong hands, who knows what will happen? We must get it back as soon as possible." He nods at her and asks her what they can do to help.

Hemera opens her mouth to speak again, but suddenly stops, before stepping back a little. Her eyes look out into the distance, as if she is looking across the horizon.
Her face now looking horrified, her eyes flicker slightly, as if she is having a vision, then a strange wave pulse shudders through her body.
She manages to speak, "Oh no", suggesting that she has seen or felt something terrible.

They look at her, then at each other, wondering what it wrong. Finally, Jason takes hold of her hands to comfort her.
She looks down at her hands being held by his and her shoulders drop, relaxing a little. A small smile appears on her face as she looks up at him. "Are you OK?" Jason asks her. "I am now" comes her reply.
Alex gives Hector a small nudge with her elbow into his ribs as she smiles. Hector coughs and gives Alex a pained look.

Hemera and Jason quickly let go of each other's hands and look back at Alex and Hector. Hemera looks at all three of them and declares to Jason, "We need to get help". Jason replies, "From whom?". Hemera looks at them, then back at Jason and says, "From the other Gods".

Bring Me to Life

Meanwhile, overnight, Nemesis and Nestor have made their way to Kameno volcano on the mainland of Greece.
They made their way to the island airport by stealing a car from the complex that Nestor took.
At the airport, with the help and persuasive powers of Nemesis on two security guards who were guarding a small access gate near the runway, they stole a small two-seater plane in one of the quiet hangars.
To gain access, Nestor, now fully under the control and influence of Nemesis, killed the mechanic who was working on the plane.
The mechanic tried to challenge them, but he was no match for the twisted duo.

As they summated the slope of the volcano, it was clear to see that the surrounding area was lifeless.
None of the towns or villages seemed inhabited. Wildlife was nowhere to be seen, no birds in the sky.
The area stank of sulphur as the wind blew, giving it an eerie chill about the place.

At the summit, with Nemesis looking on behind him and with a twisted grin on her face, Nestor pulled out the tablet from a bag he was carrying to conceal it.
He turns to the pages that she instructed him to.
He begins to read the text.
Once he had finished reading, the text turns from its gold colouring to a charcoal black, as the tablet vibrates, making a low humming sound, before suddenly stopping after a few seconds or so.

For a moment, Nemesis and Nestor look on, waiting for something to happen.
Looking puzzled, they turn around to walk back down the edge of the volcano, wondering if they had done it right, but as they do, the volcano rumbles.
Rocks start to fall down the slopes.

Nemesis and Nestor go from a walk to a run, going as fast as they can down the slope, to avoid the falling debris.
As they reached the bottom at a safe distance, they turn and watch the top of the volcano explode in a shower of sparks, lava, and rocks.
Lightning hits the funnel of the volcano as hot smoke comes pouring out.
Small lava flows soon follow, streaming down the sides, and then, without warning, the volcano collapses in on itself, as if the ground was swallowing it up.
Huge amounts of smoke fill the air from where the volcano had been standing.
A strong wind comes in and blows the smoke away within a matter of seconds.
Then, in the last embers of falling ash, out steps a colossal figure of a man.
Disfigured, with black eyes and with a look of evil in them stares back at them.

Nemesis drops to her knees and bows her body to the ground and declares her undying devotion and service to the person standing before her.
Nestor sees Nemesis and then copies her, realising that he must be in the presence of someone powerful, and then he turns to Nemesis and whispers, "Who is it?".
Before she can answer, the huge being bends downs so his head is almost next to theirs, then his voice booms back at him "Cronus!".

Embers

Cronus orders them to stand up. Cronus sees the tablet and says in a calm but menacingly, "The tablet!" looking at Nestor, then he orders him "You, read again, read the tablet again". Nestor obeys and nervously opens it up to the page he was at and hurriedly reads it again as Cronus stands over him.
Nestor reads the words again, the ground rumbles and shakes, followed by a massive sinkhole that appears near where they stand, almost engulfing them, as they quickly step back several paces to avoid falling in.

As the rumbling around the sinkhole settles down, the clouds above crackle with lightning, and then a huge fork of lightning hits the hole.
Steam rises from the hole, as a stench fills the air, and then the steam moves out of the hole and onto land, where it twists into a small tornado.
Elements from the ground pick up and get caught in its vortex. Then, as the steam settles, a figure appears from it.
"My boy," Cronus says to the figure.
The figure, now visible, flashes a sinister smile and replies to Cronus, "Hello father, it's been a long time".

"Who is that?" whispers Nestor to Nemesis. Before she can reply to Cronus interrupts and says to Nestor, "This is Hades". Nemesis and Nestor quickly drop to their knees to worship him.
"Stand up" commands Cronus, chuckling at them. "We do not have time for playing God worship".
They do as he commands, then Cronus says, "You will go back to Kolumbo. Go, now, your work here is done. Bring them back".
Nemesis and Nestor get back up and start to walk back to the plane that they arrived in.

Cronus suddenly waves his hand, lifting an enormous boulder from the ground and uses his elements to hurl it at the plane, destroying it.

Nemesis and Nestor turn and look at Cronus, as if to ask why he did that. Cronus beckons them over, then places his hands, one on each head.

Elements leave Cronus and filter into Nemesis and Nestor. Once the transference is complete, they both open their black eyes, with snarling grins on their faces.
"Now go!" Cronus commands. "You will free all my disciples. I have much to do".

For a moment Nestor's body shudders at the power given to him by Cronus, his body adjusting to the changes taking place.
Once his body settles down again, he looks at Nemesis with evil etched in his eyes as she too looks back at him, grinning menacingly.
"Are you ready for the ride of your life?" she asks him.
"I thought I already had" he replies, smirking, as she bursts out into a fit of laughter.

They look up to the sky, both faces contorted with evil thoughts, then with a small crouch they leap skywards, launching themselves up into the air, reaching the clouds in a matter of seconds before changing direction and heading back to Santorini.

Dark Room Yoga

"We are going to need their help," exclaims Hemera. "I want to help. What can I do?" replies Jason.
Hemera pauses for a moment and looks at him and his colleagues then says, "We must go to Olympus, only there will we find the help we need".
Jason looks at her and nods and says, "I will do whatever I can".
Hemera says that they must find the tablet too. Jason reminds her that they can only be in one place at a time.

As they think of what to do first, Jason's colleagues Hector and Alex announce they will track the tablet.
"We have our trackers that we use for detecting metallic elements. Could that work? If we reconfigure them to follow one specific element?".
Jason replies that he thinks it will do so.

Hector radios a colleague to bring the device to them. Alex adds that if they can have a tiny sample of an element that the tablet contains, then they will track it.
Hemera opens her hand and plucks the tiniest grain from it.
Elijah comes running over to them, holding the tracking device. "Thank you, Elijah," says Alex.
She then turns it on and places the tiny grain into the device and switches it on.
It begins to emit a beeping sound.
They turn it around and it beeps quicker this time.

"OK, this is the plan," says Hector. "Jason, You and Hemera go to Olympus and climb that thing! We will go after the tablet", "I'm coming too" exclaims Elijah, "strength in numbers".
Alex and Hector are unsure at first but then relent, allowing their junior colleague to join them.
Hemera thanks them for agreeing to help and wishes them a safe journey.

"Keep your phone and radio with you so we can contact you when we have success," says Hector.
Jason and his friends share a group hug and wish each other good luck.

Hector, Alex, and Elijah head over to the helipad in the compound and ask the pilot to take them so that they can follow the signal.
Gabriella runs over to join them. "I'm coming too, and you're not stopping me!".
They look at each other and just shrug their shoulders as if to suggest that they won't try to stop her.
Once all four of them are on board the helicopter, the pilot takes off, taking them towards the source of the signal.
All four friends look out of the helicopter and down to the ground at Jason and Hemera, their hands pressed against the window to suggest a good luck signal to them.

"Maybe we should have done that first, use the helicopter!" remarks Jason,
"We have a sea to cross, and we still have to reach Olympus by land!".
Hemera looks at him and says, "I know a way that's quicker, but first, collect the spear and bring it with you."
They head to the main building and Jason picks up the spear.
"OK, what now?" asks Jason.

"I can do this only once today, then I will need to rest. What I am about to do will take up a lot of energy," says Hemera.
Jason nods his head to understand, not quite sure what she means but agrees anyway.
"Let's find some space outside," she finishes.

They walk outside into the compound to find a clear space.
Hemera then holds on to Jason.
By now some of his colleagues have started to gather around, wondering what is going on. He looks at them and calls out to one of his senior colleagues.

"Zak, whilst I am gone you are in charge of the site".
His colleague looks back at him and acknowledges Jason.
"Don't worry Jason, she is in safe hands" Zak replies.
Hemera quickly quips, "Is he talking about the site or me?"
Jason looks at her and grins, then replies, "Both!". This makes Hemera smile as she takes hold of him to prepare for the transformation process.

Jason looks into her eyes as she looks back at him. "Do you trust me?" she asks him.
"With my life," he replies with a small smile appearing on his face as he looks at her.
Jason takes hold of the spear tightly and straps it to his back securely.

Her elements break away slowly and carefully, bit by bit, until they rotate like a vortex spinning on its axis.
Jason's other colleagues look on in astonishment at what they are seeing.

Jason's body starts to break away as elements deform, bit by bit.
He flashes her a look of slight concern, but she continues to look him in the eyes and smiling.
He relaxes and continues to focus on her.
Then, in a whirl of wind, their elements are swept up in a gust of wind, up into the sky and then shoot across the whispery clouds, creating a streak of ultraviolet colours behind them.

From the Deep

Nemesis and Nestor arrive back at Santorini, and head straight to the site where the islands of the underwater Kolumbo volcano are situated.
As they approach the top of its location, they slow down and levitate just above the waterline.
Gentle swells from the ocean just meters below their feet make their way towards the shoreline.

As Nestor reaches for the tablet from his bag, he glances across the water, in the distance at the land and harbour, near where the expeditionary dig is located.
With a sneer, he turns to Nemesis and declares that they will soon fall.
"I want to destroy them," he snarls, as he looks across the water at the complex in the distance.
"Patience!" she tells him slyly.
"All in good time. First, we need to bring back them back".

Nestor scoffs at the land once again and then turns the pages to the chosen text.
He reads them as a look of excitement creeps up over Nemesis's face.
After completing the reading of the words, he quickly puts the tablet back into his bag and they wait for a few moments.
Soon enough, the gentle swells become larger.

Below them they can see that the water is turning bright red with hints of orange, then bubbles of lava start to rise and burst on the surface.
They both continue to hover above the water and move slightly higher, allowing for the waves that are building in height.
Soon enough, they can hear the crackle of lightning above them.

They move away from the epicentre of the lava that is now spewing to the surface, making the wave fizz and bubble from the shear heat it is generating.
Nestor and Nemesis watch on as the surrounding climate darkens.
By now the waves that were swelling up and heading towards land have now turned as they crash into each other, before finally, they circle into the shape of a vortex, swirling and sinking further down into the ocean.

Finally, it spews the stench of sulphur and hot ash from its centre, sending up jets of hot air.
Then, a sinister figure arises from its belly.
The figure's stature is tall, with piercing, glowing eyes and a mixture of beastly parts that have mutated together instead of being humanoid.
The figure has horn looking protrusions on its head.

By now Nemesis and Nestor have moved much further back, staring on in gleeful wonder of who has appeared.
As the smoke lifts, the figure becomes clearer.
They have just set free one of the most feared Gods ever to have existed.
The God who commands the underworld.
Tartarus.

Tartarus looks at them both, thinking for a moment of where he is. He looks around to study the area and can see that he is now in a different time, as he notices modern day boats and the coastline with its buildings and cars.
He growls at a boat that has dared to venture near, what can only be curious day trippers.
He quickly puts his hands together and then pulls them apart slowly to reveal a ball of energy, then, in a fit of rage, he flings it at the boat, instantly destroying it, killing all those on board.
Nestor and Nemesis laugh wickedly whilst watching the burning vessel and its dead inhabitants now floating in the sea.

Leap of Faith

Mount Olympus.
It is calm with no obvious signs of life surrounding the primary base, just the immense mountain itself with its neighbouring other mountain peaks nearby.
Surrounding the base there are white walled buildings, with a small plaza, perhaps once a meeting place for those that dwelled there, perhaps once homes to people who used to worship the Gods.

Long tall trees fill the hard packed undulating landscape, especially in the valley section near the homes.
The ground comprises many areas of sparse dry grass patches, with many rocks and boulders ubiquitously filling the vast rolling countryside.

The environment changes quickly as a strong wind approaches from above.
A haze of elements drift to the ground and swirls, picking up other elements around them.
They bond together to create two humanoid forms.
Jason and Hemera finally take shape as they reappear after making the journey from Santorini.

Jason fully forms first and stands up.
Once he has done so, he looks over at himself, still not quite believing what has just happened.
He is happy to be back to feeling his normal self again.
Jason checks himself, using his hands to make sure everything is where it should be, then sighs with relief, then calls out to Hemera, "That was amazing!".
As he looks up, he sees her lying on the floor, looking totally exhausted.
He suddenly becomes concerned and rushes over to her to check her.
"Hemera! Are you OK?".
She slowly turns her head up to him as he takes hold of her to comfort her.

She smiles gently and speaks. "Jason, I have used up most of my energy. I must rest now. If I don't, I may struggle to reform".

Jason looks concerned but replies to her, "Get some rest. I will wait with you until you are better".

She replies to him, "No, you must go, you must climb, it cannot wait".

Jason struggles with his emotions, visibly upset at seeing Hemera in pain.

"I can't do this without you" he tells her tearily.

Hemera's body starts to de-phase, her elements slowly breaking away as she looks at him, affectionately into his eyes.

She takes hold of Jason's hand to reassure him, as she continues to fade slowly but keeps her eyes fixed on Jasons.

Jason's eyes begin to moisten as he holds her in his arms, then says "I will make the climb, I will get to the top, I promise you" he vows. "Then I am coming back for you. I need you," he whispers to her.

"Why?" she whispers with a knowing smile.

Jason replies, "Because, because I do, because I...", and before he can finish his sentence, she raises her hand to Jason's face to stroke his cheek. "I know," she whispers, "I do too".

As she does so, her elements finally break, as they float gently away in a small breeze, and then she is gone.

All Jason can do is watch on helplessly, on his knees, holding the dust from where she just was.

Something Human

Jason looks at the ground where Hemera was. He stays motionless, thinking about her. All he can do is think if she was still alive or if she had gone forever.
After a few moments, he puts his hand back to the ground to clutch at where she was, then he lifts his head up, slowly stands up and then turns to face the mountain before him.

He takes a deep breath, taking on board the enormity of what he must do, but most of all, where he might end up.
He stares up at the immense mountain, pondering what track or direction he must choose.
Jason then walks forward, hoping that the way he has chosen is going to be the right one, acting on instinct rather than any knowledge or facts given to him, as he has none to use.
As he scans the area with his eyes, he spots a way that looks like a good option for him to follow.

The climate at ground level is calm, with few clouds in the sky and the temperature in the mid-twenties, but as he continues to walk and climb, he can see that the weather higher up is not so accommodating for him.
Above, he can see the clouds and mists that seems to cover the top of the mountain.

Jason is fully aware from many of his previous expeditions that the weather can change instantly and is glad that he has prepared by bringing along suitable clothing and some supplies that he hopes will be enough to reach the end goal, the top of Olympus.

After what must feel like several hours of walking and scrambling, Jason checks his watch, seeing how long until the sun will set, to see how long he has been going for.
He also checks to see if there is somewhere suitable to find shelter. He knows he will not reach the summit tonight. In fact, he is apprehensive that he may not reach the summit at all.

He stops to eat some snacks to refuel and drinks from his water bottle. As he looks out from the mountain edge, he spots a small flock of birds circling together.
He thinks about his friends who have gone in search of the tablet.
He thinks about the last couple of days and how everything has been a bit of a whirlwind, but most of all, he thinks about Hemera.
Once he has rested for a few minutes, Jason packs his things away, checks his watch and continues his journey upwards. The further he climbs, the more he can feel the climate changing.

The wind suddenly picks up, the temperature drops quickly, so he stops to put on his jacket, but as soon as does, the wind disappears as quickly as it came, as if the mountain is alive, toying with him, challenging him with each step he takes.
He remains positive though by focusing on his pathway, constantly checking his directions, making sure that he can spot the safest route up, and keeps moving on.

He sees a small branch on a ledge near him and he stops to watch as a raven lands on it.
He watches the bird closely, wondering what it is doing, curiously, not much, as the bird is looking back at him.
It's almost as if the bird has paid him a visit, to see who he is, what he is doing.
The raven barely moves, doing nothing else other than looking at him.
Jason takes his bag off his back and pulls out a small piece of food from it.
He holds it in his hand and offers it to the bird.
After a few seconds, the bird hops along the ledge, over to where Jason is and takes the small piece of food that he has offered it, taking the offering from him quickly before taking off into the air.
Jason watches this curiously, with a small smile on his face, hoping that he has done something good, and, just as much for him, a pleasant distraction to keep him mentally focused.

Millennia

Meanwhile, at Mount Penteli, Cronus has made his way to the Davelis Cave.
Cronus enters the cave, walking past the derelict church that stands at its entrance.
As he enters the cave deeper, as the light from the outside fades, fire torches light the way.
He looks at them curiously and smirks at himself.

When he reaches the belly of the cave, he finds mortals in red robes, worshipping an idol on a stone altar.
All of them are on their knees, bowing forward in a satanic style prayer, chanting an older version of the Greek language.
As he steps closer, he observes pictures carved on the walls on either side.
He also notices that the idol on the altar is a representation of him.
Again, he smirks at what he is witnessing as he silently reaches the back of the congregation.

For a moment, he stands behind them as they are facing the other way, unaware of his presence.
Someone at the front of the congregation stands up to offer the idol a gift of a live goat, about to be sacrificed no doubt.
This person, assumed to be the leader for the congregation, then speaks loudly more words as part of the ritual.
The leader then speaks to the idol, stating "Dark lord of all that you rule, we offer you this gift of sacrifice" as he picks up a knife to kill the helpless animal.

Cronus cracks half a smile, his face clearly displaying amusement at what he is seeing.
He steps forward and makes his way through the congregation.
They stand up in awe and surprise at what they see.
Could this be their God in the flesh they wonder? Is it an imitation? Then, as they realise that they truly are in his presence, they all begin chanting louder.

The leader at the front offering the gift of sacrifice turns and, with a look of surprise on his face, says, "My Lord! You have returned to us."
Cronus approaches him slowly, and says menacingly, "Why worship a piece of metal when you can worship the real thing?"
The leader replies, "We have prayed every day since our creation for your return. We offer you this sacrifice, hoping this day would come for you to lead us again."

Cronus looks at the goat on the altar and says, "A sacrificed animal is worth nothing to me. If I wanted something to be sacrificed, then I will need something much bigger than a goat!".
With that, Cronus turns to the leader and grabs him by the head, lifting him up off the floor and slowly begins to squeeze tightly.

"Real worship deserves genuine sacrifice!" he says, as he continues to squeeze the leaders head more so, until it finally disappears withing his huge hand.
The room echoes with the sound of crunching bones.
He tightens his grip on the person's head even more until it is squashed into mulch within his huge hand, saying, "My name deserves genuine sacrifice!" as the blood of the leader oozes down from the bottom of his hands.

The lifeless body hangs from the hand of Cronus, who then turns and flings the dead body across the floor to the side of the cave.
Cronus then swipes the metallic idol away from the altar.
He turns to the congregation and speaks, "My followers, our time has come, and you will do my bidding", at which point they drop to their knees again in worship. Their chanting becoming louder as their faces fill with delirium. Their cheering becomes intense for the return of their depraved God that they seek to follow.

Try Again Tomorrow

Jason is now feeling the effects of his journey as the sun starts its descent from the sky towards the horizon, but still, he struggles on.
Each step becomes more difficult than the last, as he feels tiredness setting in on his body.
The distance he has travelled so far, so high up, is starting to affect his thinking.
The oxygen levels are lower the further he goes. The pressure of the climb is getting to him.

The wind is now howling around him.
His head bowed down to avoid the icy blasts on his face.
Snow drifts settle and form on the rocks that surround his chosen path.
He looks up to see how far he has gone, how far he has left, but every time he looks up, it feels like the summit becomes more shrouded in cloud and mist.
It looks further away each time.
Of course, it is not, but Jason is now exhausted from the climbing.

As he looks across the land, he can see the other tops of the mountains and can see that the weather looks a lot more accommodating on them, as they bask in sunshine, as he thinks why is it that his mountain is the only one with the weather conditions he is having to endure.
He stumbles over, then he pauses for a moment, before picking himself back up carefully to carry on.
He looks again across the sky and horizon.
The sun is sinking rapidly now. It is getting colder still.
He takes out his mobile phone, but it doesn't have any signal.
He tries his radio but that too shows no signs of a signal.

His eyes moisten as he looks at the palm of his hand, looking at the dust that is mixed in with elements that he picked up, reminding him of Hemera, and every time he does, it's like a shot of adrenalin for him.

His facial expression then changes to one of determination to keep going, to keep fighting. His thoughts remain on Hemera.

The weather's intensity now limits his vision to just a few meters in front of him.
He becomes dazed and confused, not knowing that if he steps forward, he could step off the ledge of the mountain.
Still, he fights on though, until finally his body cannot take any more, and after a few more laboured steps, he falls to the ground where he stands.
He takes his bag from his back to pull out a foil blanket and a sleeping bag but struggles to maintain focus whilst he fumbles with the contents.
He unwraps and unfolds the items, but he doesn't manage to get into them in time to keep him warm.
With no strength left, he's anxious about the weather's impact on him.
His mind becomes unfocused as he struggles with the harsh conditions.

As he lies there exhausted and drifting out of consciousness, he just about sees the sunset on the horizon, the rays of the sun disappearing from the sky and from his view as his eyes close.
"Is this it?" He thinks to himself. "Is this the way that I go out?".
He is too weak now to focus properly on what he needs to do to survive, too delirious to function.

With the sun now gone, and the weather being so intense, he will surely die.

Redshift

Meanwhile, just off the coast at the Aegina volcano, Nemesis and Nestor arrive, touching down, standing at the top of the volcano along its edge.
Nestor opens the tablet to the page needed and reads the words from it.
A few moments pass as nothing happens, quite familiar with the previous Gods they have set free so far, but he is patient, knowing it will do so.

Nemesis turns to Nestor and tells him "You are about to witness the return of a legend".
Nestor menacingly smiles at her before replying "And when he is free, I want you!".
She looks at him with a glint in her scheming, lustful eyes and replies, "Oh, you will!".
His eyes wander over her as they both wait.

The volcano eventually erupts, as hot ash and smoke fill the air.
Lava pours out from the top of it, completely smothering the volcano so that all you can see is the slow flow of red lava all over.
Lightning hits the lava as it flows down the sides.

Nemesis and Nestor by now have moved further down the slope, near the bottom of the volcano, to escape its fiery traps.
The lava pools up near where they stand, until it bubbles after several large lava bubbles have popped, the lava stops moving then rises, to reveal something buried beneath the lava, to form the shape of a very defined muscular man.

The lava starts to cool and solidify quickly into solid mass, then into granite.
Nemesis and Nestor look at the solid rock formation, then they turn to look at each other, then the rock cracks, pieces of it falling away.

From inside, a man of very good looks and physique steps out slowly, pushing away the last remnants of the rock that held his shape.

"Ares!" cries out Nemesis "I have waited a long time to see you again".
Ares steps forward, his eyes fixed on her.
As he approaches, he puts his arms out to grab hold of her, as if to move in for an embrace, his eyes burning red, and a smirk comes over his face.
At that point, Nestor steps forward with a look of jealously, but before he says anything, Ares stops, then flashes him a look as if to suggest that he will regret his actions.
Nestor begrudgingly backs off as Ares then turns his attentions back to Nemesis and embraces her.

Ares then steps back and looks at them both and declares, "It seems my grandfather is back from his slumber. We have work to do".
Nemesis looks at him with lust in her eyes. Nestor just looks away, annoyed at what he has seen.
"Don't be jealous, Nestor" she says to him, "I am yours to have still" she finishes, as she smirks at him and Ares.

"Come, we need to set the rest free," she tells Nestor.
As they stand side by side, ready to take off into the air, Nestor catches the eye of Ares, who is smirking at him.
"Be glad boy that it is not you that takes my interest".
Nestor's face changes to one of concern as Nemesis chuckles.

Once again, Nemesis and Nestor set off to free the rest of the planned Gods.

Climb Together

Jason blearily opens his eyes, looking out over the land from up high.
Disorientated and not quite able to focus properly still.
His eyes can now see snow-capped peaks and a clear moonlit sky, with the reflection of the moon giving off much light, as stars twinkle above in the heavens of space.

He doesn't move at first, so he can get his bearings, then he tries, but he is still so exhausted that he simply doesn't have much energy.
Jason can feel warmth but doesn't understand why as he can clearly see that from where he is, he should have frozen stone cold solid, especially as his sleeping bag and foil blanket are flapping beside him.
He thinks for a moment if he could paralysed, as he cannot feel the cold but clearly sees that he should be, but then he asks himself aloud, "Am I dead?".
"No!" comes a voice next to him.
Jason manages to just about turn his head, with barely enough strength to do so, to look up at who it is.
"Try not to move," says the voice.
Jason recognises it. "Erebus?" he asks.
"Yes, my friend, it is I," replies Erebus.
"Why am I not dead?" Jason quizzes him, "I should be".
Erebus replies to him, "I am sharing some elements to keep you warm. Did you forget that I appear at night?", Jason manages a weary smile and thanks him for doing so. Erebus nods at him in acknowledgement.

"You must be hungry," Erebus tells him rather than asking him. Jason gently nods.
"Do you have any food left in your pack?" He asks Jason.
"No, I ran out last night," Jason replies.
Erebus uses his other hand, placing it on the rocks at the side of the mountain.
His hand glows as he holds it in place for a few moments, then takes it away.

After a few seconds, small leaves come through the cracks and grow quickly into mountain herbs. Once they have stopped growing, Erebus picks them and then carefully feeds them to Jason.
Jason chews slowly and swallows the food. Jason clearly does not enjoy the taste of them. "This is food of the Gods," Erebus remarks, a small smirk on his face as he can see that Jason is clearly not impressed.
"Are you sure about that?" Jason replies to him.
"Unfortunately, it is not as nice tasting as your mortal beer!" Erebus says.
This time Jason breaks into a small laugh, as Erebus chuckles with him.
"How are you feeling?" Erebus asks Jason.
"I feel OK, but I just don't have any strength. The mind is willing, but the body is not able," he replies.
Erebus nods at him in acknowledgement.
"Give the food a chance to settle in your stomach so that you can absorb the nutrients," Erebus tells him.
"I might be sick before that happens!" Jason chuckles back at him, to which Erebus shares with a laugh.
"Did you see a bird yesterday?" Erebus asks Jason.
"I saw many birds!" Jason replies with a laugh, recalling what he can remember from the day before. "To be honest, I dint have too much to look at as I was concentrating not falling off the edge!" he continues.
Erebus chuckles then replies, "What I mean is did you see any in particular? A raven perhaps?".
Jason looks at him puzzled how he knows and asks, "Yes, how would you know what type when you were not here? Was that you?!".
Erebus chuckles and replies, "Sadly not! I don't have that ability".
Jason then asks him, "If it wasn't you, then who was it?".
Erebus looks at him then he motions his eyes skyward, as if to look at the top of Olympus.
"They are watching you it seems, curious who dares climb the mountain".
Jason thinks for a moment and just smiles.

Get up and Fight

After a minute has passed, Jason grunts and groans from the rigours his body has gone through from the day before. "What time is it?" Jason asks. Erebus replies he doesn't have a watch, so he doesn't know.
Jason moves his arm so he can see the time, seeing that most of the night has passed.

"How do you feel now?" Erebus asks Jason.
He tries to move a little more, but not enough yet to stand up or function properly, as his body has taken a huge beating from the weather up high on the mountain.
"Jason, we have little time. The sun will come up soon. I will vanish. I won't be able to help you, so you must get to the top to get out of this weather".
Jason struggles again. This time, he gets to his knees into a semi- crawl.

"I wish I could help you more, but up here I am already pushing the limit of my powers that I can use," Erebus tells him.
"Well, you didn't let me die overnight, so I would say you are in credit!" Jason replies to which Erebus chuckles.
Erebus blames his inability to use many powers on the curse he and his sister have, which was placed upon them a long time ago.

"Who placed it? Was it them from above?" asks Jason, looking up to suggest it was the Gods. Erebus looks at him and says, "No, if they were all here, then I would be fine. The mortals placed it a long time ago during the great wars,".
Jason feels bad about the past events, so he decides to apologise to Erebus about their past actions.

Erebus chuckles and says, "Why are you saying sorry? It wasn't you! If you had to apologise for someone else's doings, then every person in existence would say sorry for something,".

Jason replies, "Very true," as he continues to struggle to move and get up.

The sun's rays are faintly cresting over the horizon through the mist of the mountain, moments away from appearing at the top.
"Come on Jason! You can do this, get up Jason! Get up and fight!".
Just as the first glimpse of sunrise begins, Erebus starts to break away as he has done so on previous occasions, his elements deforming and floating gently into the breeze, but, just before he is gone for another day, Jason cries out from his efforts and stands up tall, his arms outstretched as he lets out a roar of defiance.

As he does so, Erebus just has seconds left to see him do it, then a big smile beams over his face, as he manages it in time to say, "Good man!" as he finally vanishes.

Jason looks around, seeing that Erebus is now gone. Sadness comes over him to begin with, but after a few seconds he then smiles to himself, knowing that he should hopefully see him later that night when it is dark again, and appreciating what his friend has done to help him along in his quest.

As he looks around, he picks up his equipment and packs it away, then he picks some herbs that were left over from what Erebus had grown for him, giving them a wincing look as he recalls their bitter flavour, then putting them into his bag as he steadies himself and continues his journey.

He pauses for a moment as he walks, seeing that the sun has risen, to see if Hemera could appear.
After a brief search looking around, especially being on a narrow path, he can see that she is not there.
For a moment he contemplates whether he would ever get to see her again, as he keeps going onwards.

Reaching

Jason feels just a little bit more revitalised now.
The herbs that he ate have given him much needed strength.
He feels much better, stronger, in fact stronger than when he first set off on the climb.
He pauses to reflect on this for a moment.

Jason continues to walk steadily on, climbing and carefully scrambling some more, and after some time, he sees a flicker of light in the distance above him.
He stops for a moment to figure it out, then as his eye's focus, he can see that it is fire.
He moves again, this time with haste.
As he moves out of the mist, he walks into the glorious rays of warm sunshine.
He takes another look up, this time seeing the flame much clearer.
It is a wooden torch, with the flames flickering away brightly and strongly.
He allows himself a smile as he moves further up the last part of his climb, closer to the flames.
He pulls himself up onto the final ledge.
Many fires catch his gaze, torches burning to his left, then to his right, all alight with flames and burning strongly.
Then he slowly looks forward and sees what he has been climbing towards.
Jason has done it; he has reached the summit of Mount Olympus.

Jason walks slowly forwards towards some impressive monumental structures.
He makes them out to be temples with vast steps and torches attached to the side and above.
Jason sees other great buildings all around him.
He sees a vast open area, probably what could be a central square, like a meeting place you'd find in large city centres, a place where people would meet.

Jason is awestruck by what he is seeing as he looks around him, taking it all in.
He continues to walk forward towards the temple, then he climbs the steps, slowly one at a time, before reaching the top step.
He walks through the giant entrance of the largest temple and into a great open space, what must be the main hall.
As he continues to walk forward, he can make out lots of large seats all made of smooth stone, all the seats placed in the shape of a big crescent, almost forming a complete circle.

At the far end of the crescent, he can see one chair that is bigger than all the rest.
He stares at it for a moment, his mind thinking about it, so he gets a little closer, and then he makes out that carved into the huge stone chair is the symbol of a crown, with a lightning bolt under it.
Jason suddenly realises who this chair must belong to.
His eyes widen and his curiosity was now in overload.
He puts his hand out and goes to touch the symbols on the chair to feel the stone carvings.

A loud voice cries out, "STOP!", causing Jason to spin around and withdraw his hand to his side as he looks for the source of the voice.
His eyes fix upon a person who is watching him from the shadows of the temple. He tries to focus on a bit more to see who it is, but before he gets a chance to study the figure more, the person quickly moves forwards to reveal themselves.
A woman of great beauty, long brown hair fixed in plaits, her white clothes rich in colours of gold and encrusted with precious gems.
She has a golden laurel wreath on her head and a long, flowing white cape.

She quickly pulls out a sword and holds it to Jason's throat, as he recoils back, wide eyed and a little afraid of what will happen next.

Figure It Out

Hector, Alex, Gabriella, and Elijah are speeding across the country in the helicopter, hot on the trail of the tablet.
The pilot, his focus on flying the craft, keeps it high in the sky so that they can get a good signal.
They stare intently at the tracking device, following the sounds it gives off, following the location of the tablet.

"It's got to be this way," says Hector.
"Is the device broken, Hector?" Alex asks while looking at it.
"It seems to come from where we started".
Elijah asks to see and takes hold of the device, examining it.
"It's definitely not broken," he declares, then handing it back to Hector.
All of them seem confused.
"I do not understand "Alex says, "It's taking us back to where we started", Hector replies "I know, I don't get it either, we have followed it and every time we get to where we thought it was, it changes".

The pilot pulls upwards sharply, making the gang of friends quickly grabbing hold of the handles inside the helicopter.
"Woah!" exclaims Elijah, chuckling, as the other three look on a little bit more nervously than him.

Elijah looks down at the ground and then back at his friends and says, "Guys, don't you think it is a little strange though that at each location we flew past earlier, the landscape now looks a lot different to what it should be?".
Hector and Alex look at him and ask how.
Elijah looks through the window of the helicopter, down to the land below.

He motions them to look out the windows of the helicopter.
"Down there. We went past this area earlier" he says.
Hector and Alex look at him again, still confused.
"On the way out, that extinct volcano we saw, it's now active" he concludes.

"What do you mean its active?" asks Alex.
"I mean its active! It wasn't earlier!" Elijah concludes.

Hector and Alex quickly look at their work iPads that they have with them in their bags. They pull out the maps of the local area to double check, to cross reference.
Their eyes widen slightly at the realisation that Elijah is correct.
The volcano in question is in fact alive and active.
They put the map down and look out.
This time, when they look more closely, they see that many volcanoes have become active.
"This isn't good," Hector says to them.
He looks worried, as do the others.
Gabriella looks at the details on her iPad, then looks down at the ground, then speaking to the others she says, "From calculations, almost a dozen volcanoes now seem to be active, based on the seismic reports coming in".

They look at her with puzzlement, but concern, too.
She continues, "the data that is showing is suggesting that many of them have become active in a brief space of time, all in under twenty-four hours".
Hector replies to her, "They have got to be linked to the tablet going missing, surely?", as they all look at each other, as if to ask the same question.
Truth be told, they already know the answer though.

As the helicopter continues to speed forward, they all look out of all available windows to now see that the sky is filled with hot ash and smoke, not just from the volcano near them, but far away in other places.

Ageless Empires

The pilot announces that they are about a minute away from being within view of their site complex.
As the site complex comes into their view, they look down in horror at what they see.
Smoke and fire are billowing out from the buildings and structures in the distance.
As the helicopter gets closer, they see the burning bodies of many colleagues, strung out across the landscape, as fires rage and smoke continue to fill the air around the site.
What they see horrifies them.

In the town by the harbour below, many people are running around screaming and crying while emergency service vehicles and personnel tend to the wounded and setting up emergency field hospital tents to help those affected by whatever has happened.
As they circle above the carnage, Alex breaks down in tears as Hector consoles her. Elijah's head drops, sobbing.
Gabriella consoles Elijah as the helicopter now drops lower, its blades helping to clear the smoke as it makes its descent.

The helicopter lands safely back at the complex.
The four of them and the pilot exit quickly to search the area to look for survivors.
They frantically search around but have minor success.
As they approach each body to check, it is clear to see that they are all dead.
Elijah screams out, then drops to his knees and sobs uncontrollably as he spots one body that is on fire.
It was his girlfriend.

Hector and Alex rush over to him and console him.
Elijah shouts out loud again in pain and anger, before letting out a blood-curdling scream.
After gathering himself up, he turns to Hector and Alex. "I will have my revenge for this" as his eyes fill with tears and anger.

From out of the burning fires and smoke, they see one of their colleagues appear.
It is Isaac.
Somehow, he has survived whatever caused the scenes of devastation.
Walking, coughing into his hand and using the other to bat away the smoke, he makes his way over to the others. Hector, Alex, Gabriella, and Elijah cannot believe it, as the scenes of devastation are enormous, and that Isaac survived.
"Oh my God!" cries Alex, "I can't believe you are alive!".
Isaac replies, "I was in the town below when it all happened. When I heard the explosions and looked up, I could not believe what I saw." Isaac then says with sadness in his voice, "I rushed back as quick as I could to help, but when we got here, this greeted us. There was nothing we could do."

All the friends are stunned by their surroundings.
All of them are thinking of how or why this has happened, was it a huge accident? What caused this?

Isaac then composes himself and says with worry, "There's one other thing. I saw Nestor. I can't explain it, but I don't think Nestor is exactly human like us anymore," pausing for breath before continuing, "I think he has the power of the Gods; He was with one of them. He helped them. I don't know how or why, but he has something to do with this".

They are speechless by this news. "I knew that man was always a dirty snake," Gabriella says.
The group all nod in agreement and then Alex says, "First, we must get the tablet, then find Jason, and then, we kill Nestor". They look at her, as her eyes are now filled with anger.

They now have the purpose to complete their goal even more so, with purpose and focus, more determined than ever to find the tablet, no matter the cost.

The Handler

Back at the Davelis Cave, it fills quickly with ungodly souls released from the underworld.
The worshippers who were there when Cronus arrived, are now going through some type of transformation, still humanoid but disfigured, their veins pumping dark blood, their limbs and torso stretching out, their hands resembling claws, with needles sticking out of the fingertips, their heads becoming disfigurements of what they were, their eyes turn dark and some of their hair falls out. Bits of skin flap from their bodies. You'd think that they had just been dipped into toxic waste.

Inside, the great caves main area, sit some of the most feared Gods ever to exist.
On three giant thrones made of stone sit Tartarus, Cronus, and Hades.
Cronus sits in the middle of them both.
All three represent the worst of humanity from each generation of Gods, each from his own timeline.

As they sit, other Gods walk inside the cave to come and greet the axis of evil.
Each God from his or her own time, each one of them a product of a time gone by when they followed Cronus into the wilderness, or who sided with him in the wars, with darkness in their hearts.
The Primordial Gods take their place inside first. Achylis, Aion, Ananke, and Thanatos.
The Titan Gods Lapetus, Atlas, Epimetheus, Typhon, Perses and Pallas soon joined them. Nemesis and Nestor stand to the side, with Nemesis glowing with admiration as they watch each God fall in line at the front, facing the thrones.
Once they are all inside, the final great God of their times walks in, the Olympian God of war himself, Ares. Nemesis looks at him with lust, as Nestor looks at her with jealously.

Cronus smiles to himself as he watches on as they all line up inside.

Hades and Tartarus watch on with interest.

"Welcome back, my family," Cronus announces to the congregation of Gods as they settle down.

They sneer, smirk, or grin and look on, glad to be back, but most of all because they know they will soon have their time to destroy and cause destruction once again if anything like the last time they were here is anything to go by.

"Ares" bellows Cronus. "Come forth". Ares walks forward, his blood-stained armour gleaming against the backdrop of the Gods. The cave lit up with torches that adorn the walls, as he walks towards Cronus.

"Welcome back Ares" continues Cronus. "It is now time. Leave this place. Go to Athens. Fulfil what you were born to do. Make War. Show them the meaning of obedience."

Ares smiles as his eyes light up red, almost as red as the blood-stained armour that he wears. "Finally!" Ares says, turning to his fellow Gods.

"Go to the cities, all of you. Make them kneel before you. Destroy their monuments to the idols they worship," Cronus bellows out.

He then continues, "Once you have made an example of them, we have other plans to fulfil."

Ares walks down the centre of the cavern and out of the main entrance of the cave, pulling out two swords that were strapped to his back, followed by the rest of the Gods, each one now brandishing their weapons of choice. As the last God walks out, a second or two later, demons pour out of the cave to follow their masters in their droves.

As the other Gods ascend to the skies and disappear in different directions, Ares launches himself skywards, hurtling through the air at tremendous speed, until he reaches the whispery clouds above Athens. He hovers above the city, looking down at the people in Athens.

Then he makes his move.

Ocean Sky

"How did you get here?" asks the woman, with her sword pushed close to Jason's throat.
At first, he feels apprehensive about the sharp blade being so close to him, but relaxes a little, realising that if she wanted him dead, he would be so already.
"I climbed up," he replies.
She pauses for a moment, looking at him, working his intentions out. Slowly, she puts her sword away.
Her stern face softens, then turns and walks away.

Jason looks around then quickly decides to follow her, confused, but beginning to understand as he follows her. She stops and turns around and says to him, "I know you're not a God by the way" as Jason smiles at her.
"I know every God that's ever lived. They are family, after all. You are not family. So, you are not a God" she quips, looking at him with a bit of suspicion but her face too softens as she can see he is not a threat to her, but it intrigues her.
"But I am puzzled as to how you got here. No mortal has ever made the climb and lived to tell the tale. Even the strongest of mortals could not survive that,".
Jason tells her he agrees, saying, "Yes, I can testify to that!".
"Then how did you do it?" she asks him.
"I had help from two people, two Gods," he tells her. "Who?" she asks him.
"Erebus helped me". The woman nods in understanding about whom he is talking about.
"Erebus is a good man," she says, her gaze fixed on Jason, studying his face and his expressions, still working his intentions out for being there.
"And the other?" she asks.
Jason pauses and looks slightly down at the ground.
"Hemera," he whispers. The woman pauses for a moment.
Her stance softens, noticing his sadness when he said Hemera's name.
"What's your name?" she asks him. "Jason" comes his reply.

She then asks him more softly "And how did she help you, Jason?". He replies softly, "She gave me hope".
She looks at him, slightly puzzled by his response, but doesn't question it. She reads the situation well and then she says, "Hemera is a great Goddess, one of the best".
Jason nods in agreement at her assessment of Hemera.

"Are you hungry, Jason?".
He looks back up again at her to make eye contact. "I am yes. I ate some herbs given to me by Erebus on the climb, and whilst they helped, I am certain I still have their rather unsavoury taste in my mouth!" as he finishes the sentence with a wry smile.
The woman chuckles and says, "I will feed you something much tastier than what our mountain goats eat!".
Jason laughs, then a with a smile on his face, he replies, "I knew Erebus was fobbing me off!".

She laughs and asks how so. Jason tells her the story of how Erebus helped him on the climb by growing the herbs to help feed him, and that they were not exactly the nicest tasting thing he has eaten before.
She laughs louder, shaking her head and says, "I do miss him, he is funny!"
"Come!" she says to him.
Jason nods and follows her.
"Oh, and by the way, thank you for feeding me too," she tells him, giving him a small wink.
Jason at first is confused by her comment but quickly realises that it must have been her that he was talking to on the mountain. She must have been the raven who paid him a visit.
"You were the raven?!" he asks her with a hint of excitement in his voice. She looks back at him and nods.

As they both walk together, he asks her, "Do you mind if I ask your name?".

"Hera" she replies.

When It All Falls Down

"Wow!" exclaims Jason, "Your stories are legendary!", paying her a compliment to repay her kindness, also in part to probably carry favour with her, after all, he doesn't want to do or say anything to annoy her.
"Really? twiddling her hair playfully, as she expresses happiness that people still know who she is, even after a few thousand years since she and the other Olympians were present, in response to Jason's compliment about her legendary stories.
"Absolutely!" he replies.
"You will have to forgive me as a lot of literature from what we had back then to what we have now is very different, but your stories in all versions of recorded text are epic!".
She ponders his comment and gives him a smile of acceptance, as she now feels proud that she is recognised after all these years still.

As they continue to walk slowly, she asks him again, "Jason, why did you come here?".
"We found something buried in the earth. Something ancient and something powerful," he tells her.
She looks at him curiously and continues to listen.
Jason continues, "These days, the past fascinates mortals, by our history. We like to look for these things to learn about our past," says Jason.
"Why did you come to Greece then" she asks him.
Jason replies and explains, "My friends and I are part of a specialist team. We travel the world to locations when something has been discovered from the past".
She looks at him curiously as he tells her about what they do in more detail.
She then asks him, "So Jason, what did you find here in Greece?".
"We found a tablet," comes his reply.

Hera suddenly looks anxious and replies to him, "Do you mean the actual tablet? Where is it now?".

Jason takes a breath of air and replies, "When we found it, we locked it up.
Hemera and Erebus were about to assist me in burying the tablet again, but someone stole it before we could.
She thinks for a moment, then asks him, "Do you know what that tablet can do?".
"Yes, I am afraid so, and that is why we need to find it, so that we can destroy it or at least hide it, so that it cannot be located, but before we could, dark forces have come into play".

Hera thinks for a moment, not sure what to say, as she searches her mind for an answer.
She is clearly concerned about the situation, knowing full well what it can do.
Hera asks him, "What is it that you want from us?".
Jason replies to her they need their help and that his friends have gone off to look for the tablet.

Jason continues, "I came here to find Hermes. I brought along his spear, too.
Hemera and Erebus said that he may be able to help."
Hera looks at him and says, "Hermes is here on Olympus with me, but what makes you think he can help?".
Jason replies, "Hemera and Erebus have told me great tales of Hermes and his abilities.
"They also said that he is one of the quickest Gods, and we need to ask him for his help as we need to act fast."

Hera looks at him for a moment, her mind thinking of Jason's words, then she calls out "HERMES!".

Our World

Hermes appears in the great hall as summonsed.
Hermes looks imperious in his attire, a white outfit laced with golden trims.
He has his shining armour on too, surrounding his clothing.
His golden boots have small wings coming off them, as does his gold helmet, with wings on the sides of them.
Hermes's cape, down to his waist and trimmed with gold.
His body armour displays the same laurel wreath crest Hera wears on her head.

He approaches Jason and speaks. "I am Hermes".
Jason pauses for a moment and looks at the God, appreciating that before him is a legend of old before him, then he replies "Hello, my name is Jason, offering his hand forward, as Hermes does too, to shake hands.
"I have come here to give you back your spear," Jason concludes.
"That's a long way for you to give me back my spear," Hermes replies, rather deadpan but showing appreciation for his efforts.

Jason tells Hermes that they need his help.
"I heard everything that you told Hera," Hermes tells him, "And I appreciate you coming here to return my spear and for making the journey here".
Jason senses he will not get much of a positive answer next.
"But?" Jason says to him, expecting it.
Hermes replies, "But, you appreciate we will not interfere with the mortals squabbling".
"Squabbling?" Jason says, looking a bit flummoxed, half chuckling as he continues, "Right now the tablet is missing, and I fear for what it can do and where it is now".

Hermes replies to him, "You have my word. I will help if needed. Jason, you must appreciate it was the mortals that did this to us" as Jason looks around to see his surroundings.
"Looks pretty impressive to me!" he says.

Hermes too glances at his surroundings before muttering, "It's looked better," raising an eyebrow.
"Besides, it wasn't us mortals from the here and now who you fought with, things are different now" he tells them, a little annoyed that they have tarred him with the same brush as the mortal from thousands of years ago.
Hera looks at him and replies with some degree of sympathy, "We do understand that, and we know that the people of today are not the same as those from the past, but some scars run deep".

Jason smiles at them both to appreciate the comments.
Jason speaks again, "Hermes, if we locate this tablet, will you then definitely help?".
Hermes looks him square in the eyes and replies, "You have my word. As you may have worked out, us Gods cannot touch, let alone hold, the tablet, but if you find it, or you know where it is, then all you need to do is call my name out and I shall appear."
Jason looks at him and replies, "You must have pretty good ears to hear me if I am miles away!".
Hermes again raises an eyebrow and replies, "You might be surprised by what I can hear!"

Hera then interjects, "Jason, we are sorry that this may seem like a wasted journey, but it is not. We are now aware of the tablet being exposed, and now that we know it will make it easier for us to help you if needed."
Jason replies, "I have a feeling that they will need you in the not-too-distant future."

Jason then explains in more details to them both about what he knows to date, as they listen to him.
They thank him for telling them and he acknowledges it.
Jason then takes another look around his surroundings and asks Hermes about what he meant earlier, when he said that it had looked better, as in Olympus.

Try Again Tomorrow

Hermes tells Jason about the splendour of how Olympus used to look like, with shining white buildings made of stone and marble, the huge pillars of flames that would roar with fire, how trees and flowers in their hundreds once adorned the great gardens of the city.
Hermes then points out areas of the city that feature, or did feature, splendid large, detailed fountains that are situated around the city centre and its streets, that many Gods used to be present and frequently visit earth, with exotic animals roaming around that you wouldn't find down on the mainland of earth too.

Hermes tells Jason how Olympus used to reach to the heavens, how it would penetrate the earth's atmosphere, scraping the boundary of space, with colourful stars and galaxies and nebulas that used to glitter and glow above them. "It truly was a stunning city to be in" he says, with a hint of nostalgia in his tone and at the way he looks around the place. Jason looks around too and can imagine what it must have looked like.

Hermes continues it was because of the great wars that decimated Olympus and how they would rebuild it, having had much of the mountain knocked down to the size it is today, but before the mortals finally ridded themselves of the Gods, the Olympian Gods created the shroud of mist and weather systems that now protects and prevents anyone, well, almost anyone, from making the climb to the top, to protect what remains of their great civilization.

"What happened in the wars that divided the Gods and mortals?" Jason asks.
Hermes turns to look at Hera, who looks back at him and nods, before turning back to look at Jason.
"To begin with we fought side by side, Gods and mortals" he explains.

"Who did you fight?" Jason asks, his curiosity getting the better of him.
Hermes replies, "People from far away places…", and as he is about to explain more, Hera interjects, "It's complicated".
"What happened to the other Gods?" Jason asks him. Hera replies for him, "Most of them are gone. They are one with the earth. Some are the stars above. They are not dead, they are still conscious, still there among us. Only a few of us remain to keep the flames burning."
Hera continues, "During the last war with the mortals, a mortal read the tablet and stripped them of certain elements that allowed them to be in the present".
"Can it break Hemera and Erebus's curses?" Jason asks.
Hera says, "Only Zeus can do that, only he is powerful enough to do that. He keeps a vast number of elements and power."

Jason asks, "Where is he now?". Hera replies, "Below you". Jason looks down at the ground, puzzled slightly, then he steps back gingerly, to which Hera and Hermes smirk.
Hermes then follows up with, "Zeus is within Olympus. Just before he became too weak to exist in our form, as you see now, he placed himself on this mountain so that one day he may return.
Jason looks at them and acknowledges what they have told him. Hera bends down slowly to stroke the ground by her feet, contemplating the past.
After a moment, she stands back up again.
"How come you both are still here then?" Jason asks them.
Hera simply replies, "We were spared, as reminders and examples apparently". Her mood changes slightly to one of annoyance of the past events.
"We cannot help you anymore more for now Jason," she tells him. Hermes follows up with, "Find the tablet and we will help." Hermes concludes with, "You can bring them back Jason, you can bring them all back". Jason looks at him, weighing up the enormity of his words. "The Gods, Jason, the Gods," Hermes says with a slight hint of sarcasm.
Jason chuckles and replies, "I think I got that!" but in his mind he is not so sure. Would they go to war again if he did?

Beyond the Clouds

Hera tells Jason that she will help him down the mountain as they can descend much quicker than for him to climb back down, especially as he almost dies on his way up, something that Jason remembers all too well.

Jason speaks to Hermes and says, "I hope I don't have to call your name out anytime soon, but I fear we may see each other again sooner than you think."

Hermes looks at him and replies, "I will be ready if you need me".

Jason thanks him as he and Hera begin to walk out of the great hall of the temple and towards the great ledge that Jason came up from originally.

Before they reach the temple entrance Hermes calls out to Jason, "Good luck. I will see you again soon" then he raises his spear upwards and nods his head to again acknowledge and thank Jason for bringing it back to him.

Jason and Hera approach the ledge, then she takes Jason's hands and faces him.

She tells him to focus on her and to not look down.

Suddenly, his feet leave the ground, as he and Hera gently float upwards and then out from the ledge and hover momentarily over the vast drop.

Jason, of course, looks down, and his face shows one of concern, but not to where he is afraid as he trusts Hera.

They descend the mountain quickly, but not too quickly that Jason couldn't see and appreciate the snow-covered rocks and sparse foliage that adorns the sides of the great beast that is Olympus, before its landscape changes to one of what you would expect from a hot climate, with lots of jagged rocks and small trees growing on the sides.

"I can see why she loves you," mentions Hera.

Jason looks at her, pretending he doesn't know what she means, and he replies, "Who's that?".

Hera laughs and says, "You know who!".

Jason smiles at Hera as she returns a smile back, with a knowing look in her eyes.

"And I can see that you love her too," Hera adds.

Jason blushes a little and another embarrassed smile breaks over his face.

Hera stops their descent about five meters from the bottom of Olympus, landing gently on a flat rock that juts out from the side.

"This is as far as I can go," she tells him.

It puzzles Jason why she cannot go further, but replies, "I think I can make the rest, but how come?" as he smiles and thanks her for helping him down the mountain.

"My curse is that I cannot leave Olympus, at least not yet anyway".

Jason understands the situations better now and then turns to walk down the final few steps onto terra firma.

He then turns to speak to Hera.

"Hera, I am sorry for what the mortals did to you,".

Hera smiles and her face becomes slightly emotional and then says to him, "In some ways, we deserved it. We became arrogant, maybe some things were meant to be".

Jason nods to show he understands but counters, "If we get this tablet back, maybe we can reconcile all the sins of the past".

Hera smiles at him and thanks him for his kind words.

"You are a man of heart and passion, Jason," she says to him, her gaze fixed on him in appreciation of his genuineness.

"Go now," she tells him.

She then begins to slowly levitate skywards again but stops after a few meters.

She turns and smiles at him, then flashes a wink and says, "Enjoy the rest of your day!".

He looks at her to think about what she meant, but he has no answers, so he smiles to himself and dismisses it.

Shadowfall

The city of Athens is bustling, with people going about their daily lives, some going to work, some people are shopping whilst others in secluded squares and alcoves sit amongst parades of shops, talking to friends, sipping coffee, eating snacks, talking about their daily activities to their friends.
Families play in the parks and green spaces. There are many people, many tourists, visiting some of the most famous places such as the Panathenaic Stadium, the Greek parliament, and of course the Acropolis, with many of its buildings and ruins full of tourists.
The ambient noises are typical of what you would expect from a modern city.

From out of nowhere, they hear a tremendous noise throughout the city, making people stop what they were doing and sit up to take notice.
An enormous explosion took place at the Aeropagus, shaking the ground for miles around.
Tremors and loud noises can be heard in the city centre and surrounding suburbs, with people coming out of their houses to see what is going on.
Vehicles stop to see what has happened.
All they see from within the built-up areas is a huge plume of smoke rising to the sky, as they try to figure out what it was.
Did an airplane or something big crash? To make that amount of smoke.
Was it a petrol station blowing up?

The city goes eerily quiet.
People concentrate on a faint repeating sound they can hear, then the noises become all too clear. It is the sound of people screaming.
Another explosion takes place, followed by many more, spread out by a few seconds each time.
The screaming gets louder and closer to those in Syntagma Square.
A look of panic and fear fills their faces.

Then, something explodes next to the Acropolis, within sight of many people at the square.
The temple of Erechtheion crashes to the ground below.
Blind panic now sets in as people in that area of the city are now scattering away from the Acropolis, as the figure of the warlord Ares moves ever closer towards them.

The people of Athens do not know who he is, nor recognize the God of war. Why would they? Throughout history his statues and features change from one century to the next.
All they know is that this person before them is causing whatever it is that is happening.

Sirens of the emergency services quickly converge in the areas affected, its personnel springing into emergency actions to help the suffering of the people of Athens.
As the root cause of the explosions and destruction, Ares has drawn the attention of the now mobilising police forces, who are quickly heading towards his reported location.
As each police car comes close to him, Ares launches devastating attacks on them, using fire as a weapon to destroy the vehicles and the brave people inside.

Anything that comes within striking distance of Ares is quickly met with a swish of his blade, as he scythes his way through the crowds of people trying to flee, as they scream in terror.

Ares eventually reaches Syntagma square, keeping his eyes fixed on his prize in front of him, the Hellenic Parliament.
As he looks at the building with menace in his eyes, he picks up one large rock after another, using his elemental powers to set them alight, then launching a barrage at the parliament building, damaging much of it.

Flocks of workers come running out, some of them are on fire, some of them screaming and running for their lives.
Ares moves to the bottom of the steps of the building.

Inside, many of its members of parliament continue to pour out, and see the warlord standing there, completely in fear of the destruction that Area has caused.
Ares then calls out, "Kneel".
Many of them are stunned and don't know what to do, then Ares fires another flame covered rock at a small group trying to run away.
"KNEEL!" Ares screams again at them.
This time, no one runs.
They listen, and slowly, they all kneel.

"Where are your leaders?" he bellows out.
From the main entrance to the building steps forward several key people of the Greek cabinet, including the President and Prime Minister.
Ares looks at them but doesn't speak.
As they look back, fear across their faces. As quick as a flash, Ares launches himself up to the doorway in a tremendous leap, his sword in his hand, and swings away, slaying all of those that stood there only a moment ago.

As he surveys the dead bodies next to him, he turns around to see all those still on their knees, too frightened to move.
He then moves towards a statue of Zeus that is on the steps.
He looks at it for a second, then with a swipe of his blade, slicing the head off.
He then looks down at them and declares, "I am your God now!"

Assassin

Many Greeks are in their homes across the mainland and its islands, as news breaks on their televisions and radios of what is happening to their capital city.
News channels who have reporters based in Greece quickly start broadcasting the news, all sharing the same story about the sudden attacks as it fills the TV screens of many people in Greece and across the world.
People sit or stand as they watch, stunned at what they are seeing.
Some cannot believe it and think it is a hoax.

Greece is not the only country affected though.

In Tokyo, Japan, a man named Takeru stands and watches the broadcasts intently as he and his family struggle to understand what is going on.
He switches channels to protect his young children from seeing what is happening, but every channel has the same news being broadcast.
The news reports take a turn for the worse.

The live news feeds show the demons that emerged from the Davelis cave running through the streets, killing anyone who stands in their way, including those who are running for their lives, and everyone whom they swipe with their razor claw-like hands.
Suddenly outside his apartment block, he hears explosions in the distance, followed by people screaming and running, and the site of demons running amok on the ground below.
He cannot believe his eyes at what he is witnessing.

In China, downtown Beijing, a lady named Sun Li watches the news in her apartment, in one of the city's tall skyscrapers, with many of her neighbours in the corridors all talking about what is going on.

They flick through the channels and get the same thing; the same broadcasts are being beamed live to them from Greece, going out across the world, with reports coming in about other cities in the world also under attack.

Then they too, hear a colossal explosion near to where they live, followed by more, and then the sight of demons scattering through the streets below.
Sun Li looks on, hardly being able to believe what she is seeing.
As she looks on, she sees a demonic creature attack but not kill a woman who was running for her life, then in a matter of seconds, the scared woman trying to get away transforms, mutating into something like the beast that set upon her just moments ago.

In many places across the world, the same thing is happening. The news is everywhere, spreading like wildfire across on a global scale.
The spread of the destruction becomes pandemic in a matter of minutes.

Across Europe, many major cities are on fire, across Africa, the same thing, across Oceania, more of the same, and across Asia it's the same thing too, many of its greatest and historical cities are on fire.
The bombings and fires have destroyed many of Washington D. C's famous monuments. The world, it seems, is now on fire.
In Paris the Eiffel Tower and other famous monuments are destroyed. In London it is the same thing, monuments and famous buildings and landmarks, obliterated.
Madrid too, Lisbon, Warsaw, Copenhagen, Oslo, Berlin, Vienna, Dublin. All of them have now suffered, along with many other European countries.

The globe has woken up to the apocalyptic devastation of the Gods.

Persecution

In cities around the world, the scenes of devastation are catastrophic.
Devastation has destroyed many buildings and symbolic monuments. Governments have quickly fallen into disarray, with many of their leaders either dead or enslaved by the attacking Gods.
Families have quickly become torn apart by the attacking Gods. Friends who have watched other friends being slaughtered in their droves.
Many people manage to get away. They are the lucky ones. The ones that didn't were about to endure the next step of wickedness from the Gods and their sadistic followers. It might be kinder to be among the dead than to suffer what the Gods have planned for them.

In downtown Rome, Italy, Pallas, God of warcraft, surveys the destruction and devastation he has inflicted upon the population.
He has taken up residence inside the colosseum as a symbolic way of saying he is the main gladiator in this town.
Many statues and monuments along the streets of Rome have also been destroyed or left in ruins.
In St. Peter's square, by the Vatican, the statues of the saints have been smashed down to the ground.
Outside on the streets, where the Roman parliament was, is now reduced to a pile of rubble and ruins.
Its citizens being savagely attacked by the hordes of demons that are under the control of Pallas.
As he watches from the sky above with an evil smile across his face and his eyes ablaze with evil, the demons are rounding up those that they have not yet killed or captured, herding them all in like sheep, moving them all slowly towards the colosseum. One cannot turn off the horror-like scene that unfolds before their eyes.
Pallas descends from above the colosseum and touches down on its floor to greet the mortals gathered, looking like lambs being brought to the slaughter.

As each mortal reaches the front of the line from their groups, Pallas offers them a choice. "Do you take me as your God?" Many of them painfully accept his offer.
They are herded along like sheep to the dungeons and ad hoc prison camps, either to be put to work or to be locked away until needed.
The mortals have quickly become slaves to the Gods and will be forced to build new temples and statues to worship them from.
Those that died in the process will be replaced by the next mortal from the lock ups.
The local forces try to free and fight against the God and the demons, but they are no match, quickly realising that they too will surely perish from trying to fight, or they too try their best to go into hiding along with the rest of the population.

Not every mortal accepts this offer, only the most defiant ones will answer no to Pallas. Unfortunately for many, it will be their last words.
From a small group brought forward to him, one such man defies him and answers that Pallas should go to hell. Pallas gently laughs at him and declares "But I've only just left!" as he raises a hand and places it on the man's head, then with a swift push to the floor with his hand, he flattens the man where he stood, into a congealed ball of flesh and broken bones, blood flooding the floor where the man just stood.
This makes the rest of the group recoil in horror. They quickly choose to accept him as their God.
In another group, one of them, a woman, defies Pallas and tells him she would rather die. "Death is not the answer for you, my child," he tells her with a sinister response to her comment.
He raises his hand up to summon a demon, who walks forth, then Pallas says to the obedient demon, "Take this creature away and sire it".
The demon growls and drags the screaming woman away, taking her to its chosen lair, deep inside the colosseum.
Soon, the others can hear her screaming as the beast has its way with her.

Choose Your Destiny

"This way, about a kilometer away," Hector says, looking at the tracker that they are using to find their way to the tablet. In the distance, they can see Athens and huge clouds of smoke pouring from the ground in various locations.
"God, look at that," Elijah says to them, as they lean over to look out of the windows of the helicopter to see in the distance the devastation caused by Ares.
They all display sadness on their faces as they see the devastation caused by Ares below.

"Land here," Alex shouts to the pilot, who nods to acknowledge her.
"It's probably best to go on foot from here, to be on the safe side," she tells the group.
"Agreed. I don't think they'll just willingly hand the tablet over if we just turn up!" Hector replies to her.

The helicopter lands down slowly and carefully.
The terrain is challenging for the pilot, but he takes his time to make sure they are all safe.
Its passengers disembark quickly and gather around.
Gabriella tells the pilot "We don't know how long we will be but keep looking in the direction that we will walk away from you, and when you see us coming back, get that bird of yours started up quickly, as we might end up leaving in a hurry!".
The pilot agrees and replies that he'll be waiting for them.
"Ok, we go on foot from here onwards, but we must keep our eyes and ears open. We don't know what to expect, so let's stay as hidden as possible until we know more," Hector says to them all.
"Hand signals only," Gabriella reminds them all.
They all nod in agreement then walk towards the location of the tablet, as they turn the sound volume down on their tracker so that the beeping is faint.

After about ten minutes of walking carefully between the dotted about trees that line the undulating, rocky terrain, they come across a huge mound of rock that stands out from the surrounding others, with an old, abandoned looking church at the foot of it as they approach a little more, they see the entrance to the Davelis Cave.
They gather around Hector as pulls out a map to look at it so that they can get their bearings.
They need to pinpoint exactly where they are, and, importantly, how to get back to the helicopter in a hurry if needed.

Alex huddles them in and whispers to them all "No matter what happens, we must get the tablet back, no matter the cost, too much is potentially at stake".
Quietly, they all nod and put their hands in the middle to wish each other good luck.
Isaac takes one more check of the tracker and looks at Hector to suggest they should turn it off the sound now as it beeps too loud, especially as they realise, they will have to go inside the cave, to which Hector agrees.
They put away anything else they are carrying so that they are free to use their hands and to make sure that they feel prepared as best as possible.
Once ready, they enter the cave slowly and carefully.

As they creep slowly inside, they stick to the shadows that are cast against the walls.
Flame torches and candles line the way in, creating enough light to see. It is eerily quiet; they feel maybe a bit too quiet.
They keep moving forward until they hear faint noises from deeper inside.
The more they walk deeper into the cave, the louder the noises get.
Eventually, they come to a large open section of the cave.
As they peer through from the corridor that they are in, they cannot see anyone, but they can still hear faint noises from somewhere, and they spot large stone thrones and an altar, and, on top of the altar, they see the tablet.

They look at each other in surprise, expecting it to be guarded, but then, why would it need to be guarded if the Gods do not think that they can find it? Especially by some mere mortals. They look at each other in the darkness of the shadows, wondering what to do next.

They make hand gestures, trying to communicate with each other, but they have trouble trying to understand what each person is saying, which does make them giggle slightly.
As Hector and Alex try to communicate, Isaac and Gabriella shake their shoulders gently to get their attention, and as they turn to look at them, Gabriella and Isaac urgently point toward the tablet.
Elijah had slipped away from them. They watch him as he keeps going.
Eventually, he makes his way to a point where he must come away from the wall, from the safety of the shadows.
Faint noises are heard in the background still, a little louder this time, and it makes them feel uneasy.
All of them stop moving completely.

After a few seconds, Elijah crouches lower to the floor and moves slowly behind the huge thrones, using them as cover, then he reaches the altar.
He stands there for a moment, looking at the tablet.
He looks around to check it is safe, then he looks at the others.
They stand there, eyes wide open, looking at him with anticipation of the next move.
He looks back and puts his hands out to take the tablet carefully from its resting place.
Elijah now holds the tablet in his hands.
He turns to look at the others and smiles, giving them a thumbs up.
He carefully puts the tablet into his backpack, then he creeps back the way he came from, making his way back to the wall for cover once again, into the protection of the shadows.
The noise they heard moments ago sounds closer, much closer.

They all freeze for a moment until it has passed.
Elijah re-joins the group, as they congratulate him with a silent and gentle pat on the back, before they turn slowly to creep out of the cavern, heading to the entrance, treading with care.

"Daylight!" Isaac whispers happily to them, as they all smile in agreement, all of them happy to be outside.
They all turn around to look at the cave entrance as Elijah walks out last behind them, holding the tablet in his backpack and smiling, then he says, "Well, that wasn't as hard as I thought it would be!".
The friends begin to walk away carefully from the cave entrance towards the direction of the helicopter.
Elijah suddenly stops walking as the others notice this and turn to see why.
"Erm, the tablet, I think its vibrating" he tells them. As he slowly turns around to show the backpack to them, they can see that the bag it is in is now glowing and a low humming noise is coming out from it.
"Ooh, that can't be good" exclaims Alex.

A blood-curdling scream comes from the entrance to the cave, followed by two of the transformed worshipers of Cronus, holding spears, and charging at them, and right behind them, one of the scowling Demons bursts out from the shadows too.
"RUN!" screams Alex, as they all turn and run as fast as they can toward the helicopter, that is still a kilometer away from them, something that crosses their mind very quickly.
The friends run as hard as they can, as the evil trio of beings behind them takes up the chase.
As one worshiper closes in on Hector, he weaves through the trees to dodge the spear thrusts coming from behind him.
Isaac runs in a straight line and twisting sharply to avoid the same thing from the other chasing worshiper.
Alex and Elijah run as hard as they can in a straight line as the demon chases after them, in hot pursuit of the stolen tablet, but most likely wishing to cause them much harm being its first objective.

Eternal Light

The pilot, still on watch as he sips water from a bottle and sitting on a rock outside his helicopter, spots his colleagues in the distance, charging towards him, frantically waving their arms at him as they shout something inaudible.
He quickly realises what is going on when he sees five has become eight, alarm bells ringing, he instantly jumps into the helicopter and starts the engine.
As they get ever closer to the helicopter, Hector ducks under several low branches of trees, then an idea springs to his mind.
The next tree he is about to run past, he grabs hold of a low branch sticking out and then lets it go, smashing one of the evil worshipers in the face, knocking them to the ground.
Isaac also gets an idea and grabs a rock from the ground and as he runs forward still, stuttering his stride to do so, then he jumps and turns his body whilst in mid-air, and launches the rock at the face of the other evil worshipper, knocking that one to the ground too.
Alex and Elijah are still running as hard as they can, but the demon is catching them up.
As they are just a few meters away from the helicopter, the demon launches itself at Elijah to grapple him to the floor, as he still has hold of the tablet in his bag, the tablet falls out of the bag and to the ground as the demon swipes its hands and arms at Elijah, who is desperately doing his best to fend off the blows being aimed at him.
Hector and Isaac make it back to the helicopter, as they spot Elijah desperately trying to fight the demon.
They rush over to punch and kick it off Elijah, doing their best to help him up off from the floor so they can all escape.
Alex spots the tablet and quickly picks it up before entering the helicopter.
As they all finally climb on board the helicopter, they can see that Elijah is badly hurt.
Elijah's face and abdomen have deep cuts, and his arms and legs have severe cuts too.
His clothes, too, drenched with his blood.

They lay him on the floor as they gather around him to help stem the bleeding.

"Stay calm Elijah" Alex tells him, "We're going to get you patched up".

Elijah is in a lot of pain but can respond to them through quick breaths and says, "Did we get it?".

Gabriella replies, "We did," says a teary Gabriella, holding his hand to comfort him.

The helicopter quickly ascends from the floor off and flies upwards and away.

"Argh!" Alex suddenly screams out.

They all turn and see the demon holding on to the landing rails under the helicopter, its face contorted with a snarl, baring its teeth, holding on with one hand and the other grabbing hold of Alex's lower leg.

As the helicopter climbs higher and moves forward, the demon holds tighter to her leg, with Alex being dragged out of the helicopter more and more.

Gabriella, Isaac, and Hector desperately hang on to her, trying to pull her back in, whilst trying to kick the hand of the demon from holding her leg.

Alex is now half hanging out of the helicopter, screaming, as the others try their best to save her.

The demon makes one final effort to pull her out to get the tablet back too, but then, in a blink of an eye, the friends are pushed aside.

Elijah throws himself at the demon, his shoulder hitting it square in the face, as his arms wrap around the demon to cling on tight.

The demon instantly lets go of Alex's leg, as the weight of a grown man is too much for it to hold.

"No!" screams Alex as she looks behind her.

Elijah, clinging to the demon, starts falling to the ground below.

Elijah twists the demon and himself around as they fall, as he looks up at them.

A small smile appears on Elijah's face as he and the demon plummet to the ground, away from his friends.

Then he is gone.

Compliance

One by one, tens of thousands of men and women have been captured in the cities across the world by the dark forces of Gods and demons.
The Grand Palace, Istanbul, Turkey. One by one, the captured men are forced to step forward, heads bowed down low, some quietly sobbing, some silent, some gripped by fear.
They have been herded in like cattle.
They all turn to one side as they walk slowly, looking at their wives, girlfriends or family members and friends, before looking forward again to the last thing that they will probably see.
Demon's growl at them, surrounding them, controlling them to keep them all penned in, like frightened lambs.
Their loved one's look on, screaming and sobbing in terror at what they are being forced to watch.
A demon stands at the end of the line snarling at them, its face staring at each mortal who stands before it, who by now are all trembling with fear and panic.
The demon just growls and has a sinister smile on its face.
The demon then raises its hand, and on its forearm, a tubular spike protrudes out, then the demon lashes it into the torso of each man that stands before it, directly at the heart.
Each man then drops to the ground in agony, then being dragged away by the other subordinate demons, as its God, Epimetheus, just laughs and revels in the pain that he is causing, not giving it a single afterthought for what he is doing.
It takes little time for the changes to take place.
After about thirty seconds, the minds of each man have already changed, unable to focus, their faces contorted in pain and confusion.
The physical features soon follow.
Each man that is stabbed by the huge demon with the tubular spike, is slowly being converted, turning into one of them, into a slave to the Gods.
One woman breaks free from the ring of demons surrounding them and charges forward and starts punching Epimetheus.

The blows, of course, have no effect on him, and he quickly restrains her from the wild swinging of her fists.

"Why are you doing this to them?!" she screams at him.

"Why not us? You may as well kill us all now; we will never help you," she rages at him.

Epimetheus just belly laughs at her, turning his head skywards, before his laugh slows down before stopping.

He then tilts his head back down and stares her straight in the eyes, and with his voice becoming lower, he says, "My dear girl, we can only but turn one man into a disciple of the Gods at a time, but you, with you my dear child, well, you will all bare the fruit of my followers, every single one of you. Again, and again, and again".

She recoils back in horror at his words, as he lets go of her. She falls to the floor, followed by a demon grabbing hold of her to drag her back to the others.

Epimetheus looks at her laughing, and then turns his head to look at the other gathered women in the groups, and he declares loudly so that they can all hear him, "And you, you will all make them for me, again, and again, and again!".

A look of horror spreads across her face, and the faces of the other women, has now turned to one of sheer dread, as they begin to sob uncontrollably.

One woman from the group finds a sharp object on the floor and tries to kill herself, to no doubt spare her a lifetime of perverse rape and slavery, but before she can bring it to her throat, a demon grabs her hand and rips the object from it, ripping her palm open too.

She screams in agony as she clutches it with her other hand to stem the bleeding.

Epimetheus walks menacingly towards her, his eyes fixed, and grabs her, and putting his face next to her face, then says to her loudly in an angry tone "NOBODY, gets to choose that option!", before moving his face away from hers by raising his hand to push her away, then pushing her to the floor.

The demons drag her back to the group she came from as Epimetheus casually walks away from her, sniggering to himself.

Unbroken

Back in Greece, Jason looks around, not really knowing what to do. He ponders the conversations he had up on top of Olympus with Hera and Hermes.
Jason looks around to assess his next actions.
He then notices the collection of houses that he saw from the previous day, then walks towards them.
He is in the middle of nowhere and will need some shelter for how long he doesn't know.
He approaches and looks at the stone houses, painted white, with terracotta roof tiles on some of them, others are flat roofed.
Some of them have window shutters. Some have porches made of wood, as are the doors.
The buildings look old, but they keep a charm and character to them.
Inviting enough for Jason to consider looking at closer.
Besides, he didn't know what else to do.
He takes his phone out to call his friends to see how they are getting on, but all he gets is an answerphone message from all of them.
Perhaps they are somewhere with no signal, he thinks to himself, as he can see that his phone has a signal.
He just has no one to call who does have a signal to get through to.
As he approaches, he can see that they are all grouped around what looks like a cobbled village square.
He thinks to himself that this must have been a good place to meet for all those that once lived here.
The village square has rocks that are carved into rectangular looking benches or seats, and other formations that look like they once could have been troughs for flowers or growing food, or maybe even for animals to drink from.
A water well sits at one end of the square, and what looks like a drinking outlet at the other, and in the middle of the square is a small fountain, no longer working, that has carvings over its plinth.

He looks closer at it and can see that the carvings are in fact the faces of the Gods from Olympus.
He affords a small chuckle to himself, a little with sarcasm, as he cannot help but feel a little let down that they don't seem willing to help.
After his chuckle to himself, he becomes thoughtful, then decides that his reaction is maybe one that wasn't deserved as he thinks about how the mortals from the past must have behaved over the years, just as much as the Gods have.
He looks at the ground as a way of remorse, even though that he really has nothing to apologise for.

Jason continues to explore the square and looks at the buildings closely, taking his time to study them.
He them moves into another section of the village with more houses and another cobbled meeting place in the middle, although this time this one is circular in design.
This one's diameter is about twenty meters, it has tall thin wooden poles, like flag poles, standing about four meters high, with each pole spaced about a meter apart each, fully encircling what must have been a ceremonial or communal place for its former inhabitants.

Attached to each pole is a crisp looking white sheet, triangular, not too different from a ship's sail, except on a smaller scale.
He sits down on one of the stone seats at the edge of the circle and watches the sheets in front of him blow gently in the breeze.
As the sun shines down, he affords himself a half-hearted smile at his peaceful surroundings, but then his thoughts turn to Hemera.
His smile disappears as he thinks about her. Jason's head bows down as he stares at the ground by his feet, gently kicking away a few small stones on the floor.
His emotions turn to one of sadness as he sits there alone.
As he does so, he can feel that the gentle breeze has picked up into a stronger one, as dust is now blown along the floor.
As he stares at the ground to watch the dust move, he spots a shadow move past his feet.

Reverie

The shadow startles him as he quickly stands up, surprised that he is not alone.
Strangely, though, he doesn't feel afraid, just curious who is there.
He can now see that someone is slowly walking on the outside of the circle between the sails, looking across in his direction, to where he is standing.
At first, he cannot see who it is, as the sheets move too quickly in the wind, too quick to reveal the person who is nearby.
Then, Jason's face turns to one of happiness, as he now realises who it is.
The wind has now died down to a small breeze.
The sails drop lower. He now sees her.

In front of Jason across the circle, Hemera stands there, her eyes fixed upon him.
Jason's face lights up, his eyes now fixed on her, his face beaming, his mouth becomes a huge smile.
She looks at him, her eyes fixed on his face, happy to see him.
Her smile radiates across her face.
They are both lost in the moment, longing for each other.
Slowly, they move towards each other while keeping their eyes fixed, neglecting their surroundings and the blowing sails.
They get close enough to reach out and touch each other's hands, then they stop and smile, like two long-lost lovers who have finally reunited after a long time apart.
She raises her hand up slowly, watching it as she places it on Jason's chest.
She then looks at him, feeling his heartbeat, as she keeps her gaze and smile fixed on him.
He does the same to her, raising his hand to her to feel her heartbeat as well.

They both drop their hands down slowly, taking hold of each other's hands, then they move in closer, their bodies touching, as they lean forward to kiss for the very first time.
An enormous flash of lightning, followed by the sound of thunder, takes place, followed by an instant downpour of rain.
They both pull away quickly, both laughing as they look up at the pouring rain, then they both run to the nearest house that has a porch over the doorway to shelter under.
Jason then uses his hand to wipe away raindrops from her face, then pushes her wet hair back, behind her shoulder.
Her eyes stay fixed on his, her face glowing as he looks back at her.
Then, they move in close together, bringing their heads closer, finally kissing each other gently and slowly, savouring the moment.
After a few seconds, they part lips slowly and move back slightly, taking in the moment, enjoying every second together.
She looks at him, all serious for a moment, as he looks at her adoringly, and then they both move in quickly this time, kissing passionately.
Her hands hold his body, moving up to his face, then to his neck, gently stroking him.
His hands hold her waist, then move up her back, and keeping one hand on her back as the other goes behind her head, gently running his fingers from her neck into her hairline.
Time slows down as they share this moment, for what they would h forever if they could.
They finally stop kissing and then touch foreheads as they catch their breath as they lift their heads to look at each other again, both grinning at each other, both committed to the moment, now clearly in love with each other.
Hemera then turns her smile into a grin, as she pushes open the door to the house that they are both stood outside.
She looks at him, stepping backwards into the house slowly as her hand reaches out to him, taking hold of his hand, as he steps forward to the doorway.
She pulls him forward quickly through the doorway as they laugh together.
As he does, the door closes behind them.

Verona

Jason and Hemera lie there, on their sides, facing each other, gazing lovingly into each other's eyes.
His hand lifts to stroke her shoulder, moving down to her arm. One of the white sails from outside covers up their modesty, as their legs entwine beneath the sheets.
She strokes his face with her hand and then pulls him in for another slow, lingering kiss.

Sunlight beams through one of the window shutters, and through a small hole in the roof above them.
They look up to see light coming through and look back at each other and smile and giggle together.
"Are we mad?" he asks her.
"No!" comes her reply sharply.
"Good!" he says back.
"I don't want this moment to end," he tells her.
"Then let's stay like this, here, forever" she counters, "besides, I quite like this house" she quips, then giggles.
Jason chuckles with her as he pulls her closer to hold her close.
"It's got potential this place," he says, as they both smile, keeping their eyes fixed on each other.

Jason's mind wanders, as he contemplates everything that has gone on since he left the work complex, thinking about the last few days, from initially losing Hemera, climbing Olympus, then being reunited with her.
"What's on your mind?" she asks him, stroking his hair, using a finger to twirl a piece, sensing that he is worried about the past events.
"It's been a bit of a whirlwind few days" he tells her, then continuing, "So much has happened, and I haven't even had time to digest it all".
"I can appreciate that" she tells him. "It has been quite a crazy time, even from a God perspective" she concludes, to which Jason looks at her and smiles in appreciation, then giving her a kiss.

"My friends, I hope they are all OK," he says. "I am worried about them; we have heard nothing" he concludes.
She looks at him with sympathy and says, "I am here with you. We will do this together".
He smiles at her and tells her he knows she will.
They head to the doorway of the house and sit down together, arms wrapped around each other, keeping themselves wrapped up in their sheet on the doorstep under the porch.
They both share another kiss as they watch the world go by.

The sun is in its slow descent from the sky now.
The moon can be seen, as can only the brightest of stars in the darkening sky above.
He looks slightly downwards to the ground, his face now looking sad.
"We have little time," Jason says to her with a look of concern on his face.
She looks back and smiles, strokes his back with her hand and tells him, "You are the reason I came back every day. I didn't have to, but when I saw you…I knew".
He smiles at her but then asks, "Knew what?" playfully teasing her for her answer.
She giggles and tells him, "You know exactly what I mean!".
He laughs with her then tells her "I do too".
They both get the giggles and share the moment with a kiss.

"Jason, I don't want to disappear from you when we are still awake," she tells him.
"Shall we go back inside?" he asks her, to which she nods in agreement.
Jason looks at her, pulls her closer to him and gives her another kiss, then he stands up, takes hold of her hand to help her up too, and together they walk back into the house to lie down on their makeshift bed.
As they lie there, they gently drift off to sleep together for the first time.

Einaudi: Nuvole Bianche

Jason and Hemera lie there silently as they sleep, having bonded for the first time.
The rays of the sun have now shifted from where they once were, shining down through the shutters of the windows and the roof.
Outside, the bottom of the sun is about to touch the horizon.
The faint sound of crickets is now audible in the background.
Inside the house, it is still, calm, and peaceful.

A small breeze blows against the door, cracking it open, as the breeze makes its way in through.
Then, as it calms, elements begin to appear and start to bind and form the shape of a man.
Eros, God of love and love and procreation, appears.
He looks at Jason and Hemera as they lie there asleep.
A small smile appears on his face as he can see how relaxed, content, and peaceful they look as they sleep.
Eros walks silently over to them both and crouches down slowly and quietly.
First, he places a hand on Jason's head and whispers, "Bless this man, let there be light".
His hand gently glows, then the glow moves down his hand, through his fingers, and into Jason's head.
Jason twitches slightly but settles quickly, unaffected, still asleep.
He takes his hand off Jason's head and then moves it to Hemera, placing it on her lower torso, around her abdomen.
As he does so, he whispers, "Bless this woman. Let her bear fruit", then his hand gently glows again, and again the glow moves from his hand, through his fingers and onto Hemera's sleeping body.
After he has finished, he stands up and looks on, admiring the two of them as they lay there wrapped up together.

The wind picks up again as more elements make their way through the slightly open doorway, as they twist and bind, forming another man.

Morpheus, God of dreams, stands next to Eros.
"Hello old friend," Morpheus says to him.
Eros smiles and greets him. "It's been too long brother". "Why are you here?" continues Eros, slightly puzzled.
Morpheus looks at Eros and tells him with a more serious look on his face, "I wish it was to give them good news in their dreams, but we need them both now, more than ever.
Great danger is on its way".
Eros looks at him, then at the two lovers asleep on the floor, then sighs and nods in acknowledgement of what Morpheus has told him.

Morpheus then moves closer to Jason, his hand outstretched, and goes to touch his head so that he can plant a dream that Jason must experience.
Before his hand reaches Jason's head, Eros quips, "You know how to ruin a pleasant moment!".
Morpheus stops briefly, half looks at him and affords a small smile and a small nod to appreciate the humour of the comment, then he focuses again on Jason, reaching out and touching his head.
Morpheus then whispers to Jason, "Forgive the visions that you are about to see".
A small ball of light travels from his hand and through his fingers, into Jason's forehead.
Morpheus then tells Eros, "I have made sure that he will not see this until after sunset has taken place.
Let them have peace for this moment".
Eros clasps his hands as a gesture of thanks to his friend.
Then, Morpheus stands up and stands next to Eros and says, "We must go, we need to be ready for what lies ahead".
Eros looks at him and nods in agreement.

After one last look at the two lovers asleep, the breeze picks up, and in a swirl of the wind, their elements quickly break down and blow away gently through the open door and away into the air, out to the fading light.

The Dark Side

Mortals worldwide are scared for their lives.
In all the major cities affected, they hide in their homes and use anything available to them when they move around anywhere outside, doing so carefully, slowly.
Sometimes it could be a brick wall, or a hedge, using cars or anything that will shield them from being seen out on the streets by the roaming demons.
Everyone needs food and water to survive, as what people have in their houses will not last long.
Many of them must take big risks.
Some are successful. The unlucky ones are not so much.
Some escape to the countryside if it is accessible to them.
Some get in their cars and head out of the cities, trying to outrun any chasing demons, if they have a clear pathway to do so.
Most people hide in their homes, apartments, tower blocks.
Some help to rescue others and pull them off the streets and into hiding with them.
There are hundreds, if not thousands, of people doing their best to escape the cities, heading to the hills and caves and forests, to anywhere that will save them from being caught, to avoid persecution.

It forces people to raid recently abandoned shops for supplies of food and water whilst demons lurk outside, continuing to roam the streets looking for mortals to convert or kill.
Some raid other shops that may provide them with a chance to survive, or for weapons they can use to defend themselves.
It's a case of do what you can to survive and not get caught.
Now and then, the unfortunate ones are captured, only to be dragged away by a demon or a group of them, never to be seen again.
Families and friends are fighting to hide to protect each other.

Eudoros, a man in his early thirties, stays inside his home with his young family, with the doors and windows all boarded up from the inside.

He is frightened for his family, but he is also a brave man as he has prepared his home for potential eventualities.
He and his family are in a high apartment block that sits on the outskirts of Athens.
Eudoros assures his wife and family that if they don't leave their home to take any risks, they will be safer.
He has observed that the demons outside on the streets do not seem to enter buildings, they just roam the streets, as if it is their domain, and if they see you on them, then you become prey to them.

Eudoros's phone vibrates as he has sensibly kept it is on silent, to not alert any unwanted visitors.
He takes it from his pocket and answers his phone and speaks to someone he knows on the other end of the line.
He looks over at his wife and two young children as he speaks to the other person.
After a minute of talking, he finishes the call by telling the person on the other end that he will rendezvous with them, and to look out for his signal.
As he hangs up, his wife looks at him, scared.
He goes to her, gives her a kiss and a hug, and then kisses both his children.
He assures them it will be OK and to not leave their home.

Eudoros goes to his room, and after a few minutes comes back out, dressed in his special force's military uniform.
He reassures his wife once again as they hug for a moment, before giving her a last kiss, then he carefully removes the boarding on his front door, tell her to board it back up the second he is gone.
She nods and understands. He then exits his home, armed with his backpack and firearms.
As he does so, she boards the door back up with one last look at him.
He smiles at her and tells her to trust him. She smiles back at him and blows a small kiss.
Then he is gone.

Across town, the same thing is happening to quite a lot of other people, taking phone calls, then preparing themselves to leave home, and then heading off to locations unbeknown to the rest.

Leonidas, a battle-scarred man in his forties, is making phone calls to several people, one after the other.
Once he has finished speaking to them all that he has called, he goes to get dressed in his military uniform and prepares to leave.
Kissing his family goodbye, Leonidas makes his way slowly outside from his home and uses his surroundings to remain concealed, using cars and walls to conceal himself from the demons that roam outside, as he makes his way to a destination yet unknown.

Many men and women all over Athens are doing the same thing, taking, or making phone calls, some of them get text alerts, but they all act upon the commands and head to the streets and surrounding areas, remaining under cover, all heading to specific locations unknown.
As they do so, they can see the chaos causes in the streets by the dark forces of the underworld.
It fills them with pain; it makes them full of sorrow for the unlucky ones, but it angers them.
It angers them into action.
This could be the moment that spurs many people into action.
They are fed up; they are hungry and scared.
There are going to be many challenges that face them in the upcoming hours and days ahead.

The trouble is life for everyone across the globe right now is going to be a huge struggle.
They don't know where or how it could end.
All they know is that if they do nothing, what they are all going through right now will continue, and, it will get worse.

Young Blood

Demons continue to roam the streets of many of the world's prominent cities.
Occasionally, people still wander outside to get much needed food and drink, desperate to feed themselves, their friends, their families.
Some are successful in their methods, having got used to operating in a certain way to avoid detection, some are not.
The ones that are not are caught and dragged away, to the dark lairs.
Everyone wants to help those captured but to do so would mean certain death or conversion.
How can they help and fight back when the dark forces are so strong?

Men continue to get captured. Their screaming can be heard as the noise of their anguish travels through the air of the days and nights, and they are still being converted into demons.
The screams of numerous women, forced to give birth to new demons shatters their souls and bodies.
Right now, the world has suddenly become a miserable place to be.
Where is the help going to come from many of them wonder.

Eudoros and Leonidas, respectively, are creeping across the city, heading to their destinations based on the instructions that were communicated to them or by them.
Each one of them, witnessing the scenes of sporadic people being caught and dragged away.
Eventually they get to their destinations, to be greeted by other members of their groups.

Eudoros is the commander of an elite force.
He rendezvouses with one of his squad members, a lady in her twenties, called Ino.
Together, they stay silent, then move on to the next destination to meet with other squad members.

Leonidas waits at the rendezvous point until Pelias, a member of his squad, arrives after a few minutes.
They whisper to each other some information about their mission before they head off carefully to their next planned destination.
As each small group of soldiers grows in numbers, in the distance they can hear the screams and anguished cried of men and women.
They know that the screams are those of people suffering but these screams sound different somehow, enough to pique their interest to investigate them further.
They decide to head in the direction of these screams but making sure they take care and precautions to do so, as they know that where screams come from, demons will be close by.

Leonidas crawls to a partially destroyed building and looks inside.
There he sees horrors he has never seen before.
He can see women that are chained to the floor, screaming in agony, and next to them he sees several demons huddled around the chained-up women.
Then he sees one of them lift from one woman, a small child.
Focusing his eyes closer, he can see that the baby is not human, a hybrid creation, a baby born for the forces of darkness.
He can barely believe what he is seeing.

At first, his body twitches, desperate to get up from the floor and rush in to kill the hoard of demons, but he knows that if he does, he will surely die.
His better judgement kicks in, knowing that the fight is not now, that it will come later.
He battles with his conscious on his decision process as he must agonisingly move on.

The Great Unknown

Jason suddenly wakes up and sits up, gasping for air, having had the most traumatic nightmare.
He takes a few seconds to catch his breath before he steadies himself.
After a moment to realise that it was just a dream, then he instantly turns to his side and sees that Hemera has, of course, disappeared.
He looks out of the open doorway to see that the sun has set, that it is dusk.
Some fading light filters through.

The moon is full, its reflections providing some basic light for him to see around his surroundings.
A small fire burns in a pot that was in his room.
He looks at it curiously, knowing that he didn't start it.
He then looks back at the space where Hemera was, then puts his hand in the vacated space next to him as if to stroke where she was.

"I don't want to know what you and my sister have been up to!" comes a voice.
He is startled, and quickly turns to face the other way, seeing Erebus sitting there with a knowing smile on his face.
Jason looks at him slightly embarrassed, then asks him "Just how long have you been sitting there!?".
"Not long, but long enough to work out this little situation!" as he smiles at Jason, pointing to the makeshift bed.

Jason gets up, the sheet wrapped tightly around his waist.
"Your clothes are over there, by the way!" Erebus tells him, still smiling.
This time Jason smiles and chuckles and thanks him for reminding him.
As Jason gets dressed, he tells Erebus of his nightmare.

"It was horrible. I saw the Gods wreaking havoc on cities, I saw demonic looking creatures, killing and slaying people, I even saw women being forced to give birth to them. It was insane, totally horrific".

Erebus looks at him, with a serious expression on his face, and tells him, "Jason, I am sorry to say, that was no dream".
Jason looks puzzled, then replies, "What do you mean? None of that can be real, surely?"
Erebus looks at him silently and then at the ground.
It is then that Jason knows Erebus is telling the truth.
"How is this even possible? I don't understand," Jason asks Erebus.
"You don't need to understand how. All that matters is that it is happening now," comes his reply.
"Erebus you must tell me, what the hell is going on?!" he asks.
Erebus replies, "As you know, the tablet was stolen, and whilst you have been gone to get help, some of the Gods have been freed, unfortunately not the good ones".
Jason suddenly becomes angry at this, picking up an object inside the room and hurling it at the window shutters, smashing them.
Erebus looks at him and sees his anger and how visibly upset this has made Jason.

The mood has changed as Jason thinks about what he has seen as Erebus looks at him with a look of sorrow for the current situation involving the mortals on earth.
Before Jason can ask more questions, his phone rings, and quickly takes it out of his pocket.
Looking at it, he sees Hector's name on it.
Jason quickly answers it. "Hector! Are you OK?", "Jason, I'm OK" Hector replies to him. "Jason, we have it, we have the tablet!".
Jason puts a hand to his head and pushes his hair back as a sigh of relief goes over him.
"That's great news! Where are you?", Hector replies, "We are heading to your location now. We are not far".

Jason is puzzled though, and asks him, "How do you know where I am?!".
"Your friend sitting in the corner paid us a visit, he told us. Stay where you are!".
Jason looks at Erebus and thanks him for his help, explaining that he has had little luck recently.
"That's understandable" says Erebus, "But I think you may now get all the help you need".
Jason looks at him confused but putting the pieces of the puzzle together, his mind goes back to what Hermes told him.
Erebus stands up and walks outside, quickly followed by Jason.
Erebus looks up to the heavens toward Olympus, then he screams out, "HERMES!"

As they look up, moments after Erebus has called out to Hermes, a small twinkle appears in the sky, then it gets bigger, and bigger, before a beam of golden light crashes to the earth beside them, followed by a dust cloud that spews up into the surrounding air.
Jason looks at it, and from the dust comes a figure walking towards them.
Hermes then appears to them both and says, "Erebus, old friend, it is good to see you".
Erebus replies to him, "Good to see you too Hermes," as the two Gods lock their hands on to each other's forearms to each other.
Hermes looks at Jason and greets him, "Hello again Jason" as Jason looks at him and greets him.
Erebus then speaks to Hermes, "Thank you for coming so quickly".
Hermes then replies to them both with, "I feel that you both have news".
Jason then speaks, "We do. The tablet, my friends have found it, they will be here any moment".
As Jason has barely finished his sentence, the noise of the helicopter his friends arrive, quickly dropping from the sky to land where they are standing in the village.

Hector, Alex, Gabriella, and Isaac all disembark quickly, the tablet held tight in Isaac's hands.

Jason rushes over to greet them and asks how they are.

Hector replies "We are OK, we barely made it here alive", then Alex says "Elijah, he didn't make it".

Jason is saddened by the news and asks how.

"All that matters right now is that he saved us. We will tell you all later, but right now we don't have time to explain it all".

Jason looks at them all, glad that they are all alive but sad at the news of Elijah.

Hector takes the tablet from Isaac and steps up to Jason and says, "I believe this is for you," handing him the tablet.

Jason takes it but is unsure of what to do with it. "What now?" Jason asks Hector.

Hector looks Jason in the eyes and says "He will know" as he then turns to look at Hermes.

Hermes steps forward to Jason and simply says, "It is time".

"For what?" Jason asks him.

"To bring them back," comes Hermes' reply.

"Are you kidding!?" Jason exclaims, "Have you not seen what they have done to us!?".

Hermes replies, "Not the bad ones, Jason. It's time to get the good ones back. If we are to fight this plague of evil, then we need everyone".

Jason looks at him, unsure. It is now his turn to look upon with distrust as he explains his dream to Hermes.

"Trust us, Jason, we are here to help. We do not stand with those that seek to destroy and conquer" says Erebus, his face more serious than ever before.

Jason looks at him for a moment, his gut instinct is that he trusts Erebus, then he looks at his colleagues, who all share the same look on their faces, then Jason looks back at Hermes and finally says, "OK then, let's bring them back".

Jasons friends all smile, knowing that he has made the right decision.

Metamorphosis

Hermes takes his spear that is fastened to the back of his armour and holds it in front of him with both hands.
He closes his eyes and speaks a language unknown to the mortals, as they look on curiously.
The spear glows and the sounds and sight of static electric.
He then opens his eyes.
"Take my spear," Hermes instructs Jason.
"What for?" he replies to Hermes.
"If we are to travel quickly, you will need my help to do so. My spear is more powerful than you know. Whilst it is in your possession, it will give you great power, but don't let go of it when we are moving, or on the moon."

"Come again!?" Jason replies, startled by his last comment.
"The moon Jason. It doesn't have an atmosphere that is compatible with mortal life," Hermes tells him.
"You've got to be kidding me!" Jason says, with a hint of apprehension about what Hermes has just said.
"Why? Just, why?!" says Jason with disbelief, and more than a hint of nervousness by now.
Hermes replies, "We must go there at some point. Selene is there. She is a powerful Goddess, and we will need her help. Besides, my life wouldn't be worth living if I didn't".
Jason is still trying to absorb what Hermes has said but looks at him with an inquisitive glance at Hermes at the last part of his sentence, but then bounces back to thinking of somehow heading to the moon.
He thinks back quickly to when he travelled quickly across the country with Hemera, then he shrugs to himself as if to suggest why not.
"Jason, you must trust me. You will be perfectly fine. Just don't let go of the spear or let it leave your body," Hermes assures him.
Jason takes in a lung full of air and takes hold of the spear from Hermes.
Jason feels a warmth and then a feeling of energy and clarity.

His eyes widen, a small smile comes over his face, and he looks at Hermes as if to suggest that he shouldn't have doubted Hermes.
Hermes cocks a half smile and then steps over to Jason.
"Feels good, doesn't it!" Hermes tells him, as Jason just smiles and looks at the spear.
Hector and the others look on, curious, as they watch the events unfolding in front of them.
"This will also give you a boost," Hermes says to him, and then, putting one hand behind Jason's head and the other on his forehead, light emits from his hands and passes into Jason's head.
It takes Jason a few seconds to adjust to what Hermes has just done, before declaring "My God!".
"Hermes will suffice", Hermes replies to Jason, deadpan, as the others chuckle.
Jason replies, "hilarious! But I feel incredible!".
"Good" replies Hermes, "Are you ready Jason?".
"I think so" comes his reply.
Hermes tells Jason, "Do exactly what I do and follow me exactly and you will be OK".
Jason looks at him, then up at the moon, shaking his head slightly and then affording a small smile, then back at Hermes.
"OK, let's do this!".
Hector and the others step back slightly, not quite knowing what is going to happen next.
Erebus tells them, "Watch this!".

Hermes begins to jog slowly away from the group.
Jason also jogs beside him. After a few seconds, Jason turns and says to Hermes and quips, "We might need to go quicker. I've run a marathon quicker than this!".
Hermes looks at Jason, unimpressed by his comment, but then raises an eyebrow and replies, "Actually my great, great, great nephew was the first to run a marathon", referring to Pheidippides.
Jason looks at him oddly and chuckles at Hermes, appreciating that he does in fact have a sense of humour.

"Besides, I am warming up; it's been a few thousand years since I've done this, you know".
Jason just grins at the comment and keeps jogging. After what is about twenty seconds of jogging, Hermes then speeds up, as Jason follows in pursuit and gets alongside him.
Hermes then glances to see Jason beside him, then raising his eyebrow, runs faster.
Jason follows him and matches Hermes's speed.
Then, suddenly, Hermes sets off like a jet engine on two legs. Jason's face is one of surprise at how quick Hermes managed to just disappear at speed, but Jason just smiles to himself as he too takes off at a ridiculous speed to catch up with Hermes.

They keep going faster and faster, speeding up, as land around them blurs, until a sonic boom can be heard, as Jason laughs at how ridiculous all of this is to him, but he isn't complaining, he is running at super speeds, faster than any mortal has ran before.
"Jason, get ready to jump!" Shouts Hermes to Jason.
They can both see that they are about to run out of land and hit the fast-approaching water of the ocean, as they are now at such a ridiculous speed, with the ground behind them being torn up, like an excavator with a huge bucket and teeth is dragging the earth up behind them, vapour trails in their wake.

"NOW!" screams Hermes to Jason, and so Jason obliges by copying Hermes.
Both men hurtle into the air, above the sea, slowly rising into the sky at an angle, and before long, they are hitting the whispery clouds above as they go faster and faster.
Jason's heart is beating fast from the sheer excitement he is experiencing.
They now hit the earth's stratosphere, shooting across its curvature, speeding through shooting stars, and the aurora, as they witness lightning below in different parts of the world.
Jason spots the moon as they fly and then sees it drifting past them.
"Er, Hermes, weren't we supposed to go that way" as he points back toward the moon.

Hermes replies, "We are still speeding up, Jason. We will do one lap of the earth, use it as a slingshot and then we head to the moon".
Jason nods, but also thinking how ridiculous that statement sounds to him, that they are still speeding up.
He is still awestruck by what he is doing.
"Move next to me, Jason," Hermes says. "This next bit will enamour you the most."

They soar at a ridiculous speed around the earth's outer atmosphere as Jason moves next to him.
Then, Hermes increases his speed, dragging Jason in his wake, so fast, that elemental dust creates a vortex behind them, and in front it feels like they are being dragged into a black hole such as the force at which they are travelling at.
The moon, from which was once a small circle in the sky to them, has become, in the matter of a few seconds, the most prominent object that they can now see.

Jason can see the surface of the moon appearing more detailed as they now plummet towards its surface at a fierce speed.
From the moon's surface, if you were standing on it, you would see a beam of bright light shooting down from space, which, of course, is Hermes and Jason, as they crash down to the lunar surface.
Dust flies up everywhere from the impact of their landing, as it floats up, then falls gently to the surface.
"Jason, get the tablet out and read the passage as I translate it to you," Hermes asks him.
Jason does as instructed, pulling out the tablet and reads the text that Hermes deciphers and repeats to him.
A few seconds after Jason completes the task, the moon dust that flew up from their landing rises and twists into a vortex, beginning to form and bind, creating a humanoid figure, as the rest of the dust settles down in front of them.
The figure takes shape and then appears to them.

Tales of the Electric Romeo

Selene looks at them, her eyes fixed on Hermes as she slowly walks in his direction.
"Hello Hermes!" she says with a suggestion of that they might have a brief history together. Hermes looks coy, trying to hide it from Jason, but it is too late as Jason chuckles at him.
"So… you've come back!" she continues.
Jason says to them both jokingly, "Would you two like to be alone?".
Hermes turns to him and whispers carefully, "If you leave, you will suffocate in a matter of seconds".
Jason says back to him, "I have the spear, so I am OK".
Hermes sharply replies, "Not if you leave, you won't!".
Jason looks at him, knowing he is joking, but still hears the words and responds to him accordingly.
"Fair point," replies Jason to Hermes, as Jason clutches the spear just a little tighter.

Selene leans in and whispers in Hermes's ear, in a suggestive tone, "Remember when you promised to love me to the moon and back? Well, you only kept half your promise".
Jason laughs at Hermes, as Hermes looks sheepishly back at Selene.
She quickly glances at Jason and snaps, "And who the hell are you?" eyeing him up and down, then continuing, "And why are you not dead? You are a mortal, yes? You know there is no atmosphere here!"
"I beg to differ!" Jason quips.
Even Hermes chuckles this time, before Selene coughs loudly at them both for interrupting her.
Hermes looks at Selene and says, "It was Jason here, who has brought you back," suggesting she should be more grateful in her responses.
"And should I be grateful for this!?" she snaps at him.
Hermes replies, "Yes, otherwise you'd be doing the same old thing, day after day, staring at the earth from space, just going around in circles.
Jason again chuckles at Hermes and says, "Good one!".

She replies without much conviction, "I actually enjoy it".
Both Jason and Hermes look at her as if to suggest that they know she doesn't mean it.
Jason then turns to Hermes and quips, "And people wonder why you're not together".
Hermes affords a small chuckle, making sure not to do so too loud to upset Selene too much.

Hermes then changes his demeanour and becomes more serious and says to her, "Unfortunately we have not come to catch up on old times, we have a serious problem on earth."
Selene looks at his face and reads the situation.
One God, one mortal, both bringing her back from her incarceration, then she too looks more serious and asks them both, "Where is the fight?".
Hermes looks at earth in the distance, points, and says, "At Olympus".
Selene looks at the earth, narrowing her eyes to see Olympus. She then speaks to Jason, "OK. You, mortal, are you ready for this?".
Jason quickly replies to her, "My name is Jason by the way, clearly a pleasure to meet you!".
She looks at him and softens in her approach to him slightly.
"Jason. Thank you for bringing me back".
"Pleasure was all mine," he replies, as he turns his head to look at Hermes and raises an eyebrow.
"At least you get to do part two of that moon and back, promise!" Jason says to Hermes.
Hermes replies, "You're quite amusing for a mortal."
Jason replies to him, "I'll take that as a compliment!".

The three of them crouch down slightly, in quick preparation, getting ready to perform a hyper jump back down to earth.
As they do, particles from the moon's surface start to vibrate and rise, and then, they perform the most incredible jump, heading skyward, creating a vortex of dust and particles behind them, as they hurtle up from the lunar surface and then arcing their flight path to head towards earth.

Spectral Dimension

Jason, Hermes, and Selene hurtle through space between the moon and earth, and in a matter of a few seconds, they perform a controlled crash landing back down on earth.

"Where are we?" asks Jason.
Hermes replies, "We are at the Attica mountains, there are many Gods at rest here".
Hermes asks Jason to get the tablet out from his bag and to read the same passage of words, as he did to bring back Selene.
In a matter of seconds, rocks fall down the side of the mountain they are standing on, as particles start to swirl and bind, creating the shapes of several humanoids.
As the dusts begins to settle down, several Gods start to appear one by one before them.

The first one to appear steps forward to greet Jason first, which surprises him.
"I am Hypnos, God of sleep, thank you mortal".
Hermes corrects the God by saying, "His name is Jason".
Hypnos looks at Hermes and smiles and then turns back to Jason and says, "Thank you, Jason."
Hypnos looks a little embarrassed for his first comment.
"That's OK," Jason replies with a smile.
Jason then turns to Hermes to silently mouth a thank you to him, to which Hermes speaks so that all can hear, "Respect is a two-way street".

The next person steps forward and again, to Jason first.
"I am Nesoi, Goddess of all islands," she says to him softly.
Jason greets her kindly with a smile and a nod, followed by a handshake.

Then the next one steps forward to greet him.
"Hello Jason, I am Pontus, they call me the God of the seas" he declares, as he goes over to shake Jason's hand to thank him for bringing him back.

The last one in the group steps forward.
"Thank you for bringing me back, Jason. My name is Thalassa, I am known as the Goddess of the seas".
She leans over and kisses his cheek for bringing them all back.
Jason blushes as he smiles back and thanks her for her kind words.
She then walks over to stand next to Pontus.
Selene walks over to them to greet them after such a long time apart.
Hermes addresses the new additions to their growing group and tells them briefly about how and why they have been brought back, with Jasons help and how the dark forces Gods were able to be in the present again.
Jason looks at Hermes and asks, "Where to next?".
Hermes looks at him and replies, "Follow me".

Jason puts the tablet back in his bag and on to his back and then, under the commands from Hermes to all of them, they all crouch down slightly, ready to launch off from the ground.
The dust swirls beneath them, particles vibrate, the ground shakes, then they all shoot up skywards in a flash and head to the next destination.
Before long, they approach their next port of call.
To anyone standing on the ground and looking up, they would see eight small dots moving quickly across the sky.
They suddenly stop moving, then violently plummet down to earth like meteorites.
They hit the ground, sending dust flying outwards from the impact zones that all the Gods and one mortal could make from the immense speeds that they were travelling at.

Uprising

Tokyo, Japan. A man called Takeru keeps his eyes fixed forward, crouched.
He doesn't make a sound. Takeru grips the sword that's in his hand tightly, keeping it steady, then moves it into the attack position he wants.
He gives a look to his left, then to the right, and then a nod forwards.
He signals to those who are with him, silently watching, crouching with him ready to pounce.
They jump up and move forwards, instantly thrusting their swords into the torso and head of a demon that has been prowling the street near them.
The demon gives out an almighty cry, trying to slash its hands outwards, trying to swipe them, as it writhes in agony, also in defiance, still trying to slay anyone within its reach.
Takeru and his gathered group thrust their swords at the demon again with another volley of stabbing movements into the beast, then two of the group swiftly move behind the demon to slash at the back of its head and neck, trying their best to kill it.
Eventually, the demon gives up the fight, dropping to the floor. Takeru's group violently slash their swords at it to make sure that it is dead.
He looks at the slain beast and spits in its face.
It has taken seven of them, using their strength and force several times over to bring just one demon down, something that he considers as he looks at the motionless beast.
He wipes the demon's blood from his face, then wipes some from his uniform, and puts the sword back into its sleeve, still stained with the blood of the beast, as is his custom.
Takeru and his Bushi then move off silently, onto their next target.

Elsewhere in Tokyo, Yusuke crouches down low, hiding in the shadows of the tall buildings surrounding his area.
He is up on top of a small rooftop, two hands gripping tightly on his sword, ready to leap into action.

Simultaneously, he and three others with him jump off the rooftops, quickly plunging their swords into the head, neck, and upper torso of a demon they were preying on.
The beast screams out in pain, but this one doesn't have much chance to swing and fight back.
This one they have done well to kill at the first attempt.
As they stand up and take to the shadows to hide once more, it is clear to see that previous encounters have left physical scars on them all.
Yusuke has scratches down his face and on his arms.
On the ground near the slain beast lies the body of someone in the same uniform that Yusuke wears, the uniform of the Shinobi and Jonin.
An unfortunate victim of a previous attack.

In China, Sun Li has also left her building, receiving a phone call previously, to join up with the Jiaolong, one of the most feared forces in the Chinese army.
She too, along with her group of soldiers in her area, has gone on the hunt for demons, silently moving from place to place, keeping quiet and moving slowly with purpose and commitment to slay the beasts.
Sun Li and her group also strike down a demon before moving to the next one.
Their movement pattern suggests that they have a pre-determined destination to get to.

Back in Athens, Leonidas, and Pelias move slowly from street to street, keeping hidden from the obvious dangers, making their way to their planned destination.
They come across a demon feasting on the corpse of a young girl, perhaps who was in her early twenties.
Both men draw two daggers out each from their pouches, then creep slowly from behind, then quickly start to slash and stab the demon in the back of its head, as quickly as possible.
The beast waves its arms around, trying to stop the frenzied attack.
Eventually it gives up the fight and slumps to the ground.

Leonidas wipes the demon's blood from his hands and uses his sleeve to wipe the blood from his uniform.
They silently move on, heading towards a new destination.

Eudoros and Ino have done the same thing as the others mentioned, their group getting together, moving across the city slowly and silently, doing their best to kill demons they encounter.
Ino is a fierce soldier with a proud history, the only one from her group that has direct descendants to the ancient Myrmidons, the legendary group of soldiers whose roots can be traced back to the time of Achilles.

In Istanbul, Turkey. A man named Acamas, and his second in command, a woman called Medea, have met up with other people from their special force's unit.
They have surrounded each beast that they have tracked, using their immense firepower to bring them down, although as they have dearly found to their cost of a couple of their unit members, the beasts take a considerable amount of bullets before they can be killed.
Acamas and Medea also share a special bond, as both have bloodlines that can be traced all the way back to the days of Troy.

Each of these specially trained people and their units have had enough of what has happened to them, to their families, to their friends, to their communities.
The people of the world have started an uprising.
The only question that they have been asking is, what's happened to the Gods that started this?
Where and why have they gone?
As only the demons remain.
It seems as if the Gods have gone as quickly as they arrived.

The Devil's Army

Ares hovers above the ground, about ten meters up, moving along, looking forward.
An evil smirk across his face as he moves forward, sending fireballs from rocks he is picking up and launching at anything he comes across.
The other Gods are behind him, as they have converged all together again, having been in the cities that they arrived at, created chaos and destruction, then left demons to wreak havoc in.
They move along with haste forwards, all heading in the same direction with sinister intent, killing everything and everyone that they come across in their path.
They destroy village after village, obliterate buildings, and chase down and slaughter its people.
Town after town is left in ruins as the Gods march mercilessly onwards.

Cronus observes from the back of the pack of Gods that lead the advancement, his face doesn't display much emotion, he doesn't seem to show anything really; he is focused on his goals and that is all that matters to him. He is happy for his force to do the dirty work whilst he pulls the strings to orchestrate and carry out his intentions.
Cronus has all but one primary goal on his mind, too.

He had sent the Gods across the globe to hit hard at the cities, to create a distraction so that his principal goal can be achieved.
Cronus only cares about one thing and that is the one thing that he knows could stop him. He hates Olympus. He hates the Gods who sided with Zeus. He hates the mortals too.
He also knows that the tablet is now gone from his possession, having been informed by one of his followers.
Cronus knows it can be used, and that it will be used. In fact, he kind of knows that it already has been used.
These things cross his mind, but that being so, he keeps to himself.

From behind Cronus and the Gods, there is an almighty dust storm that follows, looking like a huge sandstorm in a desert with no end in sight of where it finishes, stretching to the horizon behind.
It seems so vast to anyone who would be watching from afar.
Within that tremendous storm of dust, it is being created by the creatures within it, creatures of the dark forces, vast quantities of demons and lost souls of the underworld.
It is a collection of everything that your nightmares are made of.
Cronus has assembled the largest army of darkness, or any army for that matter, that the world has ever seen or known.
He also has only one place on earth that he is taking them all too.

"Father," speaks Hades, "We do not have far to go now".
Cronus looks at Hades and affords him a small smile, keeping his eyes fixed forward as his huge army advances, with apparently no one in sight prepared to stop them.
With Cronus and his army on the march, and with the most powerful Gods not around to stop him, who could argue against the outcome of earths destruction and the end to all mortals?

It is a worrying time for earth and all its inhabitants. Mortals and Gods alike.

Another Planet

Jason looks up from where they have just landed, to work out where they are, so he asks Hermes where they have come to.
"We are at Mount Othrys," comes Hermes' reply.
This is where the good Titan Gods are dwelling".
Jason does not question further and does not hesitate in pulling out the tablet from his bag and goes to the same passage of words as he has done so before.
Hermes again helps him to decipher and to repeat the words after him.
Jason does this and then, as soon as he has finished, he puts the tablet back in his bag.
A few seconds later, the familiar sounds of rumbling happen, with the ground shaking beneath their feet and the dust and particles around them rise, swirling around, with several vortexes forming from the ground up.

As the vortexes lose their spin and disappear, before them stand, and hover just above the ground too for good measure, some of the legendary Gods of folklore that Jason has only ever read about, believing that they were of course just myths, and each time his expression is still one of disbelief as he watches these powerful beings emerge from the dust, brought back to life, by him, holding what seems like a bit of metal and him reading some words on it, that it can do all of that.
He is still in awe and surprise at all of this.
Not that long ago that he was bringing back even older legends of the past, having resurrected the Primordial deities, and now he has Titans appearing.

Each God looks around to get their bearings and see Hermes.
He greets them all, telling them they do not have time for formalities as they are facing great dangers.
They all look at each other and sense that they know what is going on.
Hermes then calls them forward to meet the man who has brought them all back from their incarceration.

"Jason, let me introduce Crius, God of the constellations that fill the skies". Crius then descends to the ground.
Jason is in awe as he greets the God, shaking his hand.
Crius is pleased to see Jason and thanks him for what he has done, bringing him back, as do they all.

One by one, they shake his hand as Hermes introduces them. Hermes continues with each one.
"Jason, this is Coeus, God of resolve and intellect". Coeus touches down to the ground to approach Jason to greet him.
"This is Phoebe, the Goddess of prophecy".
She walks over and embraces him with a warm hug, then leans back a little, looks at him for a moment before she steps aside for the others to greet him.
Hermes notices this and asks Jason to greet the others himself.
"Jason, please introduce yourself to the others," he asks him, as Hermes approaches Phoebe to talk to her.
Jason steps forward to meet the rest of them. "I am Themis, Goddess of justice," she says to Jason.
"Hi, very nice to meet you," he replies to her.
She replies, "Last time they did not get the justice needed. This time we must make it different".
Jason looks at her, not exactly knowing what happened in the past, but acknowledges her statement as she continues to hover, looking quite serious in her nature.
He turns to greet the next one.

The next one descends to the ground. "I am Mnemosyne. I am the Goddess of memory," she tells him softly.
"How long have you been gone?" Jason asks her.
"I don't know" comes her reply, jokingly, to which Jason laughs, getting the joke.
Her face is warm and welcoming, which puts Jason a little more at ease, considering what he is doing.
Probably something that no mortal has ever done before on this scale, at least not in his time.

Above him hovering the highest, the next God speaks, "I am Helios, I am the God of the sun".
Jason's eyes widen as he has heard all about Helios from the myths and legends before.
He is quite star struck, scarcely able to take this all in.
Jason mumbles a hello as Helios continues to hover above the ground.
Jason has studied these Gods from his days of university, and now they are here.
"Hello Jason, my name is Eos. I am the Goddess of the dawn," she tells him.
Jason smiles and greets her as she descends to the ground and walks to him to do so.
"I am Leto, Goddess of the young," comes the next one to him as Jason greets her, too.
"Asteria, Goddess of the falling stars and skies," comes the next one.
Again, Jason keeps grinning as he meets God after God.
By now, Jason is feeling a bit like a rock star on stage with adoring fans, almost!
"My name is Metis. They call me the Goddess of wisdom," she tells him.
The next one descends to the ground "Astraeus, God of the winds, nice to meet you Jason," he says, as Jason shakes his hand and smiles.
The Primordial Gods all step forward and gather around to greet their family of Gods of the past. After all, they are all related.

Whilst Jason was meeting and greeting the other Gods, Phoebe had approached Hermes to talk to him quietly out of earshot of Jason.
"Hermes, when I greeted Jason, I saw a vision. It is hard to describe and understand for me right now, but I saw him, holding a magnificent weapon that I have never seen before," she tells him.
Hermes has a slightly puzzled look, then asks her, "Was it a terrible vision you had of him?".

She replies, "I didn't get the feeling it was a bad thing, I can tell from it he is pure of heart, and he was helping us, but apart from that I can't explain the rest of it, not yet anyway, as it was a vison from our future."

Hermes considers her words and reassures her with, "Whatever it is, time will come soon enough to find out."

She ends the conversation with "Whatever is going to happen, he is more important to us that any of us can understand and appreciate right now, that was the feeling, this mortal is extremely special, and it is essential that we keep him from harm."

Hermes nods at her in agreement, adding, "So far he has been quite good for a mortal."

After they have all met and spoken, Hermes then announces that they all need to rescue the final assortment of Gods from their family tree.

Jason approaches Hermes and asks him, "OK Hermes, we have some of the world's greatest legends here. What's next?"

Hermes replies, "Now, Jason, we get the last members of my family".

Jason looks at him, he thinks, and knows who Hermes is talking about.

Jason looks at him and grins, then says, "Where to?" Hermes looks at him and even manages a wry smile and a raised eyebrow, then says, "We go to free my Olympian brothers and sisters".

Jason smiles back at him, thinking how awesome that just sounded to him, whilst trying his best to remain as calm and collected as possible.

For a man who does his kind of work, this is his holy grail of discoveries, meeting the myths and legends who until a few days ago were mere stories in the pages of history.

Blockades

Across the globe, in all the major cities that the dark Gods have bombed, the mortals have now risen, taking to the streets.
The Gods that initially occupied them, have already gone, as quickly as they turned up.
Something has either changed in their plans or they have simply gone, as this is what many of the people must have been thinking.
They do not know for sure. But they see this as an opportunity to take to the streets armed with any weapon or instrument, they can get their hands on.
Not everyone does so, as many people are still frightened and scared. Some need to protect their loved ones.
Those that take to the streets have seen some dead demons before doing so, and this has given them the strength and confidence to see that the demons are not Gods, they bleed, and they die, albeit with a lot of difficulty.
Not every raid by mortals on demons ends in victory, as the dark forces still kill many. But they are rising.

Across the globe, military leaders continue to operate and plan their fightback and countermeasures, even though many government leaders and officials have been killed.
The news continues to operate on a limited scale.
Major military airbases and ports across the world mobilise with soldiers getting prepared for what lies ahead.
Many of them were on their bases, with many more arriving at their bases, some of them alone, some bringing their families to safety.
Airplanes are being loaded with supplies and weapons, bombs, and missiles and other assorted supplies.
Helicopters are being laden with as much weaponry as possible.
At the ports, warships are being loaded up too with supplies, weapons, and personnel, all getting ready to depart.

From Japan, Takeru and Yusuke have taken their groups through the streets of Tokyo and have made it to their military bases to join up with the rest of their squads and battalions.

Sun Li in China has made it to her military base to join up with her special forces outfit and armed forces that are mobilising.
Leonidas and Pelias have made it to their military base to gear up and join their comrades to travel the relatively short distance across Greece to their planned destination.
As have Eudoros and Ino, having made it through the streets to reach their target zones to meet up with the rest of their special force's outfits, to prepare for the quick journey across land.
Acamas and Medea have mobilised their forces in Turkey, and they have contacted their other squad members from the Forces of Troy unit. They, too, are on their way, travelling across land on the brief journey.

The question is, where is the destination? But this is an answer that they already have worked out.
The news pouring in from different countries is reporting the same thing.
Military forces from different countries are verifying the intel being shared.
This too is a first for many of them, shared intelligence to help combat a power they have never faced before.
Alone they will not win, but by sharing and fighting together, they just might have a chance.
All reports coming in are that the dark force Gods are in Greece and confirm to be heading in one direction.
News footage shows it from a distance.
All media on the internet has gone viral.
Everything in the world is showing only one thing, the forces of darkness on the march.

All compasses point in one direction.

Olympus.

Kashmir

Hermes, Jason, and the Gods quickly shoot up to the sky as they soar towards their next destination.
By now, the dawn of the day was approaching, daylight would be soon.
This wasn't lost on Jason, as he looked over at the horizon as they all speed to the next destination.
His eyes watching, waiting for the sun to come up.
He yearned to be with Hemera again.
He hopes she will appear again.

The Gods and Jason come back down to earth with a tremendous thud, sending the usual dust clouds up in the air and a mini crater, created by their impact.
"Jason, the tablet please," Hermes asks him.
He takes it out and reads the same passage as before.
As they wait the few seconds for a God to rise, Jason asks Hermes where they are.
"We are in Ephesus," he tells Jason.
Jason nods and thinks about it for a moment before realising he is in Turkey.
The dust swirls around, creating two vortices. Elements bind, many colours forming together as they make humanoid shapes.
As the vortices dissipate, two people step forward. "Hello sisters," says Hermes to them both.
They both greet him with a hug each and remark how good it is to see him again.
They turn around and are surprised to see the other Gods among them, but they both smile and greet them all.
Finally, Hermes introduces them to Jason.
"Jason, meet Hestia", as Jason goes to greet her.
He then turns to face the other one.
"Jason, meet Artemis" Jason meets her and tells her he has heard everything about her tales from the past.
She smiles at him politely and thanks him.
"We must keep going," remarks Hermes.

Jason and the other Gods prepare to travel to the next destination.
They prepare in the usual position, ready for take-off, then they all launch into the sky, hurtling to the next destination, following Hermes's lead.

They land on the island of Naxos, thumping the ground all together as they land.
Jason gets the tablet out and reads it.
A few seconds later, the ground shakes and dust forms vortexes, creating shapes. When the dust settles, two more Gods appear.
"Welcome back, my old friends," Hermes says to them both. "Jason, this is Demeter".
He greets her politely, and she responds in kind. "Jason, this is Dionysus," Hermes tells him.
Jason shakes his hand and says, "I hope when all of this is over, you can throw us all a wonderful party!", referring to the tales of old that he knows about Dionysus.
The God laughs and replies, "The best!". Hermes addresses the recent additions and says, "We have little time, Demeter and Dionysus.
I will brief you on the way." Demeter and Dionysus look at him seriously, showing that they understand it is not a joyous occasion that they have been brought back for.
They nod at him in understanding.
Then, they launch once more skyward like ballistic rockets, setting off to the next location.
The sun's rays show on the horizon.
As they hurtle through the sky at ridiculous speeds, Demeter turns to Jason and asks him, "How does this feel?".
Jason looks at her and laughs and replies, "Enjoying it while it lasts!". She acknowledges the response with a smile.
Jason sees the sunrise as the tip of the sun peeks its crown over the horizon.
Jason immediately thinks of Hemera and when he will get to see her again.

Reborn

Jason and the Gods all hurtle towards the ground, creating the usual enormous thud and crater beneath them, and each time the crater gets bigger, as the numbers swell in the group.
Dust, rocks, and stone fly up everywhere.
The group all step forward, following Hermes' lead.
Jason takes out the tablet so that Hermes can tell him how to read it.
Hermes speaks the first line of the text, but Jason says nothing.
Hermes waits a few seconds and then repeats what he just said, but Jason still says nothing.
"Jason are you OK?".
Again, he says nothing.
Hermes looks at him, then looks in the direction that Jason is looking in, then he realises why.
The sun is directly in front of them as they face the temple, and they can make the figure of a person out, and when the person walks closer, it is plain to see why Jason is not speaking.

"Hey!" says Jason.
"Hello!" Hemera replies to him.
Both have their eyes locked on each other, huge smiles on their faces, both walking slowly towards each other.
Their hands come up from their sides and they take hold of each other's forearms.
"Ah, I see Jason has already met Hemera then," Dionysus remarks, smiling at a few of the other Gods standing by him.
Hemera then leans in and kisses Jason as they both embrace with a hug and a lingering kiss.
"I think they might have met a few times more than we've known!" remarks Phoebe, as a broad smile appears on her face.
Some of the other Gods look on, amazed, as they have not been present over the recent days for obvious reasons.
"Is that even allowed?" remarks Artemis, with a small smile on her face.

"Is it actually possible?" replies Metis to her, also with a wry smile on her face.
Hermes walks past them both and replies, "More than you know," in his usual dry wit.
Both Goddesses smile and giggle at his reply and then look on smiling, both looking glad that Jason and Hemera are happy to be reunited.

"I thought I'd lost you again," Jason tells her.
"No, you cannot lose me that easily, I will always come back!" she replies, assuring him, "But we must break this curse!".
Jason nods at her and tells her he will do everything they can.
"I hate to break the reunion up, but we have important tasks that need doing," remarks Hermes to Jason.
Jason quickly snaps back into what they are supposed to be doing and he reads the words back to Hermes.

As he finishes, a few seconds later, as they look on, they look around them, but nothing seems to happen.
Jason looks for the usual vortex of dust, but nothing.
As he looks out to sea, he and the others see something, a huge tornado-like shape making its way to the shore.
The water recedes back from the shoreline and then comes in again as huge waves crash upon on the rocks near them, and the tornado breaks up to reveal one of the legendary Gods of all time.
The Gods all stare in awe as they watch a magnificent beast of a bearded man walk out from the water's shore.
Behold, the legend that is Poseidon.

"HERMES!" cries Poseidon, his face beaming with delight at seeing his brother.
Poseidon has with him his legendary trident, a fierce-looking weapon, held in his right hand,
Jason just stands there open-mouthed as the Gods, all welcome him.
Hermes goes over to embrace his brother.
"It's been a long-time brother," Hermes says to him.

Poseidon then looks at Jason and says, "And what is your name, mortal?".

Jason gives a small laugh and cheekily replies, "I am the mortal known as Jason!".

The other Gods give a small chuckle as Jason then quickly addresses the God of the seas, "Poseidon, I am most happy that you are here, but earth is in great danger, not just the mortals, but all life, Gods included, we really could do with your help".

Poseidon looks at Jason, then looks at Hermes, who nods in agreement with Jason, then looks at his family members, old and new, and all of them with serious looks on their faces.

He then looks back at Jason and says, "How many?".

Jason thinks for a quick second, and assuming Poseidon is talking about the dark forces, he replies with a sullen, serious face, "Probably all of them".

Poseidon recoils back with some alarm.

Keeping his eyes fixed on Jason. "In that case then, we will need the rest of my brothers and sisters, especially my youngest brother".

Hermes addresses everyone to tell them of the next destination that they need to go to.

They all agree with him like they have done previously, get themselves set ready to fly.

Jason looks at Hemera as she comes to stand with him, taking his hand and smiling at him as she tells him, "You've been busy since we were last together!" then planting a small kiss on his cheek.

Poseidon glances over and sees this, then looks at Hermes and remarks "How long have I been gone?!".

Hermes gives Poseidon a raised eyebrow and a wry smile, as if to say don't ask.

The Gods and Jason then set off skywards, like jet propelled rockets and head towards their next destination.

No Retreat, No Surrender

Jason and the Gods arrive over the skies of Athens, shooting down like meteorites, all of them striking the floor within seconds of each other, sending huge plumes of dust into the air.

This time there is no crater below their feet, for they have landed carefully due to where they are.

"No need to tell me where we are this time," Jason remarks to Hermes. "Indeed not," comes his reply.

In front of them is the Parthenon and all the other temples, on top of the Acropolis in Athens.

They take a second to look around them, witnessing the destruction caused by Cronus and his forces that took place prior to their arrival.

"Ares," says Poseidon, "This is the work of Ares. His thirst for war is insatiable." Poseidon doesn't look happy, more remorseful, looking over at how the mortals have developed and evolved over the centuries, and yet they still maintained the temples of the past that are dedicated to the Gods.

"We have let them down," Poseidon declares to the other Gods. "I know we had our differences with them, but we always had a common enemy."

Jason looks at him and replies, "Poseidon, us mortals have been far from perfect. It has taken us many centuries to get to where we are today, but wars and conflict still take place today. We are getting better, but we have a long way to go still."

Poseidon nods at him in appreciation.

"You are wise, Jason. Step forward to me".

Jason looks at him a little confused but does as asked.

Poseidon then puts his left hand behind Jason's head and his right hand on Jason's forehead, then he closes his eyes.

Poseidon's hands glow with the light from both, moving into Jason's head.

"Wow!" Jason exclaims, his face lighting up with a feeling of euphoria. "What did you do?" Jason asks Poseidon.

"I thought I would give you a helping hand," he replies, with a small grin, and then looking at Hemera and giving her a nod as she smiles back.

Hermes speaks, "Jason, the tablet. We are running low on time. I can sense that Cronus and his forces have amassed and are heading towards Olympus".

Jason nods and immediately gets the tablet out of his bag and reads the text, but this time, he doesn't need Hermes to help.

As Jason looks at the text, it surprises him he can understand what it says, as if they wrote it in simple English, so easy for him to understand.

He speaks straight away, confident in what he is saying and doing.

As Jason speaks, he looks up and catches the eye of Hemera and Hermes, who both smile and encourage him to keep going.

Jason finishes reading, then puts the tablet away as all of them look forwards at the ruins.

From around them, several vortexes spin and twist, picking up dust, rocks, anything in its pathway as the power inside the vortexes is immense.

All the vortexes spin violently inside the Parthenon before they settle down and dissipate.

From the settling dust, walk forward five figures. Five legends of old.

Poseidon greets them all, "Welcome back my family!" as he goes over to them all to hug each one.

The other Gods come over to greet them and welcome them back too.

Jason looks on in awe as usual, with Hemera holding his hand by his side to make sure he is OK.

He gives her a look to suggest that is he good, and he kisses her on the cheek in appreciation.

Poseidon introduces each one to Jason. "Jason, meet Aphrodite," as she steps forward.

Aphrodite then walks past Hermes and greets him with a knowing smile and suggestive tone in her voice, like Selene did back on the lunar surface.
Hermes greets her with a slightly embarrassed reply.
Jason looks at Hermes and tells him, "You're quite the dark horse aren't you!" as two other Gods nearby hear him and chuckle.

"Jason, this is my brother Hephaestus", followed by, "And this is Nike".
Jason collectively says to them, "It is an honour to meet you all".
Nike walks over to Jason and looks down at his shoes and sees her name emblazoned on them, then she asks him with a puzzled question, "Why do your shoes have my name on them?".
Jason smiles and tries to explain that they named a sports company after her.
"So, they have built thousands of these temples to honour my name?" Jason chuckles and replies, "Something like that".

Jason looks up to the sky, smiling. The Gods notice this, and all look up too, following his lead, unsure why but copying him.
Just then, the ground shakes.
As they watch on, two huge beams of light crash to the floor like spotlights coming down from the heavens.
Huge amounts of particles swirl around like tornadoes, at first violently, with particles and elements crashing and colliding, before the spinning slows down, slowly, before they then seem to float in the air, and then, they are pulled together, as if a magnet has pulled them together, binding with great colour and light.
Then, from the floating dust, walk forward two of the biggest mythical legends known.

Jason doesn't need introducing as he confidently walks over to them, as bold as you can get, but with dignity and respect, and is the first to speak to them.

"Athena, Apollo, this is one of the greatest moments of my life to meet you both".
Athena and Apollo step forward, slightly confused by who he is but seem to smile back at him, as they feel in no danger as they have spotted their fellow Gods behind him.
Hermes and Poseidon step forward to greet them both.

"Uncle!" Apollo and Athena say in unison to Poseidon as they step forward and hug him, as he hugs them back.
"It's good to see you both. It's been so long!" Poseidon replies to them both.
"But unfortunately, the family reunion festivities will have to wait," Poseidon says in a more serious tone.
Hermes comes over to explain to them what has been going on and where they are currently at with everything.

"We had a feeling this wasn't a jolly get together seeing all of you gathered here," Apollo says to them all, looking over at two dozen Gods, all gathered around.
Athena then declares, "Whatever the cost, we must not let the forces of darkness win.
There is more at stake than there has ever been before".
"Looking around, I feel like most of us are here," Apollo says, followed by Athena replying, "Only one more person to bring back".
"Do you think he will help?" Apollo asks Athena.
Poseidon comes over and replies to her, "If we are to prevail, then yes, we need him or we will surely lose". Apollo then looks at the rest of the Gods, then looks at Jason and then declares, "OK, Let's wake up, father!".

All the Gods and Jason crouch down slightly, then take off, like beams of light leaving vapour trails behind them as they set off, to bring back, and try to convince the biggest mythological God of them all.

Look to the Sky

From all over the world, armed forces, and other militaries with capable firepower and resources, are moving overland, in the skies or are or have set sail.
The U.S Navy and air fleet based in Europe and East Asia and North Africa, every ship in their fleet is heading across at full speed, destination, the Mediterranean, specifically, Greece, to Olympus.
China has sent every long-range airplane at their disposal, setting off, sending out every trained pilot and combatant stationed closer to Europe.
They also have an array of ships in the local area to Europe, that are heading towards Olympus.
Japan has also done the same, sending over special forces, via long range airplanes and launching from their overseas bases to all head off in the same direction.
As have South Korea, and many more are following their lead.
The British military is sending all warships, long-range bombers, fighter jets, and special forces to Olympus.
They have also recalled all military personnel from leave and put every subscribed soldier on red alert and mobilised them.
Israel has mobilised all their fighter jets and army and are heading off toward Greece.
Saudi Arabia has an enormous force on its way, making its way overland and by air.
Turkey is sending a vast army of troops across the border into Greece, especially their special forces outfits, including their fabled Forces of Troy.
India and Pakistan forces are on their way too, with a huge number of soldiers, all mobilised and heading across.
Russian forces with a huge number of troops and weaponry are on their way too, heading south through the eastern European countries by land and air.

All the NATO forces based in Europe have received briefings and mobilised.

They are now travelling overland from central Europe and from the nearby edges of Africa and Asia that are within reach of Europe.

But that doesn't stop more troops from being deployed from any of the countries and organisations that are sending them.

They are being mobilised in the U.S and are on their way from North American bases.

They are being sent from mainland China, from mainland Japan, South Korea, all the countries in Europe, from Africa, from East and South Asia.

From all over the world, every country has identified the level of danger posed to them, that humankind is under an extinction threat on a global scale.

They know everyone must fight. Many will die trying, but to not try will mean certain death, anyway.

Every country that has a plane or ship capable of carrying soldiers is sending them to fight and is on its way.

It is a sight to behold to see so many planes in the sky, all flying side by side and heading towards Olympus, all of them for once not flying with suspicion about each other, but now fighting under the banner of earth.

Many land-based vehicles join up as they travel from each direction.

Many jeeps and people carriers sound their horns to welcome each new vehicle that joins them, no matter from what country they have come from.

This is now about humanity. Old enemies have now become allies.

On the Shoulders of Giants

The army of Gods that Hermes and Jason have brought back to the world have now arrived at their planned destination.
They shoot down from the sky, all landing at the same point, in the middle of the vast open space of the city centre.
They all take a moment to look around and appreciate what was once a glorious place to be, here at Mount Olympus, home of the Gods.

Hera appears to them all and is astonished to see so many Gods to be standing there before her.
She turns to Jason and gives him a smile and remarks, "You have been very busy it seems" as Jason chuckles and nods in agreement, Hera then goes to greet all her fellow Gods.
Once Hera has greeted to them all, she heads back to Jason and says, "To see so many of them back again can only mean one thing" as her smile fades, knowing that this isn't an ordinary house call.
Hermes interjects and replies, "You are correct, there is a great darkness coming this way, we must be ready".
Hera looks at the assembled Gods and declares, "Then you will all need to be armed".
She looks over at a building near to the temple, and lifts her arms upwards, palms facing upwards too, as she does so, a hidden doorway on the building begins to open, as dust fall from the cracks of the building.
The doorway opens fully, and a treasure trove of weaponry is on display.
The Gods watch and smile at each other, then head over to pick up their choice of weapon.
Some choose the ones they used from the days gone by, and some pick up new ones.
They all pick up all the weapons available one by one so that it fully equips them.
There are swords, shields, spears, daggers, bows and crossbows, double-edged spears and more, but none of them are just ordinary weapons.

These are the weapons of the Gods, that are much more powerful than most mortal weapons.
Once they have all finished arming themselves, Athena and Apollo turn and talk to the Gods to say that they must plan for the fight.
Apollo tells them, "We must not give up, even if it means your life, because if we lose, there will be no coming back for any of us".
Poseidon quickly pipes up, "Unless Jason reads his tablet again!".
The Gods and Jason all laugh together to ease the tension.
Apollo laughs with them but then replies with more seriousness, "If they get the tablet back and kill any of us, then this is it. This is the last time we will be".
The laughter slows as they become more serious, listening, and taking on board what he has said.
Athena then speaks "All of you, try not to fight against a God that is not suited or matched based on your talents and abilities, if you can help it. This isn't an ego thing, fight the Gods that are like for like. If we get the upper hand, then the two of you together will be stronger to take on a God with more powers."
They all agree with a nod or reply that they agree.

They head to the main ledge on Olympus, the same one that Jason had climbed to reach the top, the ledge that looks out over the vast miles of space below.
In the distance, they can make out what looks like an enormous cloud of advancing dust on the horizon, to what looks like the clouds from the sky have fallen to cover the land, and it is moving across the land in their direction.
They turn and look back, watching Jason and Hermes, Poseidon and Hemera, as Jason gets out the tablet out once more, and begins to read with haste.

He is about to bring back the King of the Gods.

Reign of Vengeance

Cronus and his forces have finally arrived.
The vast army stretches across the land as far as the eyes can see, almost as if it spills over the horizon.
They stop and stare at Olympus in the distance.
Cronus is emotionless.
He just stands there looking at it.
The Gods with him are impatient.
"Why do we wait? Let's destroy them now!" cries Hades.
"Patience Hades" replies Cronus, "We must see what is before us. We need to know if anyone is home, to appreciate how much we are going to enjoy this".
Hades smirks but shuffles impatiently, as does Ares, who keeps adjusting the grip on his weapons, aching to be set loose to fight.
Behind the Gods, it is a wall of noise, as demons and other creatures stirred up by the Gods snarl and cackle, desperate to advance forward.
All they want to do is kill.
That is their level of intelligence.

Tartarus comes over to Cronus and looks in the near distance with him.
"It seems they have come prepared," Cronus remarks as he looks at Olympus.
"Yes, they have, but they do not have your son". Tartarus replies.
"Do not rule it out," Cronus says, as Tartarus nods in agreement and replies, "I do not doubt it for a second".
Cronus turns and addresses the Gods by saying, "Do not underestimate them, you all know what happened last time".
Some of them take on board what he has said, some seem to not care, they just want to fight.
Nemesis and Nestor appear before Cronus.
"What would you like us to do, my Lord?" Nemesis asks Cronus.

He turns to look at them both and smiles menacingly, then replying to them both, "I want you to kill every mortal that you see".
Nemesis and Nestor revel in the reply, moving their hands all over each other like love struck teenagers, turned on by the thought of destruction.
Cronus then turns back to face the Gods beside him, then to look behind at the dark army under his command behind him, then he moves forward.
The other Gods move with him. The dark forces behind him snap and snarl as they, too, move forward, letting out almighty roars as they do so.

Back on Olympus, Jason speaks the words of the ancient tablet as the Gods watch on, still monitoring the advancing force in front of them, hearing the roars of the underworld now becoming louder as they get closer.
"Today could be a dark day, lets introduce some light," exclaims Apollo.
Athena then looks to the sides of the advancing army of darkness, narrows her eyes, then they widen in disbelief at what she is seeing.
"What is that" asks Hephaestus, as he and the other Gods look on to focus and make out what it is they can see.
One by one, the Gods smile as they all realise what it is.
What they see are the advancing forces of the mortals coming to join the battle.
"What are they all doing here?" remarks Hera.

Jason sees this as his moment to address them all.

"They have come here to fight. To fight for their lives, for their families, for their very existence. They have come here to fight with you, for you, side by side." He continues passionately, "They could have stayed at home, hiding, leaving the fight to all of you, but they have all chosen to take up arms, and they have come a long way to get here to join you in the fight. We may be mortal, but they are brave. They will die for something that they believe in."

Hermes leans over to Jason and whispers, "Nice speech!" to which Jason chuckles at his remark.
Even Hermes affords him a small smile, appreciating that a little humour is currently is much needed.
Hermes stands up, turns to look at Jason, and making sure the other Gods can hear him, and says to Jason, "I will fight these Gods and their forces, and I will fight alongside the mortals, all brothers and sisters in arms".

All the Gods seem impressed with Jason's impassioned speech to them, and then one by one they take Hermes' lead and announce the same thing.
Every God promising to help.
"I will fight along side you Jason" says Apollo.
"As will I" declares Athena.
"It would be an honour to charge into battle alongside you" speaks Artemis.
"I will prepare the after party!" Dionysus says, laughing.
At this point the tension is broken, and everyone bursts out laughing.
Once the laughter lessens, they quickly turn their attention back to the advancing forces.
"They are going to need as much help from us as possible," Poseidon declares.
Hermes, with his eyebrow raised, leans in to whisper to Jason again, "Don't forget to finish the reading of the tablet", to which Jason looks at him and smiles at his dry humour, and obliges straight away.
Jason reads the text, ignoring the huge roaring and rumbling that they can all hear, coming from the terrain below them in the national park that Olympus resides on.
He speaks the ancient tongue and is word perfect, as Hermes and the others looks on nervously, hoping that it will work.
Jason finishes reading the text as it glows before his eyes, then the text stops glowing, and tablet returns to a dormant state.
Now, they wait.

Thunderstruck

The Gods on Olympus continue to watch on. Waiting.
It is silent, apart from the noises coming from the dark forces in the distance.
A small breeze begins to blow, then it becomes stronger, blowing some leaves and dust across the centre of Olympus.
Clouds up high begin to gather, becoming darker, swirling, and circling around, above the gathered Gods and Jason.
The sound of thunder then cracks above them.

The wind now picks up to a storm, increasing in strength, as it condenses and forms into a huge tornado-like shape.
The bottom of the funnel is several meters across on the floor, increasing in diameter as it reaches up to the circling clouds above.
Thunder crashes again, then again, then sheet lightning flashes across the sky, at first just above them, then spreading across the seeable land.

As Cronus and his army march on, seeing what is taking place, still unsure of what is happening, but doubt start to creep in.
Jason, Hemera, Poseidon and Hermes watch with intent, eyes transfixed on the tornado.
Hera comes over to join them.
The Gods at the ledge are all watching with small smiles beginning to appear on their faces in anticipation.
Their faces fixed on the events before them, ignoring what was behind them.

The advancing army of the dark forces can see all the commotion taking place.
Cronus suddenly stops, and the Gods with him all stop too, as do the amassed forces behind them. "I knew this would happen," Cronus announces to his assembled Gods.
Hades and Tartarus look on, both slightly nervous.

Some of the Gods with Cronus still don't appreciate what is unfolding before them, such is their arrogance, even Ares, who still fidgets, aching to go to war.
Fork lightning strikes the surrounding ground all, then more fork lightning flashes and crashes inside the tornado, then lightning comes up from the ground, hitting the clouds and sky above.
The tornado sucks in earth, water, fire, and air.
It then pulls elements from the sky into its vortex at incredible speeds.
All the Gods on Olympus continue to watch the amazing scenes unfolding still.
Dozens of lightning crashes per second, revealing a figure inside it that grows bigger and bigger with each flash.
The image starts as a blur, but with each lightning crash, it becomes clearer.
Jason watches on with excitement beginning to show in his eyes, as do the others.

Jason turns to Hera and says, "Is that him?".
Hera looks at him as the winds swirl around them, and she replies, "Yes, that's him!".
Jason's face now has a broad smile over it, as the Gods stand there imperiously, waiting to welcome the last arrival.
The tornado, thunder and lightning are now making the most incredible noise and light from its belly.
The figure from within it then steps out.
He is glowing, imperious looking, as lightning continues to crash around him.

The Gods faces all beam with delight, all smiling, some of them cry out with cheers and roars.
This is a moment in Jason's life that he will never forget.
Behold, the King of Kings has risen.
Behold, the God of Gods is back.

Zeus.

Invincible

The armies of north America march onwards with Olympus in their sights.
To their left, the forces from Asia come into sight.
To the right, the armies from Africa arrive.
The armies from Europe and Oceania also join the enormous collection of forces, coming in from all directions.
All the worlds' armies begin to fill in from different directions.

Each battlefield commander from each elite unit, special forces outfit, battalions and regiments from across the globe, has communicated with their counterparts from each of the other countries, as each force comes into contact with each other, each wearing their own uniforms, they join up and march on, drive or fly side by side; they are now a united front of fighters, armies, working in unison, brothers and sisters in arms, all with a single goal.
To defend earth until the last has fallen.

Tanks roll across the terrain together, from all corners of the earth.
Planes circle the skies, coming from all corners of the earth, flying side by side, each group looking over at each other who are from all different nations, nodding in appreciation at each other, giving the thumbs up to each other, they are no doubt glad to have each other side by side.

Military vehicles scream across the terrain side by side, like a swarm of ants coming from all corners of the earth.
No longer operating as independent nations, now they are operating and cooperating as one.

Commanders from different forces greet each other when they meet in person, shaking hands, locking arms, embracing, and welcoming.
Leaders from nations that would previously be enemies or at least be cold towards each other in the normal world embrace and welcome each other openly.

Every troop present can see this taking place all around them, and it lifts their spirits to know that they are now joined in the biggest fight of their lives, for everyone's lives.

Helicopters hover in the skies above them, moving forward slowly, waiting for orders.
As they move slowly forward, they talk to each other over their radios and speak about military tactics, what the plans of action could and would be, but they also exchange dialogue that shows their human side, too.

About twelve miles away, just off the eastern seaboard of Greece, a huge armada of ships of all shapes and sizes sit there, ready to go to war.
There are battleships, aircraft carriers, destroyers, submarines, gunboats, and heavy cruisers, all waiting for their orders, and as the minutes pass, more and more of them turn up, coming from all corners of the seas of the globe in terms of nationalities.
The ships display flags of many countries.
Sailors and marines line up on the deck, waving to their counterparts on other ships.
Amphibious vehicles launch from the ships, heading towards the battlefield that awaits them on the shore.

Snipers from all over the world's fighting forces, from all countries, take up positions in the hills above the battlefield, ready for action.
They communicate with each other to let each other know their positions so that they can plot and plan what they do, their potential target areas and where not to fire at so that they can avoid friendly fire.

Everyone from the ground to the seas, and the air above, have now all arrived in one place, one common purpose.
To fight for the very survival of humanity, and into battle, they will all go.

Building Smasher

Cronus surveys the mortal forces that have gathered.
He sneers at them, scowling and screaming a roar of defiance, then laughs, "Inferior beings!".
Hades asks Cronus, "Why are they here?".
Cronus replies, "It doesn't matter, they are a minor distraction. Besides, our forces will wipe them out".
Hades gives a nod to acknowledge, but deep down he is not as confident as before, he has seen the power of what mortals can do from the past, whereas Cronus has not.
Cronus turns his back on the mortals to ignore them, turning back to look, declaring "It is time".

His army roars, ready to attack.
He commands part of his army to begin the scale of Olympus to attack, but also to test it.
He then commands vast number of demons to attack the mortal forces that are behind them.
Cronus then orders Tartarus to open a huge portal in the ground, so vast and deep that it leads down to the underworld itself, so another huge army of underworld demons and other assorted evil beings can pour out, like a huge swarm of locusts.

Tartarus summons and uses his elements to shake the earth where they stand, making it quake and split, before the ground drops like it has fallen into a sinkhole.
The hole in the ground measures a diameter over two hundred meters wide, with sloped edges for demons and other trapped dark souls to climb out from.
The hole emits sounds that can be heard for miles around.
As the noises get louder, the sight of hundreds of demons and other figures can now be heard coming from the portal, then soon to be seen.
The mortal armies see this and begin their advance at a rapid rate.

The screams of the mortal battlefield soldiers are sounded as they charge at the dark forces, their guns fire, rockets and grenades launch.
The sky, filled with planes and helicopters unload their weapons of bullets and missiles at the dark forces below.
In the seas, the guns of all ships move upwards before releasing an arsenal of weaponry and firepower never witnessed on this scale before.
Ballistic missiles launch from beneath the waves of the sea from the submarines below.
Rail guns on the ships unleash volleys of firepower, all aimed at the dark Gods.
A vast fleet of bombers in the sky release drones, armed with mini missiles and mini machine guns, dropping to the battlefield below to target demons of the dark army.
Cronus and the other Gods continue to ignore the mortal forces as they all join to start the firebombing at the base of Olympus, using all their ungodly powers to do so, creating a barrage of artillery at it.
Occasionally missiles launched by the mortal forces will strike a dark force God, momentarily knocking one of them off balance, before they turn toward the mortals and unleash a fury of retaliation, before turning back to their goal, to bring Olympus to its knees and to turn it into a pile of rubble.

"CHARIOT!" screams Apollo from on top of Olympus.
Suddenly, two huge beams of light shine down in front of him, as elements combine quickly to reveal two giant beasts of horses and a golden carriage.
He jumps on and screams at them to dive as he takes up the fight with the dark Gods.
Athena also screams for her chariot and descends straight away, too, her weapons branded in both hands, ready to strike.
The other Gods perform a gigantic leap upwards over the edge before diving to join Apollo and Athena, unleashing their arsenal of weaponry towards the dark forces below.

The fight is now truly on.

Stockholm Syndrome

Demos are now scaling Olympus at an alarming speed, clawing at the rocks, and leaping upwards, scowling, screaming, desperate to get to the top with the only aim that is to kill everything they see.
On top of Olympus, Hermes approaches Zeus.
"Zeus, welcome back" before bowing and dropping to one knee, head bowed, as does Hemera.
Hera approaches and smiles at him then says, "Darling, it's been a long time".
Poseidon bellows out, "Brother! We don't have any time to explain. We need your help NOW!".

Zeus stands before them, dressed in the finest white and gold armour that covers his body like the magnificent warrior that he is, with his cape bellowing in the wind behind him.
His body fizzes with static, his fingertips crackle with lightning cursing through his veins.
He looks at his surroundings and then he smiles as he looks at his fellow Gods, then turns to see Jason, then his smile turns to a straight-faced look.
"Why is this mortal here?" he scorns.
The Gods look on in surprise, but Hermes speaks "My lord, he is the one who brought us back, all of us, including you".
The comment annoys Zeus. "Have you quickly forgotten what the mortals did to us?" he bellows.
Hera approaches his and says, "Zeus! A very long time has passed, thousands of years, things have since changed".
Hemera gets up and calls out, "Zeus, look below you. Look at what the mortals are doing. They fight for us. They are fighting against Cronus and his forces".
Zeus turns to look below at the raging battle.
His face softens a little then says, "They will not win this battle", Hera jumps in straight away with "But with us, with you, we can, we must, we will!".
Zeus then looks at Jason, his expression changes, as if he somehow recognises him.
He becomes a bit more welcoming towards Jason.

Jason speaks "Please, they need your help, we need your help".
Jason keeps his eyes fixed on Zeus, as Zeus himself looks back at Jason.
Hemera gets up and goes over to Jason, taking his hand to show her support and declares "Zeus, Jason is a great man, he is pure of heart and soul" before declaring before them all "And I love him, with all my heart, so much so that I will die for him".
Zeus looks surprised at first, having just heard that a God is in love with a mortal, but quickly remembering all the activities he has got up to over the years, he looks slightly down at the ground, then up again at them, as his stance now softens, then looking at Hera and gives her a smile. "The things that we do for love, no matter what we are," she says to Zeus, with a gentle smile and a welcoming demeanour.
Zeus then turns back to Jason and smiles and says to Jason, "If one mortal can do this, then I admit to being impressed".
Just then, demons crest the top of the mountain and charge across the open land, sprinting past the temples and monuments that make up the city centre of Olympus.
The Gods and Jason quickly see them and stare back for a split second.
Zeus looks at the Gods and Jason, smiles, and then he turns to face the demons and laughs at them, as they continue heading their way.

Zeus rises off the ground and hovers in the air.
From behind his back with his right hand, he pulls out his legendary thunderbolt.
His left hand reaches back and pulls out the legendary sword of Olympus.
His eyes turn a brilliant ice white, his veins light up ice white too.
Lightning from the sky above strikes the ground.
Lightning spits from his fingertips, then he opens his mouth and screams an almighty scream that pierces the ears of the attacking hordes.

For a moment they stop to hold their ears in pain, before screaming themselves and continuing to charge forward.

"You are about to witness something very special," Hermes says animatedly to Jason and the others that are with him.

Hermes brandishes his spear, and it glows with a golden aura.

Hera pulls out her daggers that light up and glow.

Hemera pulls out a sword and shield that glows magnificent gold.

Jason looks at them and suddenly feels vulnerable compared to what they have.

"What about me?!" Jason says, looking a little nervous at not having anything to fight or defend himself with, and that he is mortal too.

"Take this!" Poseidon says to him, as he hands over a glowing golden bow with no string.

Jason looks at it, and quickly understands what to do, then pulls back at an invisible string that appears when it's under tension.

An arrow appears, ready to be released.

Jason smiles and thanks him.

"You will also need some of this!" Poseidon says again, before putting his hands on the back and front of Jason's head, sending a pulse of light into his head, Jason gasps as he gathers himself to realise that he now possesses some powers to give him more strength, power, speed, and agility.

Poseidon then reaches behind his back and pulls out his infamous trident and shakes it, making it grow double its length, its three prongs emerging from the end.

Then Poseidon's usually happy demeanour changes dramatically. Staring at the demons, he screams out, "You think you can kill me? The great Poseidon? All you have done is come here to die!" He concludes his tirade at the demons with, "I will messing kill you all!"

Jason looks at Poseidon and chuckles, thinking this is the first time he has heard a God curse.

"My boy" Poseidon starts, "This will not be the worse of words that you will hear today!".

Jason then breaks into a laugh and nods his head in appreciation of Poseidon's humour.

Tantra

Zeus launches himself forward directly into the middle of the enormous pack of demons and ferociously swings his sword so quickly that it becomes a blur, slicing every demon near him in, cutting them in half or severing their limbs.
He uses the lightning bolt weapon in his other hand to stab demons through their hearts and heads, then waves it around and sends bolts of lightning through multiple bodies of demons that are in its way.
Lightning continues to strike the surrounding ground, almost like a protective force field, striking and instantly killing any demon they hit.
Zeus is the ultimate warrior, and as he battles, he slaughters dozens of demons, his armour becoming blood-soaked.
The top of Olympus quickly filling with demonic bodily parts, sent flying in all directions by the King of the Gods.

Poseidon, Hermes, Hera, Hemera and Jason charge into the vast hordes of demons, screaming their war cries as they smash into the wall of demons now before them, slashing away, swinging swords to slice and stab the dark creatures of the underworld.
They thrust spears deep into the chests and heads of demons that dare to be near them, killing them with a lust for rage that has now gripped them, taking them on with the same bravery as the mortals below.

As Jason battles alongside the Gods, he can see that once docile people have now turned into the ultimate killing machines, he has only ever read about.
Never did he think, or anyone, that he would get to witness this.
It fills him with confidence to do battle alongside them.
Poseidon charges at a large group of demos as he screams blue murder at them, his trident spinning in his hands so fast as he stabs and throws the demons about like rag dolls, then waving it in a circle above his head to decapitate those that venture in his path.

He grabs one with his hand and squeezes its neck so hard that it snaps.
Its head rolls limp beside its body. With other demons, he stabs their necks with his trident, lifting it up quickly to rip their heads off from their bodies, decapitating one after the other.

Hermes is a blur as he moves so fast, so quick that the demon's eyes can't keep up with where he is or was, as he moves around them, stabbing them in their chests and heads, and before they even slump down to the ground, he has already slayed the next one near him.

Hera lets out an ear-splitting scream as she charges at the demon masses.
Her face contorts as she changes her physique and looks from a beautiful woman to some type of mutated monster.
Her teeth grow long fangs like a wild cat, her hair fizzes and turns to electric and her eyes light up ice white as smashes into the demons like a possessed banshee, daggers in both hands, slicing demons, stabbing them, and slashing at them.
As demons try to battle her, she leaps up many times on their shoulders and stabs them ferociously at the tops of their heads, killing them instantly.

Hemera also becomes a Goddess possessed.
Her eyes turn ice white, her clothing lights up a brilliant ice white, with light emanating from her body.
As she swings her sword at demons, flashes of sunlight come off it like an echo of the blade, cutting through demons caught in its wake.
She leaps up high before smashing back into the ground on top of a demon, crushing its body, then she opens her mouth at one of them as pure light comes out and blinds the demon enough for her to pivot and swing her sword to cut its head clean off.
Jason, who is busy fighting demons next to her, flashes her a look and shouts "God, I love it when you're angry!".

She gives him a quick glance and laughs at his comment, then blows him a kiss, before she continues to slay the other demons that attack.

One by one, the demons on top of Olympus fall, being pulverised, slain, killed, dismembered, destroyed.
It is total carnage as the Gods have burst into life to show their true fighting nature and powers.
Jason takes a quick moment to watch them in awe of what they can and have done, and affords himself a quick smile, glad that they are on his side.
The Gods have finished the demons off.
They turn to look around to check that there are no more, and then turn to look at each other as they afford a quick smile to each other.
They all turn to head to the ledge to survey the war below.

Suddenly, from the floor, one demon that was unnoticed and still alive quickly jumps up, and runs at them, and as it does, it leaps up in the air, its mouth wide open, about to fully consume Hemera's head.
Jason spots this and reacts quickly by running and jumping in between Hemera and the demon.
Hemera is knocked to the floor with Jason on top of her, and with the demon on top of him, Jason pushes his sword into the demons open mouth, and thrusts hard as he screams, with the sword now pushed through the back of the demons' head.
He lets go of the sword and quickly puts his hands inside the demon's mouth, using his fingers to push through its skull, gripping either side of its head, and pulls his hands outwards to split the head of the demon clean in half.

The Gods are stunned for a moment but then sigh with relief that Jason and Hemera are OK.
Jason pushes the beast off him and turns his body around, whilst still on top of her.
Hemera at first is shocked but then she looks at Jason in the eyes, her breathing heavy, but then she smiles and says to him "Thank you!".

She leans her head up and plants a kiss on his lips. "I would die for you too you know!" Jason tells her with a smile, as Hemera laughs, recalling her comment to Zeus about Jason.

After they have killed the last demon, Zeus helps Jason to his feet and declares, "We will never abandon the mortals again" before smiling at Jason and nodding at him.
Jason drops to one knee and thanks him.
"No time for that Jason" Zeus declares, before giving him a small smile.
Jason stands back up and smiles back at Zeus and nods in appreciation.

Zeus then turns his attention to the battlefield and summons lightning from the sky above, raising his hands high as if to collect the bolts, and as they fire down into his hands, he thrust his hands forwards at huge packs of demons down below, instantly striking dozens of them, killing them instantly, to help protect the mortal forces that are beginning to be overwhelmed in numbers.
Hera tells him, "Zeus, we need to join them, they need our help down on the lands".
Zeus smiles at her and nods, before saying, "I have missed you my love", to which she smiles at him, as the others look on, waiting to take his lead.

Zeus turns his attention back again, looking below at the war now raging on the battlefield, then back up at the others with him, nods at them all, then he leaps up into the air, with turbulence beneath his feet, as he arcs his trajectory and launches himself at an incredible speed to the fighting down below on the battlefield.
The other Gods of Hera, Hermes, Poseidon, and Hemera, with Jason, pursue his lead, as they too jump off and dive to join the fight below.

The Fate of Our Brave

The fighting has now become fierce as Gods fight other Gods, mortals fighting demons.
Infantry soldiers are working together in groups just to kill one or two demons at a time, such is their strength and endurance.
The fighting mortal soldiers throw rockets and grenades, scattering around, as soldiers try their best to repel the demons that swarm around them amongst the challenging landscape.
In the elevated positions in the hills and peaks, hundreds of snipers from dozens of armed forces take fire at the demons to help their comrades.
Sometimes it takes a few bullets to take the demons down fully, but the biggest problem they face is that the demons keep on coming.
The portal from the ground that they pour out from seems to feel like a never-ending supply of them.

In the Thermaic Gulf, just off the coast of Greece where all the warships are, Tartarus and Hades have summoned the sirens of the seas to attack the ships.
The sirens, who are beautiful but deadly women, who take on mermaid form when in water, obey their dark lords and swim towards the battleships in the ocean.
The radars from each ship beep with alarm, picking up multiple signals from everywhere, with a huge amount of data that the sailors report to their commanders, showing vast swarms coming towards them.

Submarines under the surface of the water also pick up on their sonars the vast swathes of sirens that are coming towards them.
The ships are unclear of what it is they are facing at first, but they quickly find out as the sirens come into view.
The sirens leap from the water, attaching themselves to the ships as they scale the sides of them.

As the crews on board each vessel looks down, they quickly deduce that these creatures are not exactly on their side, based on their aggressive nature as they approach.
"Fire at will!" comes the command from all the ship's captains. Marines and sailors and all crew members take out their firearms and shoot as many of them as they can.

Back on land on the battlefield, Takeru is fighting hard with his special forces outfit.
"We need better weapons!" cries out one of his soldiers. "They just keep coming!" cries out another, as they unload round after round of magazines, spraying bullets at the advancing demons.
"We cannot stop, fire everything you've got!" Takeru yells at them.
All over the battlefield, it is the same story.
Groups of soldiers must fire everything they have just to bring down one or two demons at a time.
They know the odds are stacked against them, but their bravery and will compel them to keep trying their best.

Yusuke and his Shinobi special forces group are about to run out of ammo completely.
All they have left is their hand help weapons.
"Sir!" shouts one of his troops, "I'm empty!".
Yusuke throws him a magazine from his belt to help his colleague to keep up the fight.
After that has run out, his colleague takes out his sword and attacks any demon coming at him.
His other colleagues, who also drop their guns and brandish their swords to go on the offensive, quickly joined him.

Sun Li's forces are now all back-to-back as they are surrounded, doing their best to fight off the oncoming advances of demons.
Twelve of them, squeezed together, all facing outwards as they hold their fingers on their triggers to empty round after round, using their free hand to have the next magazine ready to load up again quickly.

She quickly takes out some frag grenades to throw at the demons in her direction, which helps to blow and dismember a few of the demons, as others in her unit throw stun grenades to disorientate the demons to slow them down.
However, they have limited resources.
A helicopter arrives and hovers above them, as a soldier hangs out of the side door, pushing ammo down to the ground for them.

Tanks roll across the landscape, firing round after round into the packed masses that advance in the near distance to help destroy demons.
Some tanks roll over demons to squash them under their tracks.
Some demons leap up on to the top of the tanks, killing their machine gunners, and try to enter the tanks, pulling on the hatches.
Leonidas and Pelias of the Myrmidon attack forces continue to fight hard, but they, too, are running low on ammo.
One of their attack helicopters arrives and hovers above them, spraying multiple rounds of bullets into the hordes of demons to help support the ground troops.
Leonidas and Pelias quickly grab on to the helicopters' rails by wrapping an arm around it, as the helicopter circles around, allowing them to get some good head shots at the demons.
Once they have run out of ammo, they too pull out their swords and hack away at the demons' heads.

Eudoros and Ino of the Spartan forces run dangerously low.
As the final round leaves the chamber of their guns, they drop their weapons and prepare to fight, pulling out their swords.
"If today is the day we die, we die side by side," she says to Eudoros defiantly.
He looks at her, nods, and smiles, then screams out loud "We, Are, Spartans!" as a rally cry for their troops, who scream with him, all by now out of ammo and now with swords in hands.

Acamas and Medea lead their Trojan forces, all of them attacking one demon at a time, but each time they kill one, a demon kills one of theirs.

With their numbers dwindling, in good timing, a couple of armoured vehicles arrive at the scene, and they all jump in or on top.

They drive around the battlefield and toss grenades and fire whatever ammunition they have left, driving into demons as they fire. "These creatures just don't know when to quit!" she says with a hint of irony.

Acamas laughs as they hold on tight as they fire, helping to support any mortal soldier involved in a battle with the demons.

Out in the thick of the action, it looks grim for the mortal soldiers.

"At this rate, we will not last long," says one soldier to another. One of them runs out of bullets and pulls out a sword, swinging and hacking at a demon, but before he can draw his arms back to strike the next one, a demon quickly appears and crushes him with its hands and bites off his head.

The decapitated soldier drops to the ground as the troops around him recoil back in horror, before unleashing round after round into the demon. "We need help, NOW!" screams Takeru on his radio.

Hephaestus, who is involved in the fighting, looks around at the battlefield and can see that the mortals are now really struggling to hold back the continuous tide of demons that pour forwards at them.

He pauses and thinks for a moment, then his eyes focus into the distance and widen as an excellent idea comes to him.

He instantly shoots up into the sky, into the clouds above, arcing his trajectory, then he dives downwards like a bolt of lightning, directly into the middle of the portal that leads to the underworld.

"Where is he going?" Apollo asks quizzically to Athena, as the two of them rain down fire on the Gods that they are engaged in combat with.

Athena just shrugs and continues to battle the dark Gods.

Hephaestus is now inside the belly of the portal, headfirst, his arms outstretched in front of him.
He creates an energy field in front of his hands as he smashes through hundreds of demons and souls that are ascending from the depths of the portal.
As Hephaestus lands on the floor, he spots demons and souls in the distance, and their noises echoing.
He is now inside the underworld, by the river Styx.

The river Styx is one of five rivers that surrounds the underworld.
Its water holds the key to his mission.
He crouches down and places one hand into the river.
He holds his other hand skywards, pointing to the top of the portal.
At first, he strains at the sheer force of what he is doing, elements falling away from him and phasing. He screams a deathly roar of defiance as elements of gold, silver and bronze particles contained within a huge beam of light shoots out from his outstretched hand that is held skyward.
He acts like a conductor between two massive amounts of energy that now fill up the chamber he is in with light and heat, as his body lights up ice white.
He fights hard to hold his posture but does so as his will is strong.
Hephaestus does not want to let them down. He will not let them down.
Moments later, a huge flash fills the entire length of the portal and then a huge beam of light exits the vast entrance of the portal and shoots up to the sky.
A brilliant glow of whites, golds, and ultraviolet colours lights up the clouds, creating an incredible sight and noise.
Then the same colours and light strike out in all directions, like an electromagnetic pulse has been activated, making the ground shake.
The planes and helicopters in the sky shake for a moment before settling back to normal, as do the ships in the sea.

Reapers

Everyone on the battlefield suddenly looks up to the sky, to see it filled with thousands of bright tiny objects, that get bigger and bigger as they fall quickly to the ground.
Tens of thousands of weapons hit the floor, all by the feet of the mortal fighting forces.
One soldier looks down at the ground and notices what looks like an ancient version of a bow.
"What the hell is that?!" she asks, looking puzzled.
"Are we supposed to fight them with this? We might as well pick up and throw rocks!" exclaims another soldier standing next to her, both bemused.
To begin with, the mortal forces ignore the weapons, not fully understanding what they are or why they have fallen from the sky.

Sun Li looks curiously at the ground and picks up what looks like a bow with no string.
The moment she touches it, it glows gold. She moves her hand around it to see what it is.
Her hand brushes past where the string should be and as she does so, the string appears then disappears when she moves her hand away.
She quickly puts two and two together, then pulls on the invisible string.
A golden arrow made of pure light appears.
She takes aim at a demon and releases the arrow.
The arrow hits the demon in the chest, instantly melting it, then the arrow explodes, destroying the demon.
Her face instantly lights up.
Straight away she screams at anyone who can hear her, to drop their weapons and pick up one that has landed on the ground.
Some nearby soldiers hear her and do as commanded, dropping their weapons and picking up one from the ground.
One of them takes aim and fires it, destroying a demon on impact.
Everyone nearby sees this and takes note straight away.

Suddenly, everyone around her drops their modern-day weapons and picks up one of the ancient-looking weapons and uses them instead.
Instantly, demons are being killed with single shots fired at them.
Word spreads instantly throughout the battlefield as radios inform all soldiers from all forces to drop their modern weapons and to pick up one from the floor instead.
The battlefield mortals scream a huge war cry as they watch fellow soldiers killing demons with ease as they use the new weapons, all pick up the ancient weapons next to them and use them.
Each weapon when touched glows gold as they do so, lighting up, ready to fire or be used in combat.
This has quickly become a game changer for the mortal forces.

Takeru picks up an ancient-looking samurai sword that instantly glows gold, its blade crackles like static electric.
His colleagues do the same, as they set about the surrounding demons, killing them much more easily, with a single stroke of the blade from each soldier that swipes at each demon.
An array of Bushi soldiers' charge into the hordes of attacking demons, slashing, and slicing their way through the vast packs, crying out their war cries as they do so.

Yusuke picks up two daggers, they too glow gold, then he quickly stabs at many demons as he slides beneath them, then jumping up to stab many more of them in the head, using his martial art skills to dodge counter attacks.
His colleagues do the same, grabbing weapons and launching devastating counterattacks.
They use of all their martial art skills to go on the offensive to repel and push back the dark forces.

Leonidas and Pelias of the Myrmidon forces quickly pick up glowing spears and shields, making their fabled attack formations, thrusting their spears into demons that try to break through their defense's.

They hold them at bay with their shields, as they lock them tight together, holding formation, using the small gaps in between to thrust their spears into the demons, killing them with ferocity.
The demons try to break through their barricades but with little success as the soldiers hold firm and counterattack.

Eudoros and Ino of the Spartan forces also quickly pick up some spears, swords and shields and create their infamous phalanx formation, all coming together with shields surrounding their group.
Their shields resembling the ancient hoplon designs, originally used from thousands of years ago.
Their spears protrude from the small notches in the shields to allow them to stab any demon that tries to break their formation.
The spartan force all grunt in unison, their battle cry, like the regular beating of a drum as they step forward.

Acamas and Medea lead their Trojan special forces into picking up slingshots and crossbows and unleashing the ammunition they create.
He pulls the trigger on his crossbow, but instead of one arrow being fired, hundreds of golden arrows fire out per second, spraying and killing scores of demons.
Acamas turns the weapon from side to side, killing demons that flank his forces, not even needing to let go of the trigger.
The arrows keep on coming as a huge smile appears on his face.
Medea swings her slingshot and lashes it towards demons, with small golden balls of light that hit many demons, instantly melting them before they explode into many pieces.
Her face lights up at her new toy.

Every soldier who bravely showed up to fight on the battlefield, regardless of their country or origin, has now abandoned their modern weapons in favour of using one of the ancient weapons provided by Hephaestus.

Up high in the sky, huge bomber planes open their cargo bay doors to release thousands of drones.
They spill out from them, whirring into life and plummet to the battle below, and as they do, they unload an immense arsenal of weaponry attached to them.
Tiny sidewinder missiles shoot across the sky, twisting and turning as they lock on to their targets below, blowing up demons on impact.

Every time a drone has deployed its payload of mini rockets, it unleashes golden bullets from its small machine gun attachments, sending bullets spraying into hordes of demons.
When they have completely run out of ammo, each drone then locks on to a target and propels itself towards its target, detonating and exploding on impact, killing that demon.

Fighter jets in the sky nosedive near to the ground and unleash a volley of machine gun fire to strafe the vast packs of demons, creating mass devastation to the dark armies' resources, before they pull up and come about for another volley of fire, their engines screaming as they do so.

Hundreds of mortal forces run towards and line the perimeter of the portal to fight and strike down any creature that dares to come out of it.

With their newfound weapons, the mortals have revitalised themselves.
They now have the confidence to fight the dark forces as equals on the battlefield.

All the battlefield commanders from all the armies receive messages and instructions from their generals, warning them of an imminent missile strike from the warships just off the coast.
They relay the messages to their on-field troops who take action to avoid the impact zone.

About sixty warships turn their guns skywards and release a vast arsenal of missiles, all of them being fired within seconds of each other.
The sky suddenly becomes full of them, all screaming inland towards their targets.

The leaders of the mortal armies quickly give the order to the troops on the ground to evacuate the rim of the portal, as they have two minutes to get to their minimum safe distance.
The troops look up to the sky as they run as fast as possible away from the portal, spotting the missiles in the distance heading their way.
Demons continue to pour out of the portal as the mortal's sprint as fast as they can, aware of the incoming arsenal of rockets.
The missiles, now overhead, turn direction and head directly towards the portal, with dozens of them shooting directly into the hole.
Two seconds later, multiple explosions take place that shake the ground like a huge earthquake.
A blinding flash spills out from the hole, filling the surrounding area.

The noise of the explosions is immense, deafening.
Fire and smoke spill out from the portal just as fast as the speed of the missiles had travelled at.
Hundreds of demons and other creatures trying to get out are instantly wiped out.
The demonic creatures just outside the rim of the portal are also burned to death, not standing a chance to escape.
The shockwave caused by the event sends hundreds of demons off their feet and maims and dismembers many more.
The portal cracks and creaks, followed by the violent shaking and rumbling of the surrounding earth.
The portal collapses in on itself, creating an even bigger hole, one that is filled only with the dirt and rocks.
As the dust settles, soldiers cry out in joy, as they can see that no more demons coming out from it.

Destructo

Cronus is incandescent with rage at what he has seen.
He screams aloud, his anger clearly visible for all to see.
Cronus immediately unleashes a volley of fireballs, striking anything and anyone in his path, instantly killing dozens of mortal soldiers, also hitting demons, and slightly wounding nearby Gods fighting his dark forces.
Some of his forces try to hide for cover as the fireballs rain down around them.
Some of the Gods fighting for him flash him a look of anger, but do not challenge him over his actions, instead choosing to try and predict where he will fire, doing their best to avoid his outburst of anger.

"HADES! TARTARUS!" he cries out.
Both Hades and Tartarus quickly come to him.
He screams at them to release the many beasts under his control.
"Release Cratos"
"Release Cetus"
"Release Hydra"
"Release the Gorgons"
They both look at him and nod in understanding.

Hades and Tartarus obey his commands, then both turn to face the battlefield and raise their hands up.
Elements leave their hands like beams of light and fire down upon the land below them.

The earth begins to shake and rumble, then a huge split in the earth appears, spanning some four hundred meters long.
It widens more, opened by the sheer force of the impact created by the two dark force Gods.
Everyone can now hear the deafening roars as the mortal forces, Gods on both sides, demons, and other dark creatures, stop fighting to look at what is coming out.

Cratos, a huge muscular beast of a God, climbs out from the vast hole in the ground and immediately swings his deadly weapon, a huge hammer, at the mortals and good Gods, striking dead dozens of the mortal forces.
Three of the Gods from the forces of good come to fight him off.
Cratos is undeterred though, and fights them, he seems unstoppable as he takes hit after hit from the Gods, but they have little effect.

Cetus is the next beast to climb out of the huge split in the earth.
A monstrous creature, dripping with water, its teeth as large as the average sized mortal, standing fifty meters tall, as it roars and swipes its massive hands at the mortals and Gods that now fight it, stomping its feet on top of anyone in its path.
The good Gods try to direct its attention away from the mortals as they engage it in battle.

The beast Hydra is next to climb out.
This creature has multiple heads and a body not unlike a dragon.
Its heads begin to grab and bite nearby mortals, swallowing and crushing them with its jaws.
People run and scream in horror at the beast as it devours and makes its way across the battlefield.
Soldiers try their best to fight it off as Gods use their weapons to repel its attacks, but the beast is a force to be reckoned with. The Gods manage to sever one of its heads off but it quickly regenerates, another head forming to replace its previous head.

Finally, the Gorgons appear.
Three sisters, snake-like bodies with human heads and snakes for hair, led by their eldest sister, the mythical Medusa.
As they appear, they scream and glare at soldiers on the battlefield, turning anyone who looks their way into stone.
Soldiers do their best to not look at them, but many of them are caught in their gaze and suffer a stony death.

As they turn each soldier into stone, the sisters slither by and swipe their tails to destroy them, sending stones flying out at great speeds, with some pieces striking soldiers and killing or wounding them.

Panic now sets in with the soldiers as they try their best to fight off these demonic creatures.
"What the hell are they?!" screams one soldier to his colleague.
"How the hell do I know?!" he replies.
Another one screams out, "Get out of here, find cover!".

Zeus sees this and is extremely concerned by the array of monsters that his father Cronus has summoned from the grave earth they have come from.
He acts quickly, seeing that the mortal armies are suffering at the hands of these evil creatures.

"Hephaestus! Poseidon!" cries out Zeus.
Both Gods quickly come to Zeus to receive his commands.
"Bring forth Talos!" he cries out.
"Bring forth the Hecatonchires"
"Bring forth the Cyclops"
"Bring forth the Giants" he commands.

Both Gods then turn to face an area of land not occupied by mortals, doing their best to not harm them.
They lift their arms to face their palms into an unoccupied space of land just over the visible scene and fire beams of shining elements at it, using an immense amount of force to do so.

Thumper

The fighting and chaos continue on the ground and in the air as the forces for good and evil battle it out.
The evil beasts that were summoned by Cronus continue to wreak havoc, destroying many of the mortals' vehicles on the ground and in the air.
Tanks, armoured vehicles, and attack helicopters continue to fire at them.

Even when armed with stygian weapons, they still take more effort to repel their attacks.
Then a gigantic crack of thunder sounds across the land, followed by lightning, making everyone look up.
Everyone then turns to face the direction of the noise.
The noise turns from thunder and lightning to one of the sounds of falling trees and tumbling rocks.

Hundreds of trees fall, as if a huge bulldozer has run them over. Huge rocks and boulders roll along the ground from all directions.
"Oh great! What now?!" shouts a soldier to a colleague near him, as his colleague shrugs.

A giant head appears on the horizon, then emerges even more to reveal an enormous body of a bronze giant, striding forward, standing some fifty meters tall.
It is the legendary Talos, the bronze giant.
As he emerges fully from the trees, he stomps on many demons, instantly killing them with each step he takes.
As he moves across the landscape, he heads directly towards the monsters that are Cratos and Cetus to take up the fight with them.

Next to emerge is another set of colossuses, three giant figures standing some forty meters tall with more hands on their bodies that you could count.
The Hecatonchires arrive and run into battle to take on the giant monsters of Cetus and Cratos.

As they move in their direction, they use their many hands to pick up and throw demons across vast distances like rag dolls. They join Talos in directly fighting the dark monsters.

Next to arrive at the battlefield is the army of Cyclops, that bear one eye on their heads, standing some thirty meters tall, muscular, and fierce in looks and abilities.
All of them stride towards the battlefield, instantly striking down demons and dark souls who stand in their way.
They move quickly to intercept the beasts that were released by Hades and Tartarus, especially the Hydra and Gorgons.
They roar blood-curdling screams as they launch into battle with them, swiping their arms and using their weapons to knock away demons as if they were swatting flies.

Talos gets the attention of Cratos, as the two giants begin to grapple and fight each other, each one striking blows on one another.
Talos sends Cratos crashing down, then Cratos grabs hold of Talos, pulling him to the floor as the giants battle it out, trading punches and wrestling to get the better of one another.

One of the Hecatonchaeires strides over and grapples with Cetus, pulling it down to stop its attacks, using all its hands to pin and subdue the beast as it fights against it.
Another of the Hecatonchaeires joins Talos to take on Cratos, pinning the dark creatures' arms back as Talos strangles it.
In a one-on-one battle of strength, Cratos is the stronger, but with two giants of the Gods world, both using their hands to fight it, the Hecatonchires fighting Cratos uses its many hands to counter the attacks being thrown its way, using some hands to hold the arms and weapon of Cratos as Talos continues to strangle and punch Cratos.
The beast is soon overwhelmed.

Another Hecatonchire then grabs hold of the Hydra beast, holding its five necks in its hands and using its other hands to fight off the repeated attacks from the hydra, as it wrestles control of the beast, snapping one neck at a time to pull each head off its neck so that they cannot grow back.

The cyclops instantly run towards the Gorgons and take up battle with them, avoiding the need to look at the Gorgons as each cyclops has its eye shut, to avoid being turned into stone.
One useful ability the cyclops all share is that they do not need to look at their enemy as long as one of them can do the looking for them, as they have the power of shared sight, so one cyclops stands back from the battle as the others keep their eyes shut and battle hard with the Gorgons, striking them fiercely as the gorgons strike back with vicious blows of their own, using their tails to swipe blows against the cyclopes.

The battlefield is now a scene of carnage and mayhem unfolding at every corner, every scrap of land, taking place all around for everyone.
It is a sight to behold, to witness these Gods of war, fighting against each other.

Ten Thousand Warriors

Cronus sees the ongoing struggles that his forces are suffering, as every time he has sent additional dark forces to get the better of the Gods and mortals, he can see the tide has turned back in the favour of the Gods, and the mortals.

Once again, Cronus summons Hades and Tartarus to him to open another portal.
"Cronus, we only have enough portal elements to open up one more portal," Tartarus tells him.
"I DON'T CARE!" Cronus screams at him.
"DO IT!" he demands.
Hades and Tartarus obey, not even stopping to think to question him, as they too want the destruction of Olympus, but nonetheless they are aware of what they have left to offer, as they glance at each other before carrying out the command.
They will still have other tricks up their sleeves, but for now they need all the help they can get to turn the tide back in their favour against the mortal forces and Gods.

Once again, Hades and Tartarus use their powers to concentrate elements, sending them through bright beams from their hands and into the earth, creating another giant portal that descends deep down.

The earth rumbles and splits, like a massive earthquake has cut the land in two almost, then the surrounding ground collapses in on itself.
This time the portal is even more vast that the last one, its diameter stretching almost three hundred meters across.
Dozens of soldiers are swallowed up into the hole, falling to their untimely deaths, as do many demons too.
No one around it can escape the fall into it.
Cronus has once again been indiscriminate in his approach, but he doesn't care.
For him, it is now about winning at all costs.
As the ground stops shaking and the dust falls gently around the portal, muffled groans are heard in the distance.

The noises become louder and louder, followed by screams and loud knocking noises.
Hands appear on the edges of the portal, grabbing hold of the rocks and roots at the top of it.
The Gods and mortals look on, eyes staring, waiting in apprehension at what is climbing out.

The hands of demons appear, followed by hands of other beasts not yet seen to be recognised, as the sounds of knocking and clattering get louder still.
Then, the hands of what appear to be skeletal looking appear.
Suddenly, an outpouring of demons and skeletons charge out in their hundreds, spilling out from the huge portal in all directions.
An army of demons and disfigured humanoid bodies now charge into battle.
Skeletal-looking souls, followed by an outpouring of hundreds of demons and yet more skeletons charging out of a huge portal.
Behind them all, now in their thousands, the skeleton army continually climb out from the pit.
It is now wave after wave of souls, demons, and skeletons of the undead.

Hundreds of them charge toward Olympus, followed by thousands more that adorn the battlefield.
The change in tactics and directions given by Cronus is now to destroy Olympus. If mortals are in their path then they will be fought against, but for now the command is to go route one at the giant home of the Gods.

Apollo shouts out to Athena, who is fighting near him, "You have got to be kidding!".
Athena shouts back, "If they want a war, then we'll give them one!" as she lets out a war cry.
Apollo and Athena change course, circling back around on their chariots up in the air, then they leap high into the air as their chariots instantly change back into elements.

Apollo and Athena absorb the elements that were their chariots with lightning speed.
They smash down into the first wave of the dark forces attacking Olympus.
After the initial smash, they stand at the base of Olympus, defending it with all their strength, speed, and guile.
Many of the other Gods stop their own personal battles to join Apollo and Athena in the fight to save their home.

Jason and Hermes are deep in the battle, fighting off hordes of demons as they move quickly and sharply, slashing at them as they fight to protect those who bravely fight around them.
Jason shouts to Hermes, "Why do they protect Olympus and not fight with us?"
Hermes replies quickly, as they continue to fight.
"If Olympus falls, we all fall. It is a conductor for the elements that give us power. No Olympus means no power for us Gods. if that happens, we all lose."
Jason replies, "Fair point!" as he continues to fight alongside Hermes.

The dark forces continue to pour forward, as the mortal forces also race across the land to help defend Olympus, attacking any demons that they come across.
Some demons are distracted from their orders and turn to fight the mortal armies.
The order is given to all air-based vehicles to turn their fire on the advancing hordes to also help distract them, trying to divert their path away from Olympus and towards the soldiers so that they can take them on in battles.
Cronus cries out and screams at his army to ignore the mortals and to head to Olympus, they hear his commands, but they find it difficult to break the mortal defenses down as confusion sets in.
The mortals have now become well organised and each army's commander communicates with his or her counterpart to share the information, making sure that their attacks are coordinated.

Sanctus Immortale

Back at the base of Olympus, the fighting becomes intense as Gods from the dark forces make their way over to smash their way through to the home of the Gods.
The Gods led by Zeus, quickly intervene, fighting them off, one on one or in small groups, as mortal forces nearby swarm over to help in the fight to fend off, to kill the demons that are attacking.

Nemesis launches a scathing attack on Poseidon, jumping on his back and clawing at his face with her hands, trying to gouge his eyes.
He waves his trident to knock her off but cannot get the right angle to do so, so he drops it to use his hands instead.
He reaches up with both hands, grabbing her by the head, then throws her to the floor.
She screams at him, "I will kill you!".
He extends a hand to lift elements and launches a wave of liquid at her, soaking her all over.
She looks at herself then sneers at him, "Is that all you've got? Throwing water at me!?" as she laughs at him hysterically.
Poseidon belly laughs back and replies, "Who said anything about water?"
At which point she then realises her skin is burning, for Poseidon has thrown a wave of Stygian Acid at her.
She screams in agony as her skin starts to drip and sag, then finally, her body slumping to the floor as it melts and seeps into the gaps of the ground where she just stood.
Poseidon smiles and then continues to help his fellow Gods defend Olympus.

Ares strides over with the look of thirst in his eyes, swinging his sword around quickly, then launches an attack at his sister Athena.
She defends herself with her shield, screaming at him as she launches her own counter attacks at him.

Each strike against her shield sends her backwards as Ares is powerful, knocking her back, but each time he does, Athena counters, sending elements to burn and scold his face, scarring his looks.
Ares much admires his own looks and feels the burning of her attack.
He screams at her in a fit of rage as they continue to trade blows.

Atlas attempts to use his immense strength to gain an advantage over Apollo in their fight, but Apollo proves to be quick and evades his attacks while simultaneously firing arrows at him.
Although Apollo hits Atlas with each arrow, Atlas simply removes them from his chest and continues to advance. However, Apollo counters Atlas by capturing sunlight in the palm of his hand and throwing bright photons into Atlas's face, temporarily blinding him before continuing to fire arrows.
Apollo is no fool.
He knows Atlas is far superior in strength, so he keeps his distance to fight him, using his speed and tactical awareness.

Artemis battles with Epimetheus, who charges at her without care or consideration, and each time he does, Artemis changes shape to avoid his attacks, taking the form of a wolf to lower herself closer to the ground as he swings his sword at her.
He then changes to using a spear to stab at her with short thrusting movements, but each time she moves clear, changing quickly into a hawk, then back to human form.
Each time she does she has a split-second advantage to scratch his face, or bite his limbs, as they continue to fight.

Each time any demons attack Aphrodite, she changes her facial features and stares at them, using her elements to hypnotise and bewitch them.
Then, she switches her facial features from beauty to a horrific looking face with fangs for teeth, and turning her eyes blood shot red, then releasing the most horrific sounding screams.

Finally, she uses her scythe weapon to slash at their bodies, exposing their internal organs that spill out onto the floor, while they are still in a trancelike state.
Artemis calls out to Aphrodite and jokes, "Who says beauty is in the eye of the beholder!", both laughing as they continue to fight, finding a rare moment to see the humour amongst the carnage that surrounds them.

Hestia battles with Aion.
Hestia, a usually very mild-mannered Goddess, but not today.
This of all days her inner warrior comes to the surface.
She uses fire to repel the attacks on her made by Aion.
In return, Aion also uses fire to attempt to burn her as they spar with each other, moving around to attack and counterattack each other.
Hestia is quick, and stronger than what Aion gives her credit for.
She creates flames of fire and burning elements to wound Aion, as she moves swiftly between attacks.

Nyx attacks Hera, but Hera slashes away at her with her daggers, each time slashing at Nyx's body.
In retaliation, Nyx throws darkness at Hera, trying to cloud her vision with darkness, using her hands to send shadow and night elements.
Hera quickly changes into a raven to maneuver out of the way of her attacks, then circles Nyx before diving.
Hera transforms back to human form and plunges her daggers into the middle of Nyx's neck, slashing it then ripping her hands outwards to sever her head, sending it rolling to the floor.
Hera looks at Zeus and asks, "One of your conquests, was she?".
Zeus glances over at Hera and declares, "I never liked that bitch anyway!", to which she does smirk, appreciating his response, before turning her deadly attentions elsewhere.

Helios fights with Lapetus.
Helios uses his hands to absorb and send waves of solar flares and fires them at Lapetus, scolding and burning him.
In return, Lapetus gets as close as possible to strike Helios with his hands.
Each time his hands make contact with any part of Helios he necrotises the elements on that part of him, so Helios quickly changes tactics to fire more solar flares from a safer distance to prevent more damage to himself.

Hyperion and Ananke meet in battle.
Hyperion uses his powers of speed and light to deceive and strike at Ananke, sending her backwards and knocking her over.
Ananke quickly takes on board the attack patterns that Hyperion uses and dodges his attacks, learning from each one he uses, and before too long Hyperion realises this and must change tactics to get the better of her.
They fight in a continuous game of cat and mouse, trying to strike each other with powerful blows.

Oceanus and Tethys work together as they battle with Thanatos.
They use their powers of hydrokinesis to raise waves of liquid from the ground and air to repel and knock back Thanatos.
In return, Thanatos fires necrotic elements at them both.
Each time when hit, parts of Oceanus and Tethys turn dark and unable to function.
Thanatos is a powerful God and is more than a match for Oceanus and Tethys.
He eventually overcomes them and necrotises enough of them to incapacitate them.
As they lie on the ground looking at each other, mortally wounded, Thanatos walks over to them, smirking.
Oceanus whispers to Tethys that he loves her, but as he does so, Thanatos fires one last volley at him, turning his body into a pile of colourless elements.
Tethys screams out in anguish as Thanatos walks away laughing, leaving her on the floor, paralysed and in agony.

Theia takes up battle with Typhon.
She knows she is no match for him, but Theia has the power of foresight to predict, so as she watches Typhon's attacks. Each time she does, she can move out of the way in time. Her best chances of survival are to keep moving, to keep her distance, to tire him out.
Typhon uses all his abilities to strike Theia, using his elements to create wind and fire, spitting poison from his hands at her, but each time she can predict his movements.
Another game of cat and mouse ensues with these two Gods.

Selene doesn't wait to defend her position; she goes straight into attack once she realises Perses has her in his sights.
She grabs and throws shadows and darkness at him, then she launches elements that make him drowsy, to daze and confuse him, whilst at the same time wielding her sword to slash at Perses.

Like Ares, Perses is delusional with a thirst for war and destruction, as his only strategy is to attack no matter the cost, so he does not back down.
Selene and Perses engage in a bitter battle as each one strikes blows at each other, drawing ichor in the process from each connection they make on each other's bodies with their weapons, inflicted by the other.
Selene, though, is powerful, and gets the upper hand, wounding Perses to the point that he must retreat or face certain death.

Nike and Pallas lock eyes on each other.
Nike looks at him and says, "Is this the way you want things to end, father?".
Pallas looks at her with a look of remorse and regret, but then replies, "I cannot change the way I am daughter. Cronus controls me now. I am sorry,", then he charges at her with his sword drawn as they lock weapons in a fight of father and daughter at the bottom of Olympus.

Pallas is strong, very strong, but Nike is too quick for him, fending off his attacks and moving swiftly to get out of the way as he swings his sword at her.
Nike only half-heartedly fights back at him to begin with, as Pallas was once a good God, but his head was now turned to the dark forces.
Eventually Pallas realises he cannot catch Nike, she is too quick.
He finally drops to his knees, exhausted, giving Nike the advantage.
"I cannot stop daughter. If I get back up, I will have to kill you. Now is your chance. Forgive me in the next life," as he looks up at her, waiting for the final blow.
Nike has no choice as she steps forward, raises her sword, and slays her father down, as she knows he would never stop.
That is the curse given to him by Cronus for once fighting against him.
As she kills her father she weeps briefly, her hand stroking his cheek as he fades, but quickly realises she must fight on, helping to defend Olympus.

Asteria is fighting off the attacks of many demons and ungodly souls when she is suddenly attacked by Achlys.
She immediately turns to fight, swinging her sword as they both clash blades and grapple.
Asteria gets the better of Achlys and sends her sprawling to the floor.
Achlys immediately thrusts her hands forward to create a mist around Asteria's face to cloud her vision, then quickly tries to attack her.
Asteria though immediately brings down a shower of meteorites that strike Achlys, sending her into a rage and screaming.
Asteria clears the mist around her as the two Goddesses continue to fight.

Zeus and Cronus finally come face to face.
The two most powerful Gods on the planet.

"You have grown strong, son," Cronus says to him, as he eyes Zeus up.
"Why do you insist on this madness?" Zeus asks him. "Why do you wish for this power obsession?"
"You are a fine one to ask that question son," Cronus replies, "Are you not King of these mortals and your Gods?"
"I am not perfect, father, but I do not wish to destroy these people, nor you or the rest of our family, but your thirst for power is blinding you," Zeus tells him. "You can stop it now!".
Cronus thinks for a moment, then declares to his son, "You know that will never happen".
Zeus senses Cronus is about to attack, so he clutches his blade of Olympus and his thunderbolt weapons tightly.
Cronus steps forward, then breaking into a sprint and charges at Zeus, attacking him by using his hands to fire an immense beam of energy of elements at his son.
Zeus counters by holding up his sword to absorb the attack before thrusting his thunderbolt forward, sending a gigantic bolt of lightning at Cronus, who holds up his hands to use his energy as a shield to protect himself.
The two circle each other, looking for weak spots.
Cronus charges at Zeus as they both fall to the floor.
Zeus reaches up to the sky and pulls down fork lighting that hits Cronus on his back, making him scream out with rage.
The two of them continue to battle away at each other, creating shockwaves that spread out across the battlefield, as Hephaestus and Tartarus come face to face.

Tartarus snarls at him, then raises his right hand upwards. This summonses many demons who instantly attack Hephaestus, but he too instantly clasps his hands, then pulls them outwards, creating an enormous ring of elements that surrounds him, instantly cutting the attacking demons in half.
Tartarus tries again and summons the skeletons to attack.
As they do, the wily Hephaestus uses his hands again to create a weapon that resembles an electric shield, that he crashes into the floor to make the most incredible sound and shockwave, which spreads around him and shatters the bones of the skeletons that are trying to attack him.

Hades sees Hermes and attacks him, trying to stab him with his bident weapon.
Hermes, though, is too quick and dodges each thrust from Hades' weapon.
Hades then points it skywards to bring down demons that are on the side of the mountain that jump off to plummet toward Hermes, but again, Hermes moves out of the way quickly, each sidestep he takes he plunges his spear into the body of a falling demon.
Hades then whistles loudly as his beloved three-headed dog. Cerberus comes over to him, snarling with blood drooling from its teeth.
Each time that Hermes side steps and moves, Cerberus counters, with each of the creature's heads looking in different directions, trying to follow the movements of Hermes, trying to sink its teeth into him.
Hermes, though, is just too quick, and one by one, he stabs each head of the beast with his spear, ramming it down each throat of the beast, which lets out a shriek of pain, before pulling out his spear one more time to plunge it into the chest of the beast, finally killing it.
Hades briefly weeps in despair at his loss, before becoming enraged and once again fighting with Hermes.

On the battlefield, Jason and Hemera fight together, side by side as the fight to help protect the mortals and Olympus rages on around them.
Out of the corner of his eye, Jason sees Nestor, who is slaying mortal soldiers.
Nestor attacks the mortals from behind, as he takes advantage of them fighting demons facing the other way. After Jason has killed his latest victim, he walks towards Nestor and screams at him, "YOU COWARD NESTOR!" as he swings his sword around, ready to do combat with him.
Nestor sneers back at him, "What makes you think you are any better than the rest of us?".
Jason replies to him, "If anyone thinks they are better, it is you, you are power hungry. You are the one who killed our friends, you started this".

Nestor scowls at him. "Look at yourself, the high and mighty Jason, Jason the righteous, Jason the hero".
Jason replies to him, "If you didn't steal the tablet in the first place, none of this would have happened. Look around you. You have been a fool".
Nestor then holds his weapon in front of him, then points it at Jason saying, "I'm going to enjoy this, killing you", as Jason prepares to do battle with Nestor.
Above them, a loud noise suddenly erupts.
They both look up to see what it is.

An enormous explosion takes place exactly where Nestor was standing, instantly blowing him up, sending parts of his body flying out in all directions across the battlefield.
Jason looks up through the smoke to see a helicopter hovering above him.
He sees Hector, Alex, Gabriella, and Isaac hanging out of its open doors, all armed with weapons, smiling down at Jason as they come to join the battle.
Jason laughs and smiles and waves back at them to thank them.
"That's for Santorini!" Hector shouts, as they all descend on ropes that are attached inside the helicopter, followed closely by a dozen special forces troops behind them.
Jason observes that friends have been equipped with full body armour too, so that they can help join the fight.
"Thank you, my friends," Jason says as he goes over to embrace them all.
"What can we do?" Alex asks him.
"Stick with me!" Jason replies.
They all look at him, then Gabriella remarks, "Something's different about you".
Just then, several demons come to attack them.
Before they react, Jason immediately draws his sword and instantly attacks the demons, using his enhanced strength, speed, and agility, side stepping then slashing away at the demons, killing them, then for the final one, he jumps at least five meters into the air and lands on top of the final demon, plunging his sword through the top of its head.

Once he has finished, he turns around to reply to them, as they stand there stunned, with their mouths open, looking at what he has just done.
Gabriella then breaks the silence with "It's your hair, that's what it is!", as they all break into laughter.
"A lot has happened since I last saw you," Jason says.
"You don't say!" Hector replies sarcastically whilst laughing.
Jason quickly re-joins the battle alongside his friends and Hemera.
Hemera continues to slay yet more demons as she welcomes them all to the fight.
"What took you so long?" she says to them, smiling. They laugh with her as they brandish their weapons and begin to fire at the oncoming hordes of demons.

One alpha demon launches itself at Jason, wrestling him to the floor.
As Jason lays on the floor with the demon on top of him, he grabs the demon's arms and headbutts it in the chin, then using his legs to throw the demon over his body as he quickly jumps up.
Jason quickly pulls out his sword and a dagger and stabs the demon to incapacitate it, stopping it from being able to move.
Hemera, as quick as a flash, swipes the blade of her sword through the demon's neck, cutting its head off.
"Teamwork!" Hemera calls out to Jason, who smiles at his beloved.
Hector joins them and kicks the head of the demon across the floor and spits on it.
Jason and Hemera have enough time to exchange a quick kiss and a smile as they quickly continue fighting side by side with their friends.

Mercurial

The Gods continue to battle each other for the fate of the earth.
Soldiers fight with demons and other ungodly looking creatures.
Tanks and other armoured vehicles continue to fire volley after volley of their ammunition into crowded pockets of demons and skeletons.
Fighter jets and helicopters occupy the smoke-filled sky above them, sending rockets and bullets into the packed crowds of the dark forces.

Cronus by now has now broken off his fight with Zeus.
He looks around, sensing that he is not winning the fight, as mortals fight back, holding their ground, as too are the Gods that he is fighting against.
He needs another response.
He commands Tartarus and Hades, who both quickly break away from their fights to respond to his command.
"Command whoever we have left to come to the surface," he tells them.
They both obey his command and send their final waves of elements across the battlefield and into the portal.
The portal rumbles, with sounds of screams spewing out from its depths, as another vast wave of creatures comes out of it.

The legendary Minotaur's come out first, followed by an army of giant scorpions, their huge pincers and deadly tails attacking the mortals by stinging soldiers to death, and grabbing them in their giant pincers, squeezing them tight, severing soldier's bodies in half.
Once again, mayhem is everywhere, as soldiers become separated from their platoons and battalions, trying to escape and avoid the mayhem that surrounds them.

The Minotaurs rumble into battle by stampeding over mortal fighters, using their brute strength to overpower them.
Once again, the tide has turned in favour of Cronus.
The good news for the soldiers is that their commanders from all fighting forces have acted quickly enough to foresee these eventualities.
Up in the sky, the incredible sound of planes fills the ears of everyone on the ground.
Hundreds of huge carrier planes fly overhead, opening their cargo doors and side doors.
Hundreds of paratroopers drop quickly from the sky, looking like a massive collection of small dots that get bigger and closer the more they fall to the ground.
As their parachutes open, all the soldiers floating down unleash a huge amount of firepower on the demons below, killing many of them, filling the sky with the sound of gunfire and the swooshing of arrows being fired.
They also take aim at any other ungodly creature that attacks their comrades on the battlefield below who dare to venture nearby.
As they land one by one, they quickly unhook their chutes and join their colleagues in battle.
The battle to win is now at a critical point, finely balanced.
But still more dark souls pour out from the portal.

From the depths of hell even more souls pour out, like a never-ending conveyer belt of demons, ready to fight, ready to die.
They too are joined by more from the skeletal army.
From moments ago, the soldiers and the Gods of Zeus had the upper hand, now, they are not so sure as they now must fight off this new wave.
Zeus knows that they do not have the same resources as the dark forces, he knows that he cannot summon the same never-ending supply of soldiers to help their cause.

Zeus senses tells him to act, and to act fast.

Knights of Cydonia

Zeus looks out and surveys the battlefield, observing the brave soldiers, fighting alongside the Gods, sacrificing themselves for the greater good.
He doesn't waste another second.
He has seen enough.

"CRIUS!", Zeus screams out.
Immediately, the God Crius comes to Zeus.
"My Lord," he says to Zeus.
"Send in the Zodiacs!" Zeus cries out to him.
Crius clenches his fists and strains, making them as tight as possible.
He looks up to the sky and throws outwards and upwards dozens of small balls of light, no bigger than small marbles.
He does this twenty-four times, one after the other, using both hands, sending them off in different directions.
The small balls of light hurtle out from earth at an immense speed, then once in space, they hurtle away at quantum speeds, taking them a matter of seconds to reach their destinations.

One by one, the small balls of light strike into the hearts of many distant stars.
Some stars are yellow, some white, some red, or blue, some purple, and many other colours and types of stars.
As the balls of light impact the stars that they are aimed at, each one instantly reacts and collapses.
They react in a cosmic way that makes it look like a giant wormhole or black hole is ripping them apart, distorting them and sucking the solar masses into an extremely thin vortex in space.

Each star morphs quickly into huge tightly packed beams of solar light, hurtling at quantum speeds towards earth.
From each region of space that these stars came from, they begin to all converge in the same area of space just outside the solar system as they move closer to earth.

From one region of the solar system, nine beams of solar light that were stars, morph into tight beams of light that meet and combine into one giant beam.
In another region, four stars have completed the same transformation.
Twenty-four regions of space have had their stars collapse into the solar beams that are now all hurtling ever closer towards earth.
Twenty-four handfuls of balls for twenty-four beams of light.
Those solar beams that began from all the corners of the galaxy now all meet alongside each other as they hurtle towards earth in a line.

As earth comes into sight, each beam transforms again by becoming shorter until all twenty-four condense tightly, forming a brilliant gleaming figure in each one.
The figures emerging from each beam cannot yet be recognised because of their brightness, but they all appear to be humanoid or similar in shape, as they go through the final phases of transformation.
Twenty-four beings now penetrate earth's atmosphere.

On the battlefield, as the fighting between good and evil rages on, clouds instantly form over their heads.
A massive crack of thunder is heard by all, followed by horizontal fork lightning that seems to shoot out and expand across for miles in all directions.
In confusion, everyone stops fighting and looks up.
From the sky above, in quick succession, one after the other, beams of light hit the earth.

A tremendous thud from each being that was in space seconds ago, smashes onto the ground, accompanying each beam that struck the earth, followed by enormous clouds of dust, making it difficult for anyone to see clearly.
These twenty-four beings have just hit the earth directly in the heart of the battlefield.
If they wanted everyone's attention, they have now got it.

Everyone on the battlefield is now staring at the enormous dust cloud, watching it float gently back to the floor.
The fighting has stopped, no one is moving.

For a moment, all that everyone can is all see is twenty-four bright figures, all placed in a perfect circle, all facing outwards, crouched down from the impact.
Slowly, each one of the new arrivals that are crouched down emerges from the bright light, showing their new form, and stands up.
One by one they stand there motionless, until one of them opens their eyes, followed by the rest of them, all of them now opening their eyes to look out into the battlefield.
It is then that all the Gods recognise who they are looking at, some Gods are happy, the dark force Gods not so much.
The demons, looking at the twenty-four new arrivals who stand in a circle, snarl at them, hissing and posturing.
Zeus looks over at the circle of warriors he has brought forth and smiles before looking over to where Cronus is and simply states, "Best of luck!".

Before everyone on the field of battle, stands the legends of the stars, the legends of the zodiac and the constellations:

Achilles, Perseus, Theseus, Heracles, Aries, Taurus, Andromeda, Pegasus, the twins Gemini, Aquila, Cancer, Leo, Draco, Virgo, Lupus, Libra, Ursa, Scorpio, Aquarius, Capricorn, Lynx, Sagittarius, and Orion.

Each one, a legend of their time, revered by the mortals, feared by the Gods.
All the new arrivals, quickly draw out their weapons, letting out an almighty scream, as they charge into battle, smashing the heart of the demons that stand first in their way, then the next, and the next, each zodiac and constellation God demolishing their victims with pure aggression, speed, and power.
Zeus and the Gods send out another war cry.
The mortals roar in delight, instantly filled with confidence, and charge once again into battle.

Spiritus Omnia

Achilles. One of the best-known legends that ever lived, moves quickly, and fights his opponents with frightening speed, power, and agility.
No one can get near him as he strikes down demon after demon.
After clearing a small area of demons, he stops briefly and looks over to see Hector fighting near him.
Hector looks and nods at Achilles, shouting "I am Hector, nice to meet you!".
"Achilles" comes the reply from the God.
Hector then quips, "Nice boots. A bit chunky around the ankles, aren't they?".
Achilles gives him a look of confusion then replies to him, "Do you have a brother called Paris?".
Hector chuckles and replies that he does not, and looks at an incoming demon, but not before giving Achilles a puzzled look, then Hector laughs, working out what Achilles has said to him.

Perseus jumps on the back of Pegasus, the two old friends reunited after several millennia apart.
"Hello old friend!" He speaks to his winged horse, which replies with a neigh to Perseus, and they soar into the sky before swooping down to the action below, gliding just above the surface of the battlefield.
Pegasus glides and gallops over the heads of demons, crushing many skulls with his hooves as Perseus leans to one side of Pegasus, one hand holding onto Pegasus, the other holding his blade steady, cutting many demons heads off as they sweep the field.

Theseus, master of disguise, charges into the masses of demons and skeletons, disguising himself as a demon.
He moves around them completely incognito, stabbing them one by one in their chests and killing them dead before any of the other demons around him notice.

One demon observes what is happening, and moves to attack him, but Theseus is cunning and instantly disguises himself as a skeleton, joining the army of the walking bones that are intertwined in the scenes of fighting, using his cunning stunts to use a sword and hammer to smash their legs to disable them from fighting.

Heracles, the man, myth, and legend.
An enormous beast of a muscular warrior.
This man does not use weapons often.
His hands are his weapons.
He charges at the dark forces, grabbing them by their heads and squeezing them until they crush and explode in his hands. With others, he grabs their bodies and throws them around like rag dolls, smashing their bodies to the ground or using them as a weapon to smash other dark force fighters.
Heracles roars and laughs every time he kills one.
Even when demons grab hold of him, the moment they manage to do so, he grabs whatever part of their body he has access to and squeezes so hard that it breaks, snaps, or explodes.

Aries, the ram.
Taurus, the bull.
Both Aries and Taurus are Gods that, if you didn't know better, you could mistake them for the animals themselves, such is their stature as Lords of the beasts.
Both run and charge at anyone from the dark forces that are in their way.
They do not need or use weapons, their horns are their weapons, as they charge and trample over everything in their path.
They are near unstoppable as they go on the rampage, stomping and trampling demons and skeletons in their dozens, crushing and spiking them. The dark forces stand near to no chance when they are rampage.

Andromeda, a battlefield combat warrior, and leader, she is one of the best tacticians that ever lived, in her time or ours. Her skills are unrivalled on the battlefield.
She charges at the dark forces, smashing her way through them, cutting, slicing, stabbing, and slaying all that stands in her way.
She is as fierce as they come, and her insatiable drive to fight for her fellow warriors is unmatched.
Even demons look and think twice before attacking her, such is her ferociousness.
She sends fear into their dark hearts.

Gemini, the twins Castor and Pollux, a formidable pair who are so in tune with each other that they connect when they fight. One of them will start the attack and the other finishes it.
As they attack the dark forces, they merge as one person, which confuses the dark forces, then they instantly split into two people again, delivering the decisive blows to kill their opponents, attacking them from opposing angles and sides.

Aquila, a lean and athletic man, with gold and bronze wings attached to his back, his fingers like the claws of an eagle, his helmet shaped like a beak.
He jumps high above ground and glides into battle, and as he flies in at head height, using the razor-sharp edges of his wings to slice off many heads of demons, then soaring back up to dive again for another attack.
His agility is superb.
Demons try to grab him as he swoops down, but all they end up with is getting their arms sliced off by Aquila's wings.

Cancer. A beast of a man who has giant, oversized razor-sharp hands.
He grabs hold of demons and ghouls with his hands before they can even get near him.
He tackles demon after demon, squashing them in his giant hands and breaking and slicing their bodies before discarding them to the floor before grabbing the next one that comes within his reach.

Leo, the great lioness of a warrior, she runs at the dark forces and leaps high into the air and sinks her claws into her prey, then instantly biting their heads off, and others by sinking her teeth into their necks and biting hard until the heads of demons snap clean off from their bodies, leaving nothing but a blood-soaked field, and a blood-soaked mouth.
She is fearsome and her thirst for tasting demon blood in her jaws is insatiable.

Draco. This God has scales for skin as his armour.
He repels attack after attack from the demons who try to grab him, trying to dig their claws into him. A pointless task for them.
Draco lets them attack him as his armour is so thick, he then grabs them with his hands and breathes elemental fire at their faces, scorching and melting them as they scream in pain.
Draco moves slower than most of his peers but only because of his skin armour being so heavy, but nearly impenetrable.
Any dark force that he casts his flames upon cannot withstand his fire breathing elements.

Virgo. A beautiful woman.
Her stunning looks mesmerise many, but as she approaches the demons, she opens her mouth and directs her screams at them, killing them instantly, with her screams so high pitched and wild, like a banshee attacking them.
The demons try to hold their ears to block the sounds, but their brains explode inside their skulls.
Blood pours out from their heads via their ears, nose, and mouths, as they fall to the floor lifeless.

Lupus, half man, half wolf, covered in fur, fangs for teeth, claws for fingers.
He runs at his enemies on all fours, using his hands and feet to cover much ground quickly, attacking his prey by biting their necks and limbs, violently shaking them until they can struggle no more.
His bite is so strong that not one demon can escape his jaws and grip.

His claws slash and slice his opponents, causing them to spill blood everywhere.
On many demons that he attacks, he bites them directly on their stomachs, instantly ripping out their intestines, flinging them across the battlefield like a blood crazed warrior.

Libra, scales of justice, charges at the dark forces with her sword.
Each demon she encounters, she swings her sword once.
She does not need to swing it a second time, such is her accuracy of attack.
She is the deliverer of justice, and every swing of her sword never misses, and every swing of her sword delivers justice to those that oppose her chosen values.
Every demon that tries to attack, one swing of the sword, one death, always. She is ferocious.

Ursa. Half man, half bear. Covered in hair, giant arms, and a giant jaw to match.
He runs at the dark forces, charging into them, bear hugging them, crushing them in his arms, each one he grabs, he sinks his teeth into their faces, using his jaws to rip off their faces, rendering them mutilated, clutching their heads in anguish, unable to function.
Ursa then tramples over their bodies and smashes them into the ground by thumping them with his arms before moving on to his next victim.

Scorpio. A beast of a creature, a huge hybrid with arms and hands oversized for his body, and a tail with a deadly sting.
He sets about the demons with vigour, swiping aside and using his tail to sting and kill demon after demon.
He uses his hands to grab them and crush them as moves around the battlefield picking up any and all dark souls then using his tail to kill them, and once he has, he slings them across the floor like a bowling ball, knocking over demons and skeletons too as he continues his attacks with frenzy.

Aquarius. Unassuming in build, youthful, and handsome looking.
That should fool no one.
He is deadly.
Aquarius runs into battle, picking his victims by approaching any demon nearby.
He performs metamorphosis, changing shape so that the demons cannot get a hold of him.
He puts his hand into the demon's mouth and extends all the way down, spreading his fingers so that they branch off, into the demon's lungs and stomach, whilst using his other hand to keep the demon's mouth open, to stop it from closing, then injecting thick liquid into the beasts, drowning, and poisoning them, chocking them to death, drowning their lungs and poisoning them.
Other demons try to attack him, but his body morphs and shapes at will.
They cannot stop him, he is unique, one of a kind in his abilities.

Capricorn is a fearsome warrior. He charges at the dark forces, using his spear that is tipped at both ends with golden horns.
His helmet also displays horns that symbolise the house of Capricorn, part of the ancient army that he commanded four millennia ago when fighting for the ancient Greeks.
He stabs each demon, then thrusting his weapon upwards until it comes out from the tops of their heads, splitting each one in half vertically.
Several demons try to attack him from behind, but with his spear with its horns at both ends, he is too much for them, being highly skilled in weaponry, he repels then counterattacks.

Lynx, A wild warrior who runs all fours, using her hands and her feet, she can maneuver around her prey as she slashes her victims with her hands, her fingers like razors, as are her feet. She attacks the dark forces with all four limbs, and anyone coming into contact near her head she sinks her fangs into their necks, ripping their throats and flesh from their bodies as she dismembers them.

Sagittarius, part man, part horse, gallops at his attackers using his bow to fire arrow after arrow, with a deadly accuracy as he towers above them, moving through the battlefield shooting at multiple targets.
He runs over demons, using his hooves to trample their bodies, breaking their limbs, preventing them from being able to get up and function.
He is a legendary warrior on the battlefield, and demons try their best to avoid him, but without much success.

Orion. The myth. The legend. He is the most recognisable constellation in the sky to all mortals for his infamous three-starred belt.
This belt also being his key weapon, for Orion the hunter is the hunter of hunters.
He doesn't wait for any creature to come to him.
He hunts them down, using his full array of weaponry.
Orion is a master of the hunt, using two weapons at a time, such is his skill.
He uses his bow to shoot and kill demons and souls, then rapidly switching to his sword and dagger as he runs through the crowds, chasing after his next kill, to slash and stab with frenzied attacks, then switching to a shield and sword as he bashes them and then cuts open the fearful demons, then using the edge of his shield to dismember the limbs of them, making every blow count.

The mortal forces watch as they fight, all in awe and inspired by them, as the zodiac forces turn the tide in the battle against the dark forces, as the fighting has now become the most savage it has been since the war started.

Farewell to Earth

Ares and Athena's fight comes to a halt as the masses of people fighting get in their way, thus becoming distanced from each other, both unable to see where the other one is.
Ares scans the battlefield and spots Jason.
He knows Jason is mortal but possesses some powers.
This excites Ares. He feels a challenge coming on.
Ares smiles sadistically to himself as he strides towards Jason, who in turn spots Ares coming and prepares himself.

Ares swings first as the two of them lock blades, engaging in deadly battle.
After a few swings and blows of their swords, Jason's blade just catches Ares on his arm and chest.
Ares becomes enraged that a mortal got the better of him.
He quickly produces a fireball by picking up a rock and launching it where Jason stands, sending him off balance and falling to the floor onto his back.
He quickly jumps up into the air, holding a dagger in each hand, about to land on Jason.
Jason raises his hands up in defence and closes his eyes, expecting the worst, but when he quickly opens his eyes after not feeling any impact, he sees Hemera, crouched over him, her eyes looking into his.
Her hands, planted either side of his body on the ground as he lies face up, trying to get up from the ground, expecting Ares at any moment.
Then, from behind her, he sees Ares.
A smirk spreads across his evil face, as Ares then backs away, glaring at Jason for a moment as he re-joins the battle elsewhere.
Jason quickly realises that something is terribly wrong.
Looking at her face, he can see Hemera is in pain, a lot of pain.
She looks at Jason and whispers to him, "I'm sorry", as ichor soaks her clothing, running down both sides of her body, coming out from two stab wounds on her back.

She slumps to her knees as Jason holds her up with his hands to steady her.
Jason quickly becomes upset as he gets up to see that she has two daggers still planted in her back, left there by Ares.
He lays her down carefully, holding her in his arms as she looks up at him.
She raises her hand to stroke his cheek as she struggles for breath.
"Hold on, don't you leave me," Jason sobs whilst holding her. "You can't leave me, Hemera, I need you. I love you,"
She gently smiles at him, her eyes fixed on his, continuing to stroke his face with her hand, telling him, "I love you too. I regret nothing. I would do the same every day for you and for you for the rest of time".
Jason forces a smile as tears stream down his face.
He leans forward to kiss her cheek as she struggles to keep her eyes open, her breath laboured, as he screams out for someone to help him.

Jason continues to hold and comfort her as he desperately looks around the battlefield for someone to help him.
He looks across the land to spot any God that can help him, but none are in his view.
Suddenly Hermes appears along with Nike.
They look at Hemera and see that her wounds are too severe to help her.
Hermes looks at Jason helplessly as Nike also puts an arm around Hemera to comfort her.
Hemera's elements break away, slowly at first, before gathering pace, as she continues to hold Jason's gaze.
Jason holds his hand out to capture as many of them as possible.
He knows she is dying, but he is desperate to save her, he will do anything.
After a moment of Jason trying to stop her elements from leaving her body, the rest of her elements finally break away and fall to the earth.
Then, she is gone.

Psycho

"Jason. Quick, get up, we need your help!" shouts Hector.
He doesn't seem to hear him though; he is too distraught.
Slumped on his knees, his hands slowly stroking the floor where elements cover the ground where Hemera was only moments ago.
"JASON PLEASE HELP!" Hector screams at him.
Jason suddenly hears Hector, as the tears on his face continue to flow, but then his expression changes from deep despair to one of anger.
He stands up, his face filled with rage, still looking at the ground where Hemera was, then turns around, letting out a blood-curdling scream that everyone around him hears.
His eyes have a hint of an ice white glow to them.
The demon fighting Hector suddenly stops moving, then blood gushes out from it, then its torso is ripped clean in half.
The bottom half attached to its legs are thrown to one side, its top half to the other.
Behind it stands Jason, his hands soaked in blood.
Hector thanks him and continues to look at him as Jason stands now emotionless.
"Are you OK buddy?" Hector asks him, but Jason doesn't reply.
He just looks at Hector blankly, then turns around and walks directly into a crowd of demons and skeletons that surround them, pulling out his sword.
Jason swings his sword with athleticism to slay the first one to reach him.
The next demon he sees is met with a thump of a fist on top of its head, hammering the demon into a flat pile of flesh and blood on the floor where it stood.
The next one is met with another swing of the sword to chop it clean in half diagonally down from its shoulder to its hip.
Jason's eyes, now pure ice white, fights everything in his way.
The next demon, Jason, pulls back and punches it so hard in the face, his fist comes out the back of its head.

He grabs another demon by its head, picks it up and swings it so hard and flat to the floor that its body explodes on impact, sending its innards flying.

Hector is stunned by the power exerted by Jason, but he doesn't care, he has his friend back, completely overwhelming the forces of darkness that surround them, and Jason is beating down all comers.

Jason spots a shield on the floor and picks it up as he carries on walking forward.

Thanatos, God of death, sees Jason and moves to engage in battle with him.

"I will crush you, mortal," Thanatos tells him.

Jason's expression doesn't change, he just keeps moving forward and looks at Thanatos.

They engage in battle, trading blows.

Jason absorbs the blows of Thanatos using the shield he picked up.

Jason strikes back, using his sword and shield to fight him.

Thanatos laughs and declares to Jason, "You cannot win. I will be your death. No one can escape death. Your fear will kill you."

Jason replies, "Only in the presence of fear will death take you".

Jason goes on a full-scale assault of Thanatos, punching, kicking, swiping, and slashing away at him with his sword.

After a barrage of attacks, Thanatos grabs Jason's arm, thinking that he will be able to necrotise him.

Nothing happens.

Thanatos looks up at Jason, astounded that Jason's arm doesn't change.

Jason smirks at him, drops his sword and grabs hold of Thanatos' chest with one hand, pulling him closer, then grabbing his throat with his other hand and squeezes, tighter and tighter.

Jason snarls at Thanatos.

Jason then thrusts his hand holding the Gods throat upwards, decapitating Thanatos by ripping it off, then throwing the lifeless corpse to the floor.

Hector is stunned at how powerful Jason has become.

It catches the attention of others too.
"ARES!" screams Jason towards the God of war.
Ares stops fighting another God and mortals to turn around to see Jason.
He chuckles at him, declaring, "You want more? This time I will finish what should have been you!".
Jason looks at him, emotionless.
He is ready with sword in hand to fight Ares once again.
Jason becomes enraged and launches himself at Ares, smashing away at him with his sword, landing blow after blow, but Ares manages to deflect them.
Ares counter attacks but Jason fends off the blows using his shield, sword, and the armour on his arms.
Jason then sends Ares bowling over with a powerful strike from his sword, using his new strength.
Another cut, this time on Ares' face, a deep gash going across his cheek to his nose.
Ares feels his face and sees a splatter of ichor on his hand.
He screams with rage and prepares to launch another fireball like he did in their previous encounter.
He launches it at Jason, sending him flying backwards and to the ground, knocking his shield from his hand.
Ares jumps high into the air with his daggers out in both hands, ready to plunge them into Jason's body.
"JASON!" screams Athena as she hurls her shield at him.
He catches it just in time as Ares crashes down, the daggers hitting the shield instead of Jason.
Ares drops one dagger to rip the shield away from Jason's grip and tries to stab him with the other one.
Jason grabs his arm to stop him, but the dagger gets lower and lower as Jason struggles to hold him back.
"Your whore cannot save you this time," Ares says to him, his eyes full of rage, smirking at Jason as he now moves the dagger just above Jason's head.
Jason heard the words spoken by Ares, but instead of reacting in anger, he focuses on Ares, on his body position, and then he sees a bright light behind and above Ares, not knowing what it is, but Jason focuses on it as seems to give him a renewed inner strength.

He then looks back at Ares, into his eyes, then smiles at him. Jason then pushes the dagger away from his head, then he pushes Ares off him, jumping up from the floor quickly before they wrestle again as Ares tries to strike him.

Jason catches his arm again, but this time Jason is the stronger of the two, as he slowly turns Ares' arm around, then bending his arm backwards so that the dagger is now facing Ares, as the cracking of bones can be heard.

Jason pulls Ares close to him, their faces inches apart.

Even when Ares tries to strike Jason with his hands to fight him, Jason holds firm, taking every punch that he throws at him, it's as if he doesn't feel them landing.

"You took my heart, now, I will take yours," Jason says to him, almost in a whisper as they are now so close, face to face, Ares now unable to swing anymore punches.

He looks at Jason, as confusion spreads across his face.

He does not understand how Jason can do what he is doing.

Jason then slowly forces the dagger into Ares's chest, then he twists the dagger before pulling it out and dropping it.

Ares, with blood seeping from his mouth and the other wounds inflicted upon him, looks at Jason, and laughs, declaring, "You missed".

Ares knows he is beaten, but he wants the last word.

Jason smiles back, shakes his head at Ares and declares "No I didn't", then thrusts his fist into the stab wound in Ares' chest abruptly, then pulling his hand back out with tremendous force.

Ichor spills from Ares, as the God of war looks at the hole in his chest and the blood spurting out around him, now in shock.

Ares tries to focus on what Jason is holding out in front of him, only to realise it is his own heart, witnessing its last beats.

Jason then squeezes the heart tightly, crushing and squishing it in his hands so that it explodes into a ball of flesh with its ichor inside it, flying out and running down Jason's fist and arm.

Ares slumps to the floor, lifeless. Jason, the mortal, has just killed the self-proclaimed God of war.

The Final Hour

Jason slumps to the floor, aching and panting. His body is covered in cuts and bruises, with dry mortal and ichor blood over his body like a patchwork quilt.
The battles continue around him as his friends, the Gods, the zodiacs, and others continue to fight off the attacking dark forces.
Phoebe suddenly appears and comes to help get Jason back to his feet, grabbing his body and using her strength to lift him up.
She holds on to him tight, keeping him upright and steady whilst he takes a moment to gather himself.
She then receives another one of her visions, one from before. This time her vision is much clearer, with much clarity on what she saw from her first encounter with him.
Phoebe's eyes flicker as she looks forward into the near future, her eyes in a trance.

She sees five weapons, all held by five different Gods.

She sees the Blade of Olympus held by Zeus.
She sees Achilles with his Katoptris Dagger.
Hermes with his Caduceus Spear,
Heracles with his Epirus Bow,
and Apollo's Royal Sceptre.

Her vision then flashes to Hephaestus holding all five and crafting them into rings, then her vision shows Jason holding it, with burn marks on the palms of other Gods, with the assumption that only Jason was worthy to hold it.
Her vision then shows the tablet by Jason's side.

Phoebe quickly wakes from her trance and instantly flies over to Hephaestus to tell him of the prophecy she has just seen. He looks at her, knowing she is not dreaming this vision, and instantly calls out to all five of the Gods that featured in her vision to come to him.

They hear his call and leave their fights to join Hephaestus. With Hephaestus by her side, she tells them that all five of their weapons can make one all-powerful weapon, so strong that it can end the war, a war that they are no longer winning. Hephaestus asks her, "Why can only Jason hold the weapon?".
She replies to him she doesn't know why; she can only tell him what she saw.
Then she quickly remembers and says to him, "The tablet. We need the tablet, it makes the weapon work, and only mortals can use the tablet. That must be it!".
Hephaestus nods in agreement. "But where is the tablet?" he asks her.
"On top of Olympus," come her reply.

No one is coming out of a portal to help the good guys, only the bad ones, and they are running out of options, fast.

Each God accepts what she has to say and hands over their weapon to Hephaestus.
"You will need help to protect you," Zeus tells him.
"CYCLOPES!" he bellows out.
The cyclopes quickly stomp over the battlefield to where the Gods are gathered.
"Protect him," Zeus commands them, pointing at Hephaestus.
The cyclops quickly surround Hephaestus to form a human shield as he quickly gets to work on the weapons, using his hands to craft and forge them into the weapon that Phoebe described to him, using his special elements of creation.

"HERMES!" cries Zeus.
Hermes appears in a flash to him.
Zeus tells Hermes "Go to Jason, tell him of the weapon. He is the only one who can wield the might of the weapon, but to do so we need the tablet. You must get that tablet now!".
Hermes does as commanded and quickly searches for Jason so that they can get the tablet back.

Ground Zero

All around the battlefield, the dark forces' numbers never seem to decrease as fresh demons and souls pour out from the portal while the mortal armies keep losing soldiers. Cronus has now engaged Tethys in battle, killing her as she fought bravely to hold him back from killing soldiers, his appetite for death and destruction insatiable. without remorse for anyone or anything, his murderous campaign slowly coming to what he hopes will be a triumphant climax.

The Gods Eos and Leto are next to be slain, killed by Hades and Tartarus, using all their dark elements and ability to kill the Goddess of dawn and the Goddess of faith, they fought well, but they were no match for the wicked duo.

In the ocean, the warships are no longer able to fire missiles. The sirens have boarded all the ships and have destroyed the rocket launchers and rail guns, by the sheer volume of sirens coming on board, overwhelming the brave souls.
Sailors and marines desperately continue to try their best to fight off the sirens, engaged in hand-to-hand combat, if need be, or by using their weapons where possible and when they can do so.
It is a near impossible task for them.

On land, Talos is defending Olympus from the dark forces that attack it.
The Zodiacs are still winning their battles convincingly, but the sheer volume of attackers never seems to diminish, thanks to the portal being open and continuing to pour out fresh dark souls from the underground.

Zeus spots then intercepts Cronus again, engaging in battle, with each God firing huge amounts of elemental energy at each other, trying to get an edge with a view to a victory.
The two most powerful Gods the earth has ever seen, in deadly combat, creating havoc and mayhem around them as soldiers do their best to avoid the Gods battle zone.

Athena and Apollo spot then engage in battle with Hades and Tartarus, to keep them at bay from Olympus and from harming the soldiers, as they fire volley after volley at the two evil Gods. Tartarus and Hades respond by throwing everything they have got at the two Olympians, but their energy is starting to dwindle, such was the number of elements they expended by opening two giant portals and then having to summon ungodly beasts.

Artemis has managed to kill Epimetheus, slaying him down with an attack that the twisted God was not expecting, with Artemis, the warrior that she is, getting the better of the fool. She was able to take advantage of his cockiness, fooling him into thinking she was badly wounded, but her cunning allowed her to prevail.

"ZEUS!" Hephaestus cries out to the God of thunder, to let him know he has created the weapon.
Zeus breaks away from his fight with Cronus and soars over to Hephaestus to join him.
"I will take it to Jason now," Zeus declares, but as he turns to do so, Cronus, who has followed him, and wounds him whilst his back was turned.
Cronus sends a barrage of elemental beams to try and kill Hephaestus too, but he is quick enough to create an energy shield to cover most of him and Zeus, but part of the attack breaks through, severing his leg off, rendering him unable to move efficiently.

Hermes, meanwhile, has rushed across the battlefield in search of Jason and finds him.
Hermes grabs hold of Jason and quickly says to him, "No time to explain" and quickly launches them both skyward, away from the battle and landing on top of Olympus, next to the tablet.
"What's going on?!" Jason shouts at him, "We need to be down there helping!".
Hermes quickly replies to him, "Jason, we need the tablet, it can power the weapon" as Hermes points at the tablet.

He is confused, though.

"Jason, please, quickly pick it up so we can get to the weapon".

Jason thinks for a moment to think about what Hermes has said, then he looks back down at the battle below.

"Now is your time Jason, you must get to the weapon".

Jason still does not know what he is talking about.

"What weapon?!" he replies.

Hermes tells Jason about the weapon they have created, that it can end the war and that he is the only one that can use it.

"What do you mean I am the only one?!" he says quizzically.

"The Gods may provide the weapons, but a mortal can only hold on to the combined power, and the prophecy says that only you can do it," Hermes explains to Jason.

Jason looks at Hermes as battles continue to be fought below.

"Why me? Why am I so special to be the only one?" he asks.

"Your bloodlines Jason, they go back further than you know," Hermes tells him.

"Yes, you are mortal, but you also have a bloodline that goes all the way back to the Gods. You are the bridge between our worlds. I believe it was fate that brought you to the tablet, to us, to this place, here and now."

Hermes looks at him with the most seriousness he has ever done so.

Jason looks back at him, not knowing quite what to say, thinking about what Hermes has said to him.

Then Hermes tells him, "I have watched you on this battlefield Jason, I have seen you do things that most other Gods cannot do, you can do this, I believe in you".

Jason looks back at him and remarks that Poseidon and Hemera gave him his current powers to help in the fight, that he is just mortal.

"Yes, they did, but only you are strong enough to use them to harness their full potential. You are the last hope to us all, Jason," Hermes says.

Jason looks at him then replies, "No pressure then!".

Hermes gives Jason a smile and even chuckles with Jason.

"Whatever happens between now and the end of this war, I will be by your side," Hermes tells him.
Jason looks back at him and smiles.
"Thank you. You are a great warrior and friend," he tells Hermes.
He nods at Jason to acknowledge the compliment and sentiment.
"Now, pick up the tablet!" Hermes says to him sternly.
Jason chuckles and says, "That's more like it!" as he grabs hold of the tablet.

They look down once more at the vast expanse of fighting raging on, the sheer volume of dark forces, still spilling out from the portal and heading in all directions of fighting, especially in their direction towards Olympus.
All over the battlefield, the mortals and Gods continue to fight as best as they can, but they are losing, this has become apparent to both sides now.
Hermes and Jason quickly spot where Hephaestus is with the weapon, and the ring of cyclopes bravely defending their position.
Hermes and Jason take a giant leap from the top of Olympus, ready to head down to Hephaestus and Zeus.

As they dive, Cronus spots them and fires a huge fireball in their direction, that explodes next to them, sending their descent out of control as they both land separately on the battlefield, instead of their desired destination.
They quickly get to their feet and look across the battlefield and the distance between them and Hephaestus, and the weapon.
"How the hell do I get through all of this lot?!" Jason asks Hermes.

Hermes nods in agreement. "We need help," Hermes replies.
He then calls out to Zeus with an almighty scream, "Zeus, here my call, help us now!".
Zeus hears the call of Hermes and sees them in the distance. Realising what needs to be done, he quickly acts.

Knock 'Em Dead, Kid

"CHRONOS!" Zeus bellows out from his position on the field of battle.
He is next to Hephaestus, wounded, but not out of the fight, as he uses his hands to heal the damage inflicted upon him and Hephaestus too.
The sky above the battlefield suddenly crackles with thunder, then a gigantic bolt of fork lightning hits the ground where the wounded Gods lie.
Chronos, God of chronology, of time, appears before Zeus.

"Give Jason the Sands of Time," Zeus commands him.
Zeus has the look in his eyes as if to say that this is the last hand he must play, the last throw of the dice, to do what they can to end the war.
Chronos does not speak but nods his head to show his understanding of the situation, then he shoots to the sky like a bolt of lightning, then another bolt to hit the floor across in the distance to where Jason and Hermes are.

Chronos looks at Hermes and nods his head to greet him.
"Chronos, it's been a long time" Hermes replies, greeting him.
Chronos raises an eyebrow to appreciate what Hermes said.
The time God then looks at Jason, emotionless, then extends his hand inside his cloak to reveal a small sand timer.
Jason has seen enough now to not question or ask; he just knows that it is going to help him somehow.

Chronos then speaks to Jason, "Turn. Time. Slow".
Jason takes the device from Chronos and thanks him, then he looks at the timer for a moment, realising what it is and what Chronos has said.
Jason looks around at the carnage then instantly turns the device upside down.
The first grain of sand hits the empty bottom half of the timer.
The noise around Jason goes from higher pitched screams and weapon fire, to a very slow-motion sound.

Jason looks around him to see that everyone is now moving slowly.
He turns to look at Hermes, who doesn't seem to be affected somehow.
"Why are you not like the others?" he asks him.
"I am the fastest of the Gods, I am able to move fast enough to assist you, but hurry, it does not last long".
Jason nods his head and says to Hermes, "Come on, we have little time!".
Jason begins to run as fast as he can, his sword drawn ready, his other hand holding the tablet.
He runs hard and smashes into the demons and skeletons, sending them flying or shattering them.
He runs through the Gorgons and Minotaur's, using his sword sideways to slice them, and his shield as a battering ram to punch a giant hole through them, to make a long gangway through the packs of dark forces to get to Zeus, Hephaestus, and the weapon they have created.
As he does so, Hermes stays by his side, running alongside him.
Every time Jason strikes someone in his way, he sends them flying, like a bowling ball launching from a cannon and knocking down standing skittles.
Demons, ghouls, and skeleton bones still shatter and scatter.
Jason then glances at the sand timer.
The grains of sands almost gone.
He is still some distance from the weapon and Hephaestus, but he has made good ground.
He knows he will have to do a lot of fighting still, to have any chance of making it.

He takes one more look at the sand timer as he sprints even harder to cover more ground.
As he looks down at it, he watches the final grain of sand fall through the gap, as it hits the top of the sandpile.
Time quickly returns to normal, as the noises and motions of people around Jason and Hermes fight and scream.
Jason quickly engages in battle with the surrounding demons.

Hermes, still loyally fighting alongside Jason, now has his back pressed against Jason's back as they fight off the attacks from all around them.
The evil souls are about to engulf them.

A dozen demons suddenly fall to the ground, dead, and from behind them is the sight of Jasons friends, the battlefield commanders Takeru, Sun Li, and Acamas, and two Gods of the Zodiacs, Achilles, and Orion, come into his view.
A huge grin appears on his face as he looks at them and quickly nods to say thanks.
"You must help us," Hermes quickly tells them. "We must get Jason to that location. There is a special weapon", as he points towards where Zeus and Hephaestus are.
Everyone looks at each other then quickly nod, then they begin to sprint towards Zeus, Hephaestus, and the weapon.

The newly formed squad of Gods and mortals run as hard as they can and power through the crowded battles taking place, as they form into the attack pattern of an arrowhead, spearheaded by Achilles.
They charge hard and fast at the demons, piercing a hole through the masses of dark forces as they approach their intended target.
Each area of battle they run through, another Zodiac joins them, the first one being Aries, who takes lead point at the front of the squad, literally steam rolling the path before him.

One by one, the rest of the battlefield commanders see what is going on and quickly join them.
Then more zodiacs join the ever-growing squad, as they run hard to their intended destination, now smashing through tightly packed areas, still slaying beats and dark souls of the underworld, to the middle of the battlefield, in the heart of the fighting, to reach the weapon.
They are nearly there.

Ode to Power

The newly formed squad of mortals and Gods manage to reach Zeus and Hephaestus.
Jason and Hermes approach the two Gods, as the commanders and Zodiacs that helped to punch the pathway through, help to repel the demon hordes that are quickly encircling, trying to get to Jason to stop him.
The wounded Hephaestus wastes no time.
He passes the weapon up to Jason.

"Take it Jason. It is your destiny," he tells him.
"Take the Circles of Chaos,".
"But I don't know how to use it" Jason replies, as he holds it, not sure of even how to hold it, let alone use it.
"It will show you how," Hephaestus tells him.
"Now is your time, Jason. Save them all, save us all".

Hermes quickly reminds Jason to open the tablet.
Words suddenly appear on it and light up in gold, as if it knew.
Jason looks at the text, understanding the word that mention a magnificent weapon, the circles of chaos.

Jason instantly reads the words aloud as he holds the weapon in one hand and the tablet in the other.
Cronus, who engaged in battle with other Gods that came to support Zeus and Hephaestus, who are defending their position, sees the tablet and tries to intercept it by running towards Jason.
Zeus spots Cronus, and intercepts him, quickly using all his strength to grapple with him, holding him back, pulling him to the floor and putting him into a choke hold.
Cronus furiously tries to beat Zeus with his elbows, trying to free himself, but Zeus holds firm, screaming at Cronus.

The final cyclops has now been killed by the dark God's firepower, and the demons of the dark forces run towards Jason to stop him.

Instantly, a ring of protection is formed around Jason, made up of Hector, Alex, Gabriella, and Isaac, as they quickly spotted the attacking hordes now focused solely on their friend.
Next to them appear Takeru, Yusuke, Sun Li, Leonidas, Eudoros, Acamas, Ino, Medea and Pelias.
In front of them come the rest of the zodiacs to defend their area.
All the remaining Gods finally join them to defend Jason as best as they can, doing their best to fend off attacks.
The whole battle has now turned to attack one, single point on the battlefield.
The dark forces are desperate to stop Jason. The forces of good are desperate to defend him.

Giant cracks appear, and splits Olympus, as giant boulders fall to the ground from above, as the dark forces, with the remaining Gorgons, Scorpions, Minotaur's, and other giant monsters all doing their best to destroy it.
This is now the last roll of the dice for the forces of good.
The circle of brave warriors and Gods surround and defend Jason's position with a ferociousness never seen before as they now give everything they have got left to give, with every bit of strength.

Jason finishes reading the text, drops the tablet to his feet and holds the Circles of Chaos weapon in both hands as it begins to unlock from one solid ring into five connected rings, each one overlapping, as it starts to buzz and hum, charging up.
A static field surrounds Jason as the power of the weapon grows stronger and stronger.
Jason screams out as the power becomes immense.
His armour catches fire, the sheer heat of the weapon burning his skin, but still, he holds firm to the weapon.
Jason steadies himself and concentrates as hard as he can, thinking and wishing the weapon to work and do what he wants it to do.
He takes one more look around at his friends and allies fighting.

It's as if everything is in slow motion again for him.
He looks at Hermes.
Hermes looks back at him, one last nod from him.
The rings violently vibrate in his hands as he slowly lifts the Circles of Chaos high above his head.
The sky and clouds above turn black, with thunder and lightning crackling away much bigger than ever before.
The clouds begin to spin around like a giant tornado.

A massive surge of energy, like a nebula, descends from outside the atmosphere, from space, hitting the earth's atmosphere, then filtering down into the massive cloud above.
A huge bolt of lightning strikes and holds its position and charge on the Circles of Chaos weapon.
Jason grips the weapon even tighter, using every ounce of strength to do so.
His eyes then begin to glow ice white.
His veins flowing ice white, his armour still alight from the orange and red flames, now turn blue from the immense heat.

The earth shakes violently around them all.
Enormous gaps appear, with splits and holes forming as smoke and vapour hisses out.
The wind picks up and quickly becomes a full-scale hurricane as it whips up dust, weapons, dead bodies, and anything else not heavy enough to stand its ground.

Small bolts of lightning fork off from Jason's body and from the weapon itself.
Tens, then hundreds, then thousands of bolts of lightning, small at first, rain down from Jason's hands and the weapon and on to the floor beside him.
All of them ice white and ultraviolet in colour.
Stunning yet terrifying at the same time.
Sheet lighting fills the surrounding air all, the sounds of the thunder roaring in their ears.
Zeus looks at Jason, as Jason turns his head to look back at Zeus.

He smiles broadly at Jason, as Cronus is still struggling to break free, Poseidon next to him, fighting back Hades and Tartarus.
Zeus puts his mouth to the ear of Cronus and whispers "No one messes with my son!".
Cronus's eyes widen at the realisation of what Zeus has just said.

Hundreds of huge lightning bolts crash down from the heavens above, just feet away from where Jason stands. Jason's whole body now glows ice white all over, as the static surrounding him grows intense, almost unbearable. He cannot hold on much longer.

"NOW JASON, NOW!" Hermes screams at Jason, not knowing if Jason can even hear him, but something happens. From the top of the black cloud that's now become a super massive hurricane in the sky, the lightning bolts hitting the floor spread outwards, striking the ground with intense ferocity.
Thousands of lightning bolts, all made from all the colours you can imagine, crash to the ground with enormous impact and noise. Rocks and boulders fall down mountains.
Trees are knocked down and are ablaze with fire.

Jason, glowing a brilliant white light and ablaze with fire, thrusts the weapon high once more, as if to fire its final load. Lighting, striking every square meter of land across the battlefield.
The black clouds above glow a brilliant white, then discharge the largest sheets of lightning ever known, hitting everything in sight.
The largest bolts of lightning ever witnessed, strike the ground everywhere, creating a noise never heard before.
A giant shockwave pulsates, spreading out from the impact, speeding across the land and past the horizon.

Then, silence.

Glow

Silence. Everywhere.
Only dust particles and multicoloured elements are the only things moving, floating gently in the air from the black cloud above, then beginning to fall slowly to the ground below.

The previously active battlefield was now dormant, occupied by bodies, buildings, and vehicles, with a scenery comprised of fallen trees, huge boulders, and rocks too.
Golden dust covers the surface of everything, as if a giant blanket has been laid over it.
The wind is no more, having gone as quickly as it had arrived.

Something then moves from within the gold dust on the floor as tiny particles of light continue to drift down, glittering.
A few specks hit something, then it moves, then it protrudes from the dust.
A hand, fingers flexing and extending, followed by more movement.
An eye opens as it looks across the landscape, flickering around to see what has happened.
The hand moves to brush away the gold dust from the face of someone lying on the ground.
A soldier stands up slowly to look around at the landscape and the devastation caused by the war only moments ago.
She smiles to herself, checking her body for any signs of damage from the fighting and from the gigantic explosions of lightning only moments ago, but she is in good health.

She looks around to watch the particles and elements float to the floor, then she spots movement around her, as more soldiers stand up and to look around, amazement on their faces that they are still alive.
Some of them look at each other in sheer happiness and grin from ear to ear at each other, extremely happy to be alive.
Dozens of people now rise and brush away the dust from their tired bodies.

They are more than tired, exhausted in fact, but all of them look around, grinning, in shock that they are alive, as more golden particles and elements continue to hit the ground, as if they are the catalyst to give energy to those it touches.

Soldiers, now in their hundreds rise from the ground, checking and looking at themselves, then looking around to see who else is alive with them.
"Am I dead?" asks one soldier to another.
His colleague playfully punches him in the arm to check, laughing.
"I guess not!" he replies to his own question, laughing.

More and more soldiers continue to stand up, all of them brushing themselves down, looking around at their friends, all extremely happy to be alive as small rays of sun now creep through the cracks in the giant clouds above to reveal wisps of sunlight.
A hand reaches down to the floor and grabs the hand of someone else lying on the ground.
The person gasps in a big lungful of air as they stand up and wipe the dust away.
It is Hector, helped up by Isaac.
He looks at Isaac and beams a huge smile before giving his friend an enormous hug.
They quickly call out to Gabriella and Alex.
Both hear their names and open their eyes and stand up, brushing the dust away, looking across at Hector and Isaac.
They all run towards each other and hug tightly.

The Gods stand up, side by side with mortals, and embrace each other warmly.
The Zodiacs stand and look around at the scenes and smile as they watch on.
Hermes picks himself up and surveys the area, to see that his fellow Gods have risen from the ashes of the war.
Thousands of people now stand up, moving around to pick up more of their comrades from the battlefield.

Zeus rises from the floor, looking around at the scenes taking place, as a smile comes over his face.
The Gods walk towards where he is to join him as they look around at the scenes of mortals celebrating with each other.
They then turn to each other; smiles fill their faces as they greet each other happily.

The battlefield commanders stand up from the spots they occupied when the giant lightning bomb went off.
They rush over to each other, hugging, smiling, and laughing.
Around them, some soldiers fall to the floor, laughing loudly as they scream and shout with joy and happiness.
On the surrounding floor are huge piles of dark, necrosed elements, to what can only be the dark army Gods.
They are gone.
No one from the dark army has survived the weapon.

Zeus looks up and raises a hand to the sky, moving his hand as if to gesture, moving the clouds sideways and gently blows upwards.
Sun light beams through the cracks in the black cloud as it begins to part more and more.
Huge rays of sunshine now beam down on to the ground below, lighting up the land, as the black clouds finally fade away and disappear into the aether of space above.
The landscape is now filled with several thousand souls, all happy to be alive.

Everyone, everywhere, is screaming with delight, some laugh, some cry tears of joy, some even roll around in the dust joyously as sunlight now fills the land.
Everyone celebrating in their own way.
They are all happy to be alive.
Hermes then turns to look at Jason, but he is not there.
He quickly looks around but cannot spot him.
There is no sign of him.
For a moment he wonders if the weapon took his friends life, wondering if Jason was the ultimate sacrifice.

Undefeated

Hermes scans the area to look for Jason, fearing the worst.
He is nowhere to be seen.
As he moves around the area to look for him, soldiers come up to Hermes, hugging him and thanking him for his help, as they in turn then go over to thank all the other Gods that are with them on the former battlefield.
He smiles and shows genuine thanks to every one of them as they move and dance around the area.
The other Gods hug each other and smile as they too thank every soldier that they speak to, knowing that they have fought alongside them, displaying bravery on a scale that they have never seen before.

But Hermes is still looking for Jason, trying to find his friend who he stood with side by side in battle only moments ago.
He approaches Poseidon to asks if he has seen Jason.
He replies that he hasn't, as Poseidon continues to talk to star struck soldiers, who still cannot believe who they are talking too, one of them holding his trident proudly as a colleague takes pictures with his mobile phone. Another soldier takes the trident and pretends to poke a dead demon, proud of what they have managed to achieve, against all the odds.

Hermes spots Alex and walks over to her.
"Have you seen Jason?" he asks.
Alex replies she hasn't.
Alex looks around, then at Hermes and her big smile turns into a gentler smile, a little concerned, as she replies again "I will help you look for him".
Isaac and Gabriella walk over and see the tablet on the floor and pick it up, putting it into a bag to keep it safe.
Gabriella puts the bag on her back as Isaac gives her a hug and a smile as they look around at the scenes of celebrations taking place around them.

Hermes and Alex continue to scan the area, looking carefully at the vast groups of people around them.
They manage to spot Hector, who is standing with a group of soldiers.
Hector then looks up at them, smiles, then walks away from the soldiers as they continue to celebrate.
Hermes and Alex watch him with curiosity as Hector stops walking to stare out across the land.
They walk over to him to check that he is OK.
He looks at them both and smiles, then hugs them both, saying, "I am fine, a bit battered and bruised, but fine", before turning away to continue looking back in the direction he was moments ago.

Hermes and Alex look at each other wondering what he is doing, and then Hermes asks, "We are looking for Jason. Will you help us find him?".
Hector looks at them and with a warm smile he simply replies, "No".
Hermes and Alex are slightly taken aback by his reply and ask him why; His comment slightly perplexing Alex, not knowing how to respond, but she and Hermes quickly discover why.
"Because" says Hector, "I am looking right at him", as he continues to smile at them both, seeing that his friend is still alive.
Hermes and Alex sigh with relief as they finally spot Jason in the distance.

Rising Dawn

They all walk over to where Jason is sitting.
They all crouch down and all put an arm around him to console him, as they sense what is going on.
Jason sits motionless, staring at the ground where his heart was broken.
Although his ears will surely hear the sounds of people celebrating around him, he blocks them out.
All he can hear are the thoughts in his head.
It is a bittersweet moment for him.
He has the look of someone not wanting to celebrate.
His eyes struggling to hold back the tears.
He desperately misses her.
They pick him up slowly, being careful with his badly beaten body that has cuts and bruises all over him, burn marks down his arms, and torn shreds of armour and clothing.
Jason looks at them both and appreciates their efforts to console him, as he too puts his arms around them and finds some strength to walk unaided, giving them both a gentle smile and squeeze of appreciation.
Zeus looks across to Jason and his friends and watches them.
He looks at Jason's anguish and feels sorrow for him.
He then whispers something under his breath.
As they walk away, a small gust of wind blows, then Jason turns around to see a man standing where he was moments ago.
"Who's that?" asks Jason.
Hermes looks over and sees the man too.
"His name is Asclepius" comes the reply from Hermes, with quite a surprised look on his face, amazed to see him there.
They keep walking, but Hermes looks back again to see Asclepius crouching down to touch the ground where Jason was moments ago.
Hermes then spots Zeus looking in his direction with a wry smile on his face.
Zeus looks at Hermes and gives him a nod, then Hermes turns around again to look back at Asclepius and stops in his tracks.

Hector, Alex, and Jason keep walking slowly away, arms around each other's shoulders, then Hector realises Hermes has stopped walking and turns to look back at him.
Jason, still unaware of what is going on, walks forward a little more but then looks up to see lots of people looking at him, all smiling at him, then they look over his shoulder.
Jason now senses something is going on and turns around to see what it is they are looking at.
"Jason!" cries out Hector.
Jason turns around and moves back to where Hector is standing and then looks in the same direction as everyone else.
He looks forward and spots it.
His eyes open wide, the widest they have ever done before; his face displays a look of disbelief, scarcely believing what he is seeing.
He sees elements from the ground change colour, then begin to rise slowly, swirling around in a gentle vortex of air, then they bind, slowly at first, speeding up as more elements create the shape of a humanoid figure.
The elements that are burnt and attached to Jason's hands fall away and drift towards the spot he was just at, joining with the figure that is appearing before them.
Jason feels a hand on his shoulder, as he turns around to see Erebus standing next to him.
Jason's face beams a huge smile, and he throws his arms around him to hug him tightly, as Erebus too hugs him tightly back, both happy to see each other again.
Jason returns his attention back to the forming elements in front of him.
Jason looks around the area quickly and sees many people watching in awe and amazement at what is happening.
He spots Zeus looking over at him with a smirk on his face and Hera standing next to him, her too with a smile on her face as they both look on.
The elements have now fully formed, as a bright glow surrounds the figure it has created.
Then, the brightness becomes less and less, to reveal the identity of who it is.

Jason drops to his knees crying, in disbelief, but with a huge smile on his face as he watches on.
Hemera now stands there, looking like she did the day they met, returning a smile back at Jason.
He instantly rushes over to her, slightly stumbling from the impact of his war injuries, as she too moves quickly to join him.

As they meet in the middle, she throws her arms around him, holding him tightly, as he does with her too, both crying and smiling, overcome with the emotion of the moment.
They soon realise the crowd that is now standing around them as they become a little coy and aware of their public display of affection, both gently giggling together.
"KISS HER!" comes the shout from one of the onlooking soldiers.
The watching crowd all laugh together, but then another voice shouts the same thing.
"Kiss Her!" comes another voice.
Jason and Hemera laugh and look a little embarrassed, but not enough to stop them!

Jason and Hemera hold each other closely as they both move their heads slowly towards each other, pulling themselves close to each other, to enjoy a tender kiss as the sun shines down on them from above.
As they do, the crowd cheers their approval.
The Gods looking on, smiling, and laughing with happiness, enjoying this newfound bond that they and the mortals now share with each other.
Everyone hugs to celebrate the joy unfolding before them.
Jason and Hemera go back to being oblivious to what is going on around them, as they stare deeply into each other's eyes, holding each other tightly, smiling.
They share another long slow kiss.
"I love you," she tells him.
"I love you too," he replies.

Sol Invictus

Hermes calls out to the mortal commanders that stood with him only a few minutes ago, who helped form the protective circle around Jason, to come and join him.
They all look at each other, a little confused but all smiling, asking each other what it is about.

One by one, they carefully walk over to where he is, as they all gather around.
Zeus approaches them and asks them one at a time to come to him.
Hector goes up first, and as he does so, Hermes drops to one knee beside him.
Hector sees this, and as a mark of respect to the God, he does the same, dropping to one knee.
Zeus approaches him and places his thunderbolt gently on his shoulder.
Upon contact with Hector's shoulder, his clothing and armour suddenly changes into a glorious new outfit, a combined mixture of ancient and modern looking white armour plating, with gold trimmings, complete with a magnificent-looking sword and shield to accompany his new outfit.
As the elements swirl around Hector, he watches them form and bind on him.
His face beaming a big grin, full of pride, as he looks over at the others with him.
They all smile back at him; they are genuinely happy for him.

Zeus then speaks "I anoint you Hector, defender of the faith, guardian of the earth. Rise, for you are now a knight in the Circle of Olympus".
His eyes widen as a huge smile appears on his face.
He stands back up and thanks Zeus, as Hermes takes his forearm and holds it, the Gods way of shaking hands in congratulations.
Hector then joins the rest of the group as they gather around him to look at his new splendour.

Zeus calls out the next name.
"Alex".
She looks up surprised and smiles at the group then walks over to Zeus.
He completes the same ritual for her, too.
After receiving her new outfit and title, she thanks Zeus and joins the others.
They all congratulate her with hugs.
"Gabriella" Zeus calls next.
She too then goes up to receive her rewards and title.
"Isaac," Zeus says next.
He looks at his friends, then at his newfound friends of soldiers, Gods and Zodiacs, and does the same, going up to do the same as his friends did before him, just moments ago.

Takeru hears his name next.
He goes to Zeus and receives his reward like the others have done so just moments ago.
Sun Li is called up next.
Followed by Yusuke.
Then Leonidas.
Pelias is next.
Eudoros soon follows.
Then Ino hears her name called.
Acamas soon joins her and the others.
Medea is last, but not least.

All of them have approached Zeus one by one.
To each one of them, Zeus knights them all, and gives them all new clothing, a suit of armour, to distinguish them as the newly formed Circle of Olympus, mortal defenders of the earth.

Hermes then asks them all to form a circle together, to which they do.
He then asks them to pull out their swords and all point them into the middle.
They all do as he asked and point them into the middle of the circle.

Hermes then asks them all to all touch the tips of their swords in the middle, so that all thirteen blades are now in contact with each other.
The blades of all the sword's glow gently and make a low buzzing noise.
They all look at each other, not knowing what to expect, but they are all smiling, knowing that nothing bad is going to happen.

A large static field forms from the middle of the circle, sending a small charge of electricity upwards.
The electricity then arcs a few meters above them, gently sending thirteen separate small charges outwards and over their heads and behind each new knight, creating a protective cage of electric around them.
Their outfits crackle as they absorb the electric.

They look around at each other, still smiling, grinning from ear to ear, feeling immensely proud.
The electrical charges that hum and fizz around them are not harming them, as their skin tingles and the hair on their arms stands on end.
All they can feel and see is that their armour glows with the sight of electricity fizzing around the joins and edges of their new suits, as if it is giving them some kind of new power.

Zeus then turns to the vast crowd watching and declares, "Behold, the Circle of Olympus, Knights of Earth!".
The crowd erupts into cheers and applause, every single person genuinely happy for what they are witnessing.

Let the Bells Rings Out

Jason and Hemera watch on, pressed close against each other, holding each other in their arms.
"Jason," Zeus calls out to him.
Jason looks at Hemera nervously, not sure what to expect.
She looks at him and just smiles, then plants a tender kiss on his cheek and says to him, "Go to him. I am with you".

Jason walks over to Zeus slowly, holding Hemera's hand, looking side to side at his friends old and new.
All of them are smiling back at him, eager to see what happens next.
Hector clenches a fist to say to Jason, "You've got this!".
Jason chuckles at Hector, then turns his attention back to Zeus.
Jason arrives to Zeus, then drops to one knee out of respect, from observing the other Gods when they have done so, but to appreciate his efforts in helping to win the war and for siding with the mortals to defeat Cronus.
All the Gods have now gathered, moving behind Zeus, including Hemera.

Remarkably, Zeus drops to one knee in front of Jason and bows his head, and straightaway, every God with him does the same, including his beloved Hemera.
Achilles, who is standing next to Hector, tells him, "This is incredible, I have never seen Zeus bow down to anyone before".
Hector looks at him shocked, then a huge smile spreads his face, extremely happy for his friend.

After a few seconds, all the Gods stand back up together, then Zeus says, "Jason, I have a very special gift that is just for you".
Jason looks at him puzzled, but in a good way, with a smile on his face, waiting in anticipation at what is going to happen.
Hermes raises an eyebrow, then gives him a wink, making Jason momentarily chuckle.

The Gods all stood behind Zeus then form a big circle around Jason.
Each one of them then holds the hand of the one they are standing next to, to create a protective ring.
Zeus walks forward to Jason and puts his left hand gently behind Jason's head.
He puts his right hand gently on Jason's forehead.
The two Gods closest to Zeus, Hemera and Hermes, let go of each other's hands, then using their free hands, place them on Zeus's shoulders, one on each side, to make the circle whole again.

A large build-up of static electricity starts to crackle and form, buzzing through each God, turning them ice white and gold as they face Jason, all of them smiling.
Zeus's hands gently glow ice white, then they become even brighter.

The energy builds up in his hands and then moves slowly into Jason's head, then, the light grows larger, and moves down through his entire body.
The scars of the war on Jason's body start to heal quickly, and in a matter of seconds, they completely vanish.
His body then begins to change, the veins on his arms no longer showing the typical blue blood found in mortals but changes to a golden colour.
Jason's veins now run true with ichor.

His muscle, skin and hair grow physically stronger.
Jason's clothing regenerates on him, changing to the same style of clothing as the Gods stood before him.
Jason looks down at himself, in shock, a huge smile on his face, but remaining humble as he goes through whatever is happening to him, as his body experiences metamorphosis.

Hector, Alex, Gabriella, and Isaac stare at him in awe, their mouths open, eyes wide at what they are seeing.
They are watching their friend Jason changing form, from a mortal and into a God.
The highest honour for a mortal.
The electricity that surges through the circle of Gods and into Jason becomes less before it finally stops.
Zeus takes his hands away from Jason's head.
He leans in close to whisper to Jason and says, "Welcome to the family!".
Jason still has a huge smile on his face, still struggling to take it all in, but he is the happiest he has ever been.

The Gods unlock their hands, continuing to grin as they keep their eyes fixed on him, grateful for everything that he has done to help them.
They all turn to watch Hemera, who takes her cue and walks forwards, past Zeus and straight to Jason.
He grins at her, almost laughing as he shakes his head in disbelief at what he has just happened to him.
She puts her hands on to his waist then leans in to kiss his cheek, then she whispers in his ear, "Not bad for a mortal my love!", to which Jason laughs.
They keep their eyes fixed on each other as they then lean in for another kiss.

Zeus turns around to address the gathered masses of soldiers that surround the Gods, "Behold, Olympus has a new God!".
The crowd roar with delight, clapping and cheering, raising their arms in celebration.

Maya

"Walk with me Jason," Zeus asks of him.
Jason leaves Hemera's side as she smiles at him.
He walks toward Zeus, looking back at her, grinning, as she blows him a kiss.
He laughs and winks at her as he then turns to walk alongside Zeus.
Zeus then says to him, "Jason, it is no coincidence that your destiny has brought you here to this moment."
Jason looks at him and replies, "I don't understand, but surely I could have been anyone?".
Zeus replies to him, "But you were not. It was fate that brought you on this journey. It was your courage, also, it was love that gave you the strength." Zeus continues, "You studied history. You came to Greece. You found the tablet, and you your actions have been exemplary."

Jason smiles at Zeus as he looks slightly downwards as they continue to walk slowly together.
"You know, of course, that she loves you, Jason," Zeus tells him.
Jason looks at him and smiles and then replies with a grin, "Good! Because I love her too, with all my heart, from the day I met her I knew".
Zeus says, "I saw how you threw yourself between a demon and her to save her life."
Jason stops walking and turns to look at Zeus and declares "I would do anything for her, I would die for her. When I am not with her, I feel empty, like a light has gone out."
Zeus smiles at him and says, "You are the only person since the creation of this earth that I have seen her fall in love with".
This surprised Jason but smiles back at the comment, quietly thrilled at what Zeus has told him.
As they continue to walk, Zeus tells him, "You also have a family history that you may be unaware of," giving Jason a knowing look.
Jason stops again and asks him, "What do you mean?".

Zeus stops with him and turns to face him, looking him in the eyes and says with seriousness, "Jason, your family bloodline runs all the way back to us!".
Jason looks confused at this statement but listens intently.
Zeus continues "I won't go into details, but one of your ancestors just so happens to be a God!".

Jason thinks about this, amazed at what Zeus has just told him, he slowly moves his head to one side and look at Zeus, slowly putting the pieces of the puzzle together, then he gives Zeus a look as if he is about to ask Zeus something.
"Come on, Jason!" Zeus interrupts abruptly whilst grinning. "Let's get back to the others".
Jason laughs quietly to himself as Zeus gives him a knowing wink, as they turn to walk back.

As they head back to the others, they see that the landscape is beginning to change.
The soldiers and other mortals look on as all the Gods have their hands pressed to the floor, releasing elemental energy into the ground.
The ground then pulsates as every colour you can imagine flows across it, heading outwards.
Everyone looks around in amazement to see the scorched grass growing through the cracks in the earth, small shoots coming up through tiny cracks in the rocks, too.
The trees that were scorched by the war gradually fill up with colour and life again, their leaves unfolding to reveal bright green colours as the bark on the trunks fills again with nourishment.
Flower stems appear before opening gently to reveal their petals, revealing a multitude of colours.
Bees and other insects appear again in the air to carry on collecting the pollen from the newly formed flowers.
Crops begin to appear and grow in the nearby fields, with golden stalks.
Poppy fields nearby also fill the landscape with a beautiful sea of red petals.

Water comes up from the ground and gently flow where the bed of a stream once sat, as streams once again show the signs of flowing water down the sides of the mountains.
Birds suddenly fly past everyone, all of them in formation, as the sun shines down below on everyone.
The nearby tops of the mountains gain a fresh layer of snow as they glisten in the sunshine.
Nearby, various animals appear from their homes, burrows, caves, or arrive on the landscape to appreciate their new surroundings.

Everyone around the area watching the events put their arms around each other's shoulders to marvel at the scenes unfolding before them.
"You did all of this, Jason. You made all this possible," Zeus tells him.
"But you gave me the power to do so," he replies.
"But you gave us hope," replies Zeus.

Eternal Flame

Up high, on top of Olympus near the city centre, Hestia and Prometheus walk down one of its major streets, looking at the surrounding buildings.
They reach the main square and look around to study the temple and other buildings that adorn the streets and walkways.

From another street nearby, Eros and Morpheus appear, and begin walking towards them.
"It looks old, in need of some much-needed renovation," Eros says to them all.
All of them nod in agreement.
Olympus is looking fragile after the effects of the war, added to by the years of neglect.
Some buildings that are made with huge finely carved rocks have cracked and have become brittle.
Some of them have crumbled and fallen from their structures.
The pillars that hold the temple roof have huge splits in them.
The parabolic dishes that sit on top of various plinths that are dotted around the buildings and temple gently flicker the smallest of flames.

Hestia, Eros, Morpheus, and Prometheus all look around at the ruins with a hint of sadness in their eyes.
All the buildings have suffered from the war that has shaken the mountain to its foundations, each one with signs of damage.
They know also that most Gods, having been absent for over two thousand years and more, could not help to maintain.
They turn to look at each other, all of them thinking the same thing, then nod in agreement, with a wry smile creeping on all of their faces.

Hestia turns and says to Prometheus, "Well, this will not do, will it?".
He turns to her and grins in agreement.

The four of them crouch down gently to the ground and place their hands to the floor, right in the middle of the city centre. They close their eyes and concentrate, as light travels down through the inside of their bodies, into their arms and then into the ground.
The ground of the city then begins to produce a rumbling sound that reverberates from the top to the bottom of the mountain.
Everyone on the battlefield below turns to look at Olympus as the huge mountain groans loudly from the vast amount of seismic activity it is experiencing.

Where the top half of the mountain had fallen slightly from a crack that spans its width, the entire top half of the mountain starts to move and shift back upwards at the angle of its huge split, until its correctly back in its original place.
Countless pieces of dust and rock lift from the ground and float gently towards Olympus, filling in the cracks and gaps that were created by the attempted destruction from the dark forces of the war.
They bind in the gaps with the elements acting like some type of glue.
Glowing and rumbling stops to reveal the face of the mountain is back to what it was.
The Gods add several lines to the main crack on the mountain's face, creating a lightning bolt shape, a symbolic gesture to recognise that it is Olympus, making it stand out from the rest, not that it would need it.
The main crack, once embossed, is now a symbolic reminder of the war.

Back at the top of Olympus in the city, dust and stones lift from the ground as a breeze picks up gently, and each particle gently floats, move in the directions to where all the damage has taken place on the temple.
Its bricks and pillars being to regenerate, with dust and rock filling in the gaps, then elements glue them all together, making them solid again.

The same thing happens to all the other buildings on top of Olympus.
They, too, start to regenerate and restore back to their former glory.
Hestia looks at Prometheus, Eros and Morpheus and says with a smile, "Something still doesn't look quite right", knowing full well what it is.
They all smile back at her as a glint appears in her eye.
She raises her arms to the sky to send elements up into the atmosphere.
Within a few seconds raindrops hit the ground, turning quickly into heavy rain.
Quickly, it turns into a downpour; the heavens have literally opened.
Prometheus, Eros, Morpheus, and Hestia look up to the sky, laughing as they quickly become soaking wet from the rain.
Buildings all around them start to self-clean from the downpour, with all the old dirt and dust being washed away to reveal sparking marble walls.
The city centre floor also shines like marble.
The mounds of earth dotted around the city, growing grass, flowers, and trees again, as the water flows away and down the sides of the mountain.

As the rain clouds dissipate, the sun appears in the sky again, then Prometheus says, "One more thing to add".
Morpheus, Eros, and Hestia all grin at him, knowing what he will probably do next, followed by Hestia telling him, "Do it!".
Prometheus looks at the two giant parabolic dishes that sit by the entrance to the temple and then extends his hands out to release red, yellow, orange, and blue elements.

The parabolic dishes instantly spark into life.
Huge flames shoot up into the air as fire's roar once again from them.
The other dishes dotted round the city then begin to light up brighter, one by one, followed by the roaring of flames, as the fires burn fiercely from each one.

Prometheus looks up to the roof of the temple and waves a hand towards it, making small circles as he does so.
Elements fly upwards from his hand to the enormous dishes on top of it, landing within the beautiful structures.
A massive explosion suddenly takes place, so loud that everyone down on the ground hears it and looks up again, to be greeted by the sight of giant flames roaring up into the sky above, thus making everyone cheer with delight.
Then, flames appear on the tops of all the surrounding mountains, flames shooting out skywards, with sparkles of elements coming out from them.
All the dishes on all surrounding mountains were now roaring with fire.

From the ground below, everyone keeps looking up, smiling, arm in arm, shoulder to shoulder, watching the huge flames spill out from the mountains.
All of them are enjoying watching the fire display taking place.

Back on top of Olympus, the four Gods look around to survey the repairs that they have made.
"Much better!" Hestia says with a smile, as all of them turn slowly in all directions to look around, all of them happy with how it now looks.
"All it needs now is to be filled with love and laughter again," declares Eros.
All of them turn their heads back toward him and nod in agreement.
Happy with their work, they then walk up the steps and inside the temple.

Welcome to the Rest of Your Life

All the soldiers on the ground look up to the sky as they hear the familiar sound of their giant troop-carrying helicopters begin to descend and land on the ground beside them.
Many of them, all from different countries, hug as they say their goodbyes to each other.
Many new friendships have now been made, many of them swapping numbers, adding each other's contact details so that they can remain in contact.
They have all gone through something unique, never experienced before.
They all now have a special bond.
As they board their respective helicopters and take off, the Gods stand and watch each one, smiling in appreciation at what they have done, at what they have sacrificed.

As each helicopter takes off, each God facing it kneels to the floor, in an act of thanks to each one of them.
The soldiers on board all smile and wave back as they lift high into the sky, heading back to where they had all travelled from.
The circle of knight warriors all gathers around, and together they make a big circle and lock arms around each other's shoulders, vowing to stay in touch and meet regularly, for they are now a special family, all of them having experienced something that no other mortal alive, except for Jason of course, has experienced before in this new Age of the Gods.
Some of them shed tears as they say a temporary goodbye for now.
Each one of them hugs one another, appreciating what they have gone through together.
They then board their helicopters, the last ones to take off from the ground.
As they do so, all the Gods, including Zeus, drop to one knee and bow their heads to honour them.
They look down and wave at them, happy and smiling at the grand gesture that the Gods have given them.
Sad to go but happy to leave, to get the chance to go back to their loved ones.

As they climb higher, Jason looks up at his friends and smiles, his heart full of pride at what he has gone through with them, knowing that they have made it through to the other side of the horrors that they have endured and conquered together.

The helicopters disappear out of sight as Jason and Hemera walk away hand in hand, as the other Gods join them.
"What now?" Jason asks Hemera.
She looks at him, smiles, then replies, "We have the rest of eternity to think about that".
Jason laughs, letting her words sink in, as he laughs and shakes his head, still not letting it sink in that he is now in fact an immortal God.

Poseidon walks over to them and shuffles himself in between, splitting them up, as he laughs and says, "Come on, you two, make way for the big P!".
Both laugh as Poseidon hugs them tightly with his arms around their shoulders, pulling them close to him, squeezing them gently before letting go and letting the two lovers walk arm in arm again.
Zeus then approaches them and with a smile says, "I feel that the two of you already know what you want to do next".
Jason and Hemera chuckle shyly as they turn and look at each other, and as they do they nod at each other, before sharing a kiss, as Zeus and the other Gods with him smile on.

All the helicopters make their way across the oceans and land, heading to their respective destinations, as soldiers look out and down below, all of them exhausted but happy to be going home.
As each helicopter nears their destination, they can see people out on the streets, seeing joyous scenes of people celebrating victory.
The helicopters descend to the ground, landing in their respective cities.

Takeru's helicopter lands gently in Showa Kinen Park in Tokyo.
As he climbs out with his squad, hundreds of people flock to greet them, throwing their arms around the soldiers, cheering and hugging.
Many soldiers see their families, who then quickly become reunited with each other.
All around there are scenes of joy, people hugging, some crying with happiness and jubilation.
It is a mixed bag of emotions for everybody, mostly relief.

Acamas and Medea touch down in Ildiz Park in Istanbul.
They too disembark their helicopter along with their fellow soldiers, to be greeted the same way, with hundreds of people clapping and cheering as they walk towards the dozens of makeshift emergency centres set up.
Their families too rush over to hug them, tears of happiness stream down people's faces in jubilation and celebration.
Many people bow down to pray at the return of their heroes.

In Athens, Eudoros and Ino jump out from their helicopter to be greeted by jubilant crowds of people celebrating the victory, with everyone running up to them to give them gifts of flowers and food, some even bring shots of spirits to share and toast them with!
As they head to the makeshift camps set up in Syntagma Square, they spot their families waiting for them.
The moment their loved ones spot them, they come rushing over to hug them, overcome with emotions to see that they have made it through to the other side of the war.
Random strangers come up to them, kissing their cheeks in gratitude for what they have done to help win the war.
Nearby, workmen are rebuilding the statues of the Gods that were destroyed by Ares, making sure that they are restored to their former glory.

The same scenes are met by Yusuke, who also touches down at the same time as Takeru, and with Yusuke spotting him, the two of them rush over to hug and bow to each other, now they are brothers in arms, as they both walk together to the military aid tents to be reunited with their loved ones.
Other military personnel bow down to pay and show respect to the two returning heroes and their returning colleagues.
From inside one of the giant marquees, a troop of imperial guards walk out, followed by the emperor of Japan himself.
He looks at them both, bows, and drops to both knees in a sign of his utmost respect to them.
Yusuke and Takeru do the same to show respect back, as everyone else around them watches on in amazement.

Back in Beijing, they greet Sun Li with the same scenes as she arrives, with hundreds of people bowing down to her as she climbs out from her helicopter.
Then the crowds begin to cheer and clap as she begins to walk amongst them.
She too bows to them all to thank them, as she makes her way to the makeshift tents set up to tend to the soldiers returning.
Many of them offer her and her colleague's gifts in appreciation, to which she struggles to carry as she smiles broadly back at them all, thanking every one of them.

Enormous crowds greet Leonidas and Pelias the same way in Sparta, with hundreds of people cheering and clapping in delight as they greet the return of their heroes.
Both smile and raise their fists in victory and celebration as the crowd roars with delight.
A small child comes up to give them both a hug, then Leonidas pulls a small rock from his bag and says, "This is for you, this is from Olympus, home of the Gods".
The small child smiles broadly and thanks them, promising to keep it safe.
They have won the war.
The war is over.
All of them can now rebuild their lives again.

The Rock Upon Which All Waves Crash

The sun is now in its final descent on the shorelines of Kavouri, near southern Athens, as thousands of people stand on the beach.
The Goddess Mnemosyne walks slowly forward, barefoot on the sand, leaving delicate footprints behind her.
She wears a beautiful laurel wreath made of gold on her head.
Her white robes shine brightly, and gold trim adorns her clothing.
A golden sash around her waist is blowing gently in the breeze.
The sea now gently caresses her feet where the land meets the ocean.
The sea is extremely calm, made so by Poseidon using his powers for the solemn occasion.

She walks across a small strip of land that joins the beach to a small island with ancient ruins in the middle of it.
She stops and stands still on the edge of the small island, facing the main shoreline, facing the gathered masses.
Low-level mists begin to form on the water's surface.
The water just about touches the hem of her robe.

Jason stands on the mainland beach, his arms wrapped around Hemera, his cheek pressed against hers.
Zeus and all the other Gods stand there too in attendance, watching on.
The new knights of Olympus stand side by side, all holding hands as they watch, respecting the occasion.
The zodiacs all stand behind them, all lined up, side by side, each one with a hand on the shoulder of the person they stand next to.

Thousands of people also watch on with them, every person, watching on silently, respectfully.
Mnemosyne puts her hands on to the sand and lets the elements flow from her body and into the ground.

Brilliant colours then spread down to the ground, as gentle waves move over them.
Beautiful ultraviolet colours filter through the seabed.
She stands back up and takes a step back.
A huge rock cracks through the seabed on the shore, rising ten meters high and five meters wide.

Once the rock has stopped growing, she then moves closer to it and gently strokes the palms of her hands across it.
A small charge of static electricity buzzes and spreads gently and slowly across the surface of it, making it as smooth as marble.
Mnemosyne then moves her hands slowly back to the rock surface, letting out more elements which spread across the rock face. As they do, the names of people begin to appear on its surface, tens, hundreds, then thousands of them, becoming embossed as they appear.
The names keep on coming, appearing, spreading across the entire rock face, around its sides from top to bottom, and on to the back of it.

Many thousands of names now adorn the rock face.
As the last name appears, every single name on the rock then lights up in a mixture of gold and bronze colours, shining brightly, that everyone on the main shore can see the rock when it is dark enough to do so.

An enormous wave then crashes against the back of the small island, sending a huge mist of water droplets and particles crashing and blowing gently over the new rock.
Mnemosyne lets out another flow of golden elements that make their way to the top of the rock and drift above it before quickly dropping.

As the sun sets and disappears over the horizon, huge flame bursts into life, reaching at least five meters, burning brightly, lighting up the entire area, now in the twilight of the day.
Huge embers of golden elements and particles spill out from the flames that slowly settle down as the flame continues to burn brightly, unaffected by the sea breeze that blows against it.

Zeus drops to one knee and bows his head, followed by Jason, Hemera and the rest of the Gods, then the knights also drop, then the Zodiacs, followed by the thousands of people watching on the shoreline, including soldiers from the war, friends, families, strangers.

Several huge waves crash against the small island as the spray drifts around before gently blowing apart in the breeze, as the fire burns on.
After a few moments, everyone rises slowly, then the families of the fallen all step forward, holding lanterns in their hands, then releasing them.
The lanterns slowly drift upwards into the darkening sky, filling it up with thousands of tiny burning lights.

Apollo steps forward, taking his bow and drawing it backwards, before pointing it up toward the lanterns.
After holding it in place for a couple of seconds, he releases it, sending the huge arrow made of light, glowing in the colours of gold, silver, and bronze, skywards.
The arrow explodes like a giant firework, lighting up the entire coastal area, as if it the sun was out shining down on them again.

Millions of golden elements spread across the night sky.
As the light fired from Apollo's arrow dims, the elements remain in the sky, still sparkling away.
Zeus gently waves a hand across, in line with the elements.
The elements above now sit in place and sparkle brightly.
The sky is now filled with thousands of new stars, each one created in memory for each of the fallen.

Stand as One

Jason and Hemera walk along together, hand in hand, across the landscape at the base of Olympus.
The sun shines down on them from above, not a cloud in the sky, perfect.
Traditional white robes with golden sashes and gold trim adorn the outfits of both Jason and Hemera.
They reach a small set of steps carved from the rocks that leads to another level of the land they walk upon.
As they climb the steps together, they give each other a quick look and a smile.
"Are you ready?" she says to him.
He looks back and gives her a big grin, then kisses her gently on the cheek and simply replies, "never more so!".

As they walk forwards, they see an enormous, whitewashed stone wall in front of them, with huge dark wooden gates that have two finely dressed soldiers guarding them, their spears blocking the gates.
Both soldiers nod and smile at them, then drop to one knee and bow.
Jason and Hemera both bow down at them too in appreciation of their gesture.
The two soldiers stand back up, pull their spears in line with their bodies and then take hold of the gates, unlocking and pulling them open slowly, to reveal an enormous crowd of people standing before them.
Again, they look at each other, grinning from ear to ear, and walk forward.

The enormous crowd of people, stand either side of an aisle, spanning four meters wide, creating perfect lines.
Then the entire crowd drops down to one knee as Jason and Hemera walk forward, smiling at the masses, and both mouth a silent thank you to everyone they can.
The entire crowd then stands back up as one, as the people closest to the aisle throw rose petals to the floor where the two Gods walk, to celebrate this joyous day.

The knights of Olympus appear, dressed in their uniforms, grinning as they walk out from the fringes of the crowd to join Jason and Hemera.
The two of them grin back at their friends, then back at each other, then look forward again as they continue to walk towards a giant temple in front of them.

At the entrance to the temple, Zeus and his fellow Gods stand on a huge stone platform, all of them with huge grins, watching Jason and Hemera walk towards them.
The two lovers reach the front of the temple then climb up a few steps from floor level to the front of the platform.
Behind the Gods stand many other people, including the Zodiacs, all finely dressed in traditional outfits laced with gold.
Several parabolic dishes burn fires brightly on the sides of the platform.

Aphrodite harmonises a sweet melody as other Gods play ceremonial trumpets and beat on giant drums.
Zeus and Hera beam with pride as they greet Jason and Hemera, then they lock arms to greet each other.
Hermes stands next to Zeus, smiling, holding two beautifully crafted golden laurel wreaths.
Jason and Hemera then drop on to one knee in front of the assembled Gods to pay their respects and gratitude.
After a moment, they stand back up and turn to face each other, their hands holding each other's forearms as they look at each other, their faces filled with happiness.

Hera drapes a golden rope over their arms and circles it over once more.
Zeus then takes the golden laurel wreaths from Hermes and places them on Jason and Hemera's heads.
Suddenly, a huge flame erupts from the top of the temple roof, with beautiful elements spilling out from them.

Aphrodite and a large, assembled choir then begin to harmonise together, creating a beautiful sound, as the trumpets and drums play louder than before to celebrate the good news, as giant banners printed with the crests of Olympus unfurl down the pillars of the temple.
Zeus and Hera embrace Jason and Hemera as soon as they stand up, as the other Gods gather around them to congratulate and give them gifts in celebration.

Hector, Alex, Gabriella, and Isaac step forward to embrace their friends, all of them with huge smiles beaming across their faces, all of them hugging one another in celebration.
Jason and Hemera then turn around to face the giant crowds of people cheering and waving at them.
The two of them raise their arms up high to wave back.
The crowds give out an almighty roar in celebration, as they release doves from the sides of the platform and from within the crowd itself, filling the sky.

Jason and Hemera turn and face each other, huge smiles on their faces, as they celebrate the best day of their lives.
The crowd quickly goes silent, not even a pin drop to be heard.
Jason and Hemera lock arms again, then they slowly lean towards each other to embrace, holding on to each other tightly as they kiss, never wanting to let go.
The entire crowd of people and Gods roar with delight in celebration, with much clapping and cheering and more throwing of petals as confetti.
Behold, Jason and Hemera, the two Gods who are so in love, are now married.

Destined for Greatness

Earth is at peace and has been for a few years now.
The world has become a united place to be.

Meanwhile, on top of Olympus, Zeus steps out from the main entrance of the temple.
As he does so, Hermes greets him.
The two of them walk down the steps, talking to one another.
Zeus laughs as Hermes tells him an anecdote, both locked in conversation, sharing jokes.
Hera appears and greets the two Gods, her face very happy.
Hera gives Zeus a kiss on the cheek, then joins them in their conversation as they continue to walk across the city centre.

Hyperion and Theia greet the three Gods and join them on their journey.
Eros soon joins them, followed by Apollo, Athena, and Aphrodite.
The group of Gods continue walking, all of them talking, smiling, and laughing together, as Hermes continues to tell them jokes.
They are soon joined by Hypnos and Nesoi, Crius and Coeus, Artemis and Demeter.
To the right of the group, Hephaestus, Phoebe, and Themis quickly joined them all too.
All the Gods walk side by side, talking and laughing, as they carry gifts in their hands, all heading to the same destination.

They come to a large white stone wall with two tall, glorious looking trees either side of a large archway.
Zeus reaches forward and pushes open two giant wooden gates as they step forward through them.
Poseidon belly laughs and throws his arms wide open to welcome his brother and greeting all the other Gods as they all enter a beautiful vast open garden.
Hestia and Nike come over to them all, smiling and laughing as they greet everyone.

Pontus, Mnemosyne, and Helios stop their conversation and turn around to greet everyone.

Dionysus comes up to the Gods who have just arrived, holding two large jugs of wine, doing his best not to spill any as he is too busy laughing, as they continue to giggle and joke with him.

Erebus is playfully wrestling, but losing, as several children jump all over him, as he breaks out in fits of laughter, as the children laugh and giggle at him.

Selene and Asteria are making a miniature galaxy in the air out of their elements to wow other children who are sitting down on the grass, watching the show in amazement as they clap and laugh.

Every type of food that you can imagine fills a huge, long marble table, full of ambrosia, food of the Gods.

Thalassa and Morpheus are deep in conversation nearby as they entertain more children who sit with them, taking hold of delicious looking slices of desserts and cakes.

Prometheus, Metis and Astraeus sit amongst the Knights of Olympus, chatting and laughing together, as their partners meet all the newly arrived Gods, smiling and talking to them with big smiles.

Lion cubs roam freely as they try to jump up and steal large chunks of food on the table.

Some children feed them too, holding food in their hands for the cubs to cheekily take from.

All the Gods and mortals then take a seat, pursued by all the children, who pull up a chair and sit down next to whoever they find one next to.

Everyone is very relaxed and comfortable in each other's company being quite the family affair that it would be.

Then two children, twins, are last to sit down at the table, flanked either side by Jason and Hemera.

As everyone eats the giant feast of food and drink, Jason and Hemera sit between the twins, passing down gifts.

The twins unwrap their gifts with big smiles, looking across at each person they came from and thanking them.

After the dinner is over, the guests all mingle and talk as Jason and Hemera stand several meters away, looking out towards the setting sun on the horizon, as Jason holds Hemera in his arms.
The twins, whose birthday it is, come up to them, and give Jason and Hemera a big cuddle and thank them for their special day.
Jason and Hemera kiss them both as the four of them share a family hug.
The four of them then look out over the land and sky, watching as the sun touches the horizon.

Jason and Hemera's twin children spot something as they look down the side of Olympus, then turn to look at each other, giggle, then quickly jump high and dive off the ledge.
Jason and Hemera burst out laughing as they watch their twins open giant golden wings on their back and join a group of birds that are gliding around nearby.
They quickly shout over to their guests to come and join them. Straight away, many of the Gods and the Olympus knights jump up laughing and run in their direction.
Wings instantly appear on the backs of the running Gods as they launch themselves off the ledge, quickly followed by the knights, who tap their wristbands, making their suits appear to instantly cover their bodies as giant metallic golden wings instantly unfurl outwards behind them.

All the other guests get up and rush over to the ledge to watch the Gods and Knights flying around in circles with the birds, following their lead, as they change direction to form an arrowhead as they fly away from Olympus.
The Gods and knights watch the birds depart as they continue to fly around, enjoying themselves, all of them laughing with each other, having the best time.
The twins then dive and twist before shooting back up towards the sky as the others follow them in fits of giggles.

Jason and Hemera then take the lead at the front of the group, creating their own arrowhead, quickly joined by the twins, the Gods, and the Knights as they soar high above and over Olympus.
Everyone on top of Olympus cheers loudly, watching on, as their silhouettes soar in front of the setting sun.

THE END

WAR OLYMPUS - THE SOUNDTRACK

(All songs in order of the chapters)

- Prologue: Birth by Audiomachine
- Supermassive Black Hole by Muse
- Map of the Problematique by Muse
- I Fear Nothing by Audiomachine
- Radius by Hi-Finesse
- The Wolf by Hi-Finesse
- Aphelion by Audiomachine
- Sport Vibes by DJ Dimension EDM
- Time is Running Out by Muse
- Algorithm by Muse
- Age of Discovery by Trailerhead
- Adventure of a Lifetime by Audiomachine
- Trouble's Coming by Royal Blood
- Equinox by Audiomachine
- Esoteric by Audiomachine
- All That We Are by Audiomachine
- Momenta by Hi-Finesse
- Anticipation by Audiomachine
- Start of Something Wonderful by Audiomachine
- Rebirth by Hi-Finesse
- Under Lock and Key by Audiomachine
- Mad Visions by Royal Blood
- These Moments by Audiomachine
- Dark Magic by Audiomachine
- Bring Me to Life by Evanescence
- Embers by Sebastian Bohm
- Dark Room Yoga by DJ Dimension EDM
- From the Deep by Gargantuan Music
- Leap of Faith by Audiomachine
- Something Human by Muse
- Millennia by Hi-Finesse
- Try Again Tomorrow by Audiomachine
- Redshift by Audiomachine
- Climb Together by Audiomachine
- Get Up and Fight by Muse

- Reaching by Audiomachine
- Figure It Out by Royal Blood
- Ageless Empire by Trailerhead
- The Handler by Muse
- Ocean Sky by Gargantuan Music
- When It All Falls Down by Audiomachine
- Our World by Audiomachine
- Try Again Tomorrow by Audiomachine
- Beyond the Clouds by Audiomachine
- Shadowfall by Audiomachine
- Assassin by Audiomachine
- Persecution by Audiomachine
- Choose Your Destiny by Audiomachine
- Eternal Light by Dirk Ehlert
- Compliance by Muse
- Unbroken by Audiomachine
- Reverie by Above & Beyond
- Verona by Muse
- Einaudi: Nuvole Bianche by Ludovico Einaudi
- The Dark Side by Muse
- Young Blood by Audiomachine
- The Great Unknown by Audiomachine
- Metamorphosis by Invisible Reality
- Tails of the Electric Romeo by Trailerhead
- Spectral Dimension by Invisible Reality
- Uprising by Muse
- The Devil's Army by Audiomachine
- Another Planet by Invisible Reality
- Blockades by Muse
- Kashmir by Escala
- Reborn by Really Slow Motion
- No Retreat, No Surrender by Audiomachine
- Look to the Sky by Audiomachine
- On the Shoulders of Giants by Gargantuan Music
- Reign of Vengeance by Future World Music
- Thunderstruck by AC/DC
- Invincible by Muse
- Building Smasher by Epic Score
- Stockholm Syndrome by Muse

- Tantra by Yar Zaa
- The Fate of Our Brave by Trailerhead
- Reapers by Muse
- Destructo by Hi-Finesse
- Thumper by Gargantuan Music
- Ten Thousand Warriors by Audiomachine
- Sanctus Immortale by Trailerhead
- Mercurial by Trailerhead
- Knights of Cydonia by Muse
- Spiritus Omnia by Trailerhead
- Farewell to Earth by Audiomachine
- Psycho by Muse
- The Final Hour by Audiomachine
- Ground Zero by Really Slow Motion
- Knock 'Em Dead, Kid by Dark Sky Choir
- Ode to Power by Trailerhead
- Glow by Audiomachine
- Undefeated by Audiomachine
- Rising Dawn by Audiomachine
- Sol Invictus by Audiomachine
- Let the Bells Ring Out by Gargantuan Music
- Maya by Audiomachine
- Eternal Flame by Audiomachine
- Welcome to the Rest of Your Life by Audiomachine
- The Rock Upon Which All Waves Crash by Trailerhead
- Stand as One by Audiomachine
- Destined for Greatness by Audiomachine

Additional songs for the credits
- Starlight by Muse
- Apollo's Triumph by Audiomachine
- I Love You Forever by Two Steps from Hell
- Translucent by Trailerhead
- No Matter What by Audiomachine
- Resurrection by Colossal Trailer Music
- Rise Above by Veigar Margeirsson
- Remember Not to Forget by Audiohead

Disclaimer:
I do not own the rights to this music.
All musical content solely belongs to the artists and/or record companies.
All lyrics, musical content, and all ownership rights, fully belong to each respective artist and any other linked companies.
Please subscribe to a reputable music streaming service or purchase the artists' songs.
Please purchase or subscribe to their music.
Don't be a pirate!
NB: No Gods were harmed in the writing of this book.

All rights reserved.

All written work in this novel is the intellectual property of the named author.

Special thanks:
To my family for supporting (putting up with!) my whimsical ideas.
To David Wardle of Bold & Noble for creating my cool front cover.
To the artists of the music that inspired a bit of writing to come up with this story.